CN00860144

Riding Solo

Nicola Jane

Copyright © 2022 by Nicola Jane

All rights reserved.

No portion of this book may be reproduced in any form without written permission
from the publisher or author, except as permitted by U.K. copyright law.

Meet the team

Editor: Rebecca Vazquez – Dark Syde Books
Proofreader: Jackie Ziegler
Formatter: Nicola Miller

Disclaimer:
This book is a work of fiction. The names, characters, places, and incidents are all products of the author's imagination and are not to be construed as real. Any similarities are entirely coincidental.

Spelling Note:

Please note, this author resides in the United Kingdom and is using British English. Therefore, some words may be viewed as incorrect or spelled incorrectly, however, they are not.

Acknowledgements

As always, thanks to everyone who has downloaded, bought, shared, reviewed, and helped spread the word. You're all amazing, and I'm thankful for each and every one of you. Keep supporting authors, we need you xx

Trigger Warning

If you're new to my books, welcome. If you're new to MC, please take caution before entering. This is not a fluffy romance, and the men are not nice. They don't buy flowers or go on romantic dinners. They're rude, unapologetic, and often bossy. If you're easily offended by poor choices, bad language, and naughty scenes, this book is not for you.

If you live for all of the above, come in, take a seat, and enjoy the ride.

Solo is waiting for you!

Contents

Playlist:

Girls Just Want to Have Fun – Cyndi Lauper
Trouble – Iggy Azalea ft. Jennifer Hudson
Radar – Britney Spears
(You Drive Me) Crazy – Britney Spears
Crazy – Aerosmith
I Fell In Love With The Devil – Avril Lavigne
I'm a Mess – Bebe Rexha
Hold My Hand – Lady Gaga
How Do You Sleep? – Sam Smith
Lose You to Love Me – Selena Gomez
Dancing with the Devil – Demi Lovato
Sorry Not Sorry – Demi Lovato
Need You Now – Lady A
Forget Me Too – Machine Gun Kelly ft. Halsey
Only Love Can Hurt Like This – Paloma Faith
Back to You – Louis Tomlinson ft. Bebe Rexha
We Belong Together – Mariah Carey
Stickwitu – The Pussycat Dolls

CHAPTER ONE

LARA

"Where in the hell did you get that?" yells Felicity, my best friend.

I spin slowly, so she can get the full effect of the leather jacket I just picked up from the back of someone's chair. "Do you like it?" I pull a pose, pouting and sticking out a leg.

"Christ, Lara, get it off now," she hisses, tugging it from my shoulders.

I grip it tighter, frowning with annoyance. "Jesus, Flick, calm down, would yah?"

"Do you know who this belongs to?"

I look at the name sewn on the right breast. "Erm . . ." I try to focus, but the amount of alcohol I've drank tonight makes it hard. "President?" I say in an unsure voice. "Oh, wait," I frown again, "Solo."

"President," she hisses. "As in, the President of The Depraved Devils MC. As in, the motorcycle club. Do you know how bloody crazy they are?"

"Why are you always so dramatic, Flick? I put his jacket on, it's not a crime."

"I actually feel sick. I think I might be sick," she mutters, fanning her face dramatically with a cocktail menu.

"Relax, I'll just take it off and put it back."

She grabs my arm in a death grip. "No, if he catches you, he'll know you took it. Oh god, what are we going to do?"

"Is it time for the grand opening yet?" Robyn's voice rings out as she approaches from the dance floor. "Oh, cool jacket. A little big, though. Did you get it from a giant?"

"Yes, good idea," says Flick, grabbing my hand. "Let's get out of here before the owner of that jacket strings you up by your throat."

We get funny looks as we make our way along the road to Maine's, the bar my brother recently purchased. The opening is tonight, and although we probably took pre-drinks a little too seriously, I'm excited to arrive.

Inside, it looks amazing. It's a warm, welcoming space with a small stage in the corner where a woman is singing something soulful. The golden lights twinkle, giving the place a glow like you're surrounded by a million tiny candles. The last time I was in here, the bar wasn't quite finished, so it's amazing to see the final look and to know all my brother's hard work has paid off.

I spot Lucas and rush over, throwing myself in his arms. He laughs, picking me up and spinning me around. "Easy, tiger, how much have you had to drink?" I smile up at my eldest brother. He's always looked out for us. He's responsible and caring, which was good considering our parents were the total opposite. The minute he turned eighteen, he worked hard to get us away from them. He's almost thirty-eight now and is finally living his dream with this bar.

"Probably a little too much. Where's Liam?" My other brother is the middle child and not nearly as responsible as Lucas, even at the grand age of thirty-three. Both of them look after me, though. They're overprotective and always make sure I have whatever I need. Being twenty-eight myself, I shouldn't need to rely on them, but I often do. It's what big brothers are for.

"He's around here somewhere. Interesting choice of outfit," he says, holding me at arm's length to take in the jacket. He frowns, spinning me around to check out the back, where there's a picture of a devil-type creature and the words 'The Depraved Devils MC'. When he turns me back around to face him, he looks panicked. "Where did you get that?"

"In the last bar. It was on a chair."

"You need to take that back right now, Lara."

"What is all the fuss about?"

"Oh fuck," he mutters in a low voice. "We're about to find out."

I glance over my shoulder and freeze. Robyn was right when she said this jacket belonged to a giant because, fuck, the guy currently standing in the doorway to Maine's is huge. I know he's the jacket's owner because there are two men either side of him wearing the same jacket while he's missing his.

"Take it off," whispers Lucas, nudging me forward with his elbow.

I can't help but stare at the man in awe. He's magnificent. As his eyes find me, they narrow, and he looks irritated but sexy as hell. It's been a long time since I looked at a guy and felt this kind of heat, and I'm not about to be quashed by him so he can just take the jacket and leave. No way. I need to be remembered.

Turning to face him fully, I put my hands on my hips and a steely glare on my face. "No," hisses Lucas from behind me when he realises my intentions. "Don't you dare sass him, Lara. Just get the jacket off."

"What is all the damn fuss? It's just a jacket."

"Oh crap, you're gonna get me killed on the first night of living my dream," he groans dramatically.

I watch as the giant moves closer, followed by the two minions who look equally as annoyed. "Welcome to Maine's. Table for three?" I add an extra-wide smile, but it doesn't do shit to break their ice-cold expressions.

"Does she belong to you?" grates out the giant, speaking directly to Lucas. I'm offended and I can't hide the fact as he stares past me. I don't know if it's because of his clear insult that I *belong* to a man or that he totally overlooked me.

"I'm really sorry—" begins Lucas, but I cut him off by standing on my tiptoes and waving my arms around.

"Hey," I shout. "Hey, excuse me . . . I'm right here!" The giant inhales sharply through his nose, and his nostrils flare. He arches an eyebrow and lowers his narrowed eyes at me. It almost takes my breath away. He's gorgeous. "It's rude to ignore me. I don't like it."

"Lara, what the fuck?" hisses Lucas, still behind me.

"I'm Lara." I hold out a hand for the man to shake, but he stares down at it with disdain. "Again, rude."

"I can't even begin to explain her," Lucas says, "but I'm so very sorry she took your jacket. Here, take it back." Lucas tries to remove the giant's garment from me, but I shrug him off.

"You need some lessons in manners," I snap. "Then you'll get your jacket back."

One of the men beside the giant sighs heavily. "Can't we just fucking kill her, Pres?"

"No, please don't do that. You'll get me shut down, and it's my opening night," says Lucas desperately. "Unless you can hide her somewhere. I mean, I won't tell anyone."

"Thanks, bro," I snap, elbowing him in the ribs.

"Lucas is right," says Robyn, moving to my side. "Give the man his jacket, so we can get on with our night."

I watch the giant assessing my friend with interest and it pisses me off. Robyn is beautiful, and somehow, all the guys flock to her over any of us, but I want this one and there's no way I'm giving him up. "On one condition," I say, folding my arms across my chest.

"You're really doing this?" she asks, her eyes wide. "You're going to try and make a deal with," Robyn's eyes take in the badge on the jacket, and she shrugs helplessly, "The Devils?"

"We really don't have time for this shit," snaps the side guy, reaching into his jacket. The giant holds his hand up, and the man keeps his hand still on whatever he was reaching for. I swallow, praying it's not a weapon of some sort.

"What condition?" he asks, his voice rumbling like he's drunk a bottle of Jack and smoked a hundred cigarettes.

I shiver. "Ask me nicely."

I see amusement in his eyes, but he hides it well. "Or I could just let my VP here put a fucking bullet in your skull and take it anyway."

SOLO

I watch the way her eyes dart to where Duke's hand is resting on his gun inside his jacket. She's a firecracker, that's for sure, but Duke's right, I don't have time for this. I left my jacket on the chair like an idiot while I was out back inflicting pain on some shithead who chose to cross me this evening.

As if on cue, that same shithead stumbles into this fucking bar, bleeding all over the place and wheezing like we popped his lung. I glance at Duke, who nods to Rock. He jumps into action right as the firecracker shoves past me and runs towards him. I grab Rock back, shaking my head discreetly so he doesn't get involved. This crazy bitch must know him. Makes sense. "Liam," she cries, hooking her arm around his waist and helping him to sit on a stool.

"What the hell happened to you?" asks the guy she called 'bro'.

They crowd around him. "Would you believe me if I said I fell over?" the shithead asks, coughing violently.

"Trust her to bloody know him," mutters Rock. "Do you want me to get him out of here?"

I shake my head. "Do you want me to kill them all so we can get back to the club?" Duke suggests. I grin, shaking my head again. It's Duke's answer to everything, but that's why he makes a good Vice President.

"Nah, he hasn't seen us. Let's get out of here and avoid the shitstorm. I'll come back for my kutte." There's something about the firecracker that intrigues me. I'll be back for what's mine. She isn't going anywhere, and now I know exactly where to find her.

We get back to the club and Kiki is mad as hell. She's pacing, still splattered in the shithead's blood. His nose sprayed us both when it burst. "What the fuck was that?" she screams, taking all three of us by surprise.

"Kiki," shrieks Siren, pulling her friend out of my reach.

"You really hurt him," she yells, and her tone is fucking pissing me off. I give her a warning glare, but she ignores it. "You make me sick!"

It's enough to get my full attention, and I haul her out of Siren's hold. "Who the fuck are you talking to?" I bellow, and she flinches. "You're not my ol' lady, so you don't get to screech at me like you are. Now, get up to my bed and be naked so I can fuck the attitude out your mouth!" I shove her towards the stairs, and she rushes up to carry out my orders. Kiki's problem is, she wants to be my ol' lady. They all do. I'm the club's President, and they don't seem to care how badly I treat them, cos they still compete to be in my bed every night. They hang around here, hoping to be claimed by a member eventually. They want a man to take care of them, and I don't blame them. None of them have had great starts in life. But the brothers here aren't looking for a whore to be their woman. Harsh but true. If a girl's already fucked her way through the club, a brother ain't gonna claim her.

Upstairs, Kiki is already naked on my bed. "What the fuck are you lying there for?" I growl. She jumps up, rushing to me and dropping to her knees. "Better," I mutter, unfastening my belt. "You wanna fuck men outside this club, Kiki?"

"No, Pres," she whispers, waiting patiently for me to give her my semi-hard cock.

"Cos you know the rules. I can't have my girls out there fucking around. He could be a cop or someone else wanting information on my club."

"I'm sorry, Pres. I was just trying to make you jealous," she admits.

"It worked, Ki," I admit bitterly. I don't like sharing my club girls, and she's been in my bed for two months now. I grip her hair, and she opens her mouth. Rubbing the head of my cock over her lips, she laps the precum. I close my eyes and the firecracker comes into my mind. I'm hard instantly. Something about her attitude, and the way her steely grey eyes challenged me, gets my blood pumping.

CHAPTER TWO

LARA

I hold the leather jacket to my nose and breathe in the musky scent of man. And he is all man. After sorting Liam out, I turned, but the giant was gone. Now, all I'm left with is his jacket covered in his scent. Its woodsy aftershave mixed with mint and smoke, and there's a hint of oil and perhaps even a touch of whiskey, or maybe that's my imagination building him up in my mind . . . because that always happens. I see a guy like that, and my mind locks him in and makes me believe he's a god. I used to think it was an illness, but now, I live for the buzz it gives me. I smile as I lie on my bed in nothing but the jacket.

I wake with a start, sitting up and looking around in the darkness. Fuck. Why does it always get me like that? I glance at the bedside clock. Four in the morning . . . again. I'm so over this insomnia.

Looking down at my half-naked body, I run my fingers over the cool leather. Laying back down, I close my eyes and enjoy the feel of it. "I've locked that image in my mind." The deep, gravelly voice comes from somewhere in the room. I almost scream, but before I can, a large hand wraps around my throat and pins me to the mattress. "Now, I would ask nicely like you insisted, but I don't really do nice." Blood pumps through my body fast, and I feel dizzy when the hand pushes tighter against my throat. "The fact you're not even attempting to prise my fingers from your throat means either you're actually liking this, or you want to die."

I squeeze my eyes closed. Do not panic. Do not panic. I open the jacket, and his eyes shift to my naked body. I try to pull one arm out, but it's difficult when I'm being held down, so I give up and stare at him. He smirks. "No funny business," he says firmly, releasing my neck. Sucking in a deep breath, I rub my throat. I remove the jacket, and he snatches it, pulling it on.

"Must be one important jacket if you went to all this trouble to find it."

"It was no trouble, Lara Maine. Sister to Lucas and Liam Maine. Orphaned but raised by Lucas. You have a total of sixty-eight pence in your bank account, but your brother will top it up tomorrow morning, which is why you continue to spend like you're a pampered princess."

I sit up, looking around for some way to cover my body. There's nothing because my sheets are a screwed-up mess on the floor, so I bring my knees to my chest and wrap my arms around them. "Am I supposed to be impressed by your stalking skills? And for the record, I enjoyed it," I say confidently.

He sniggers. "Little girl with daddy issues."

"Big girl likes kink," I correct.

He pushes his face to mine. "You've never been shown kink," he whispers. "Not properly." Goose-pimples break out over my skin as his timbre washes over me.

"And I guess you hold the key to that, right?" I laugh and roll my eyes.

"Don't bait me, Firecracker. You can't handle it." He stands. "Next time you steal from me, you'll pay."

"I'm intrigued. How will I pay?"

"Goodbye, Lara."

He leaves through my bedroom door, and I wonder how the hell he got into my house with my two brothers sleeping in the next rooms. When I was a teenager, I couldn't sneak any guys up here, not even through the window!

Flick walks into the kitchen as I'm biting into my toast. "I need coffee," she groans. She lives next door and often just turns up here uninvited.

"Is your kettle broken?" asks Lucas.

"You make better coffee than me," she whines, and he hands her his cup. Taking it gratefully, she hums her approval as she takes a mouthful. "How's Liam?"

"I checked in on him this morning and he was still asleep. He's a mess, though," I say.

"Did you find out what happened?"

I shake my head and look to Lucas for answers, but he shrugs. "You know Liam, probably caught with someone's wife."

"What are your plans today?" I ask him.

"I have the banking to do for the bar, then I'm in meetings for the rest of the day. I've transferred some cash into your account. Please stop spending like you're the Queen. And find time to get that jacket back to that guy today. Just dump it in their yard."

"Sure," I say. The last thing I want to do is alert him to the fact he came and took his jacket back last night. Nor does Lucas need to know I was naked. He smiles, kissing me on the head, then doing the same to Flick before he rushes out the door. "Look at him, all grown up," I say, grinning.

"It was a successful opening," says Flick. "He's finally living his dream."

Liam hobbles in, and I glare at him. "I didn't sleep well last night because I was worrying about you," I state.

"You don't need to. You're not my mother."

I scowl. "What did you do to deserve this?"

"Nothing. I swear. One minute, I was taking a piss, and the next, some big steroid ripped fucker beat the shit outta me."

"Taking a piss?" repeats Flick sceptically. "In an alleyway?"

"The men's bathroom was busy," he says defensively.

"Liam!" I gasp. "You weren't having sex in an alley, surely?"

He smirks, shrugging. "Actually, I didn't get that far. I don't even remember if I kissed her."

"One day, you'll grow up and settle down," I mutter.

"Nah, never."

I'm swamped at work. My boss is a wanker, plain and simple. He looks in the mirror at himself more times in one day than I have in my entire life. But the small coffee shop is tranquil and relaxed, and I love working here. Adam made me shop manager a few months back so he could free up some of his own time. Since then, he justifies the very small pay rise I got with the role by being extra wanky.

I'm telling Betsy, my work bestie, all about my night out, including the run-in with the giant when Adam places the newspaper he was reading on the coffee bar. "You do realise The Depraved Devils are an organised crime gang?"

"So," I say with a shrug. "It's just a jacket. I don't see the problem."

He laughs. "Solo is not the kind of man you want to be putting yourself in front of."

"Solo?" I repeat, frowning.

"The club President. Rumour has it, they call him Solo because he likes to kill on his own."

"Well, as you can see, I'm still alive, so no harm done. He got his jacket back, and I live to slave another day for you." I add a sarcastic smile.

"That's what he wants you to think, Lara. He's probably plotting your murder as we speak." He turns to Betsy. "You can be the manager if she disappears."

"For what you're paying, no chance," she says, winking playfully.

"How did you get the jacket back to him?" Adam asks.

I feel my cheeks blush as I think about Solo turning up in my room last night. It should have freaked me out, but shit like that intrigues me more. It's why I'm so fucked up. "Oh, I took it back to their yard on my way to work this morning," I lie.

"Yard?" Adam repeats. "You mean the clubhouse? How the hell did you get within a mile of that place? It's like London's best-kept secret. I once jogged past there and I swear they had ten rottweilers roaming the grounds."

"I left it right outside."

"How do you know so much about them anyway?" Betsy asks Adam.

"I once had sex with a member there. I can't spill the beans, though, cos he hasn't told anyone he's gay." He gives a wink and heads off to his office.

"He's such a whore," Betsy mutters, rolling her eyes.

"Have you heard of them before?" I ask her casually. I'm beginning to feel like the only one who's never heard of the club.

"I've heard rumours, like everyone else, I guess. But I'm sure he's forgotten all about the jacket incident now. Don't worry yourself."

I nod, biting my inner cheek. With everyone's warnings about the club, I wonder why I'm not even slightly put off. Instead, I'm plotting in my head on how the hell I can see him again, and I know without a doubt, we're both in trouble.

SOLO

Kiki falls back onto her arse, coughing violently. "Jesus, Solo," she gasps, looking up at me with her eyes streaming and black mascara running down her face.

I tuck my cock back in my jeans, grinning at her. "You know you love it."

"I love it at my own pace. You can't just do shit like that and ignore my signals for you to stop."

"If you're no longer up to the job, I can get Siren to take over."

She narrows her eyes and jealousy radiates from her. "I can handle you better than she can!"

"I dunno, she doesn't complain when I fuck her mouth."

I head for the door, and she rushes after me, gripping my jacket. "No, I'm sorry. Forget I said anything—" She pauses and inhales. "Is that perfume?"

I smirk. That little firecracker left her scent all over my kutte and it's gotten me off twice already. Fuck, I'm getting hard again just thinking about seeing her naked body wrapped in leather. How the hell I walked out of there without laying a finger on her is a miracle. Kiki pushes against my chest, and I laugh. Who the fuck does she think she is, my owner? "Are you ready, boys?" I yell out across the main room, and several of my men get up.

"Solo, who the fuck is she?" screams Kiki. I laugh as I lead the men out to our bikes. I'm not explaining myself to her, and I'll make sure Siren's in my bed tonight to remind her she's not indispensable.

I wait patiently on my bike for Viper and Duke to make the last collection of the night. They're taking far too long, and after a glance from Thor, who's parked beside me, I get off my bike and head inside, flanked by the rest of the men. Duke's holding his chin, and there's a guy flat on his back in the middle of the betting shop. "Everything okay?" asks Ink, bending to check the guy's pulse. "Still alive," he adds.

"Viper is out back," mutters Duke. "These fuckers were waiting when we walked in. I don't think the other guy got off so lucky."

I groan and head to the back room. Viper is washing blood from his hands when he glances over to me and shrugs. "He came at me first." I stare down at the bloodied body on the ground. There's no denying he took a good beating, but he's still breathing.

"Did you get the money?" I ask. After all, it's why we're here, to collect the monthly payments in exchange for the club's protection. We don't force people to pay for our protection, but there're a few businesses along this strip that require our help and we give it, wholeheartedly. There are a lot of street gangs wanting to make money in any way possible, and small businesses are a good target. But this fucker never seems to want to pay up. Viper holds up a cloth bag of cash, and I nod, satisfied. "Cut this place off the round. I ain't battling to get the money we earned," I say. "He's on his own from now on."

CHAPTER THREE

LARA

It's as if the good Lord himself placed Solo in my path because Flick and I are on the way to meet Robyn for drinks when I spot a bunch of his guys lingering around the betting shop. Flick grabs my hand. "Just because you've had a cocktail, it does not mean you're invincible," she hisses as we're passing the gang. I grin at her, and her eyes widen. "Please, Lara. Just for once listen."

"It's fate," I whisper.

"It's not, because fate isn't real. It was invented so we'd convince ourselves to believe in it when, in actual fact, it tricks us into doing really stupid things, like . . ." She stares on horrified as I throw my leg over the bike at the front of all the others. It has to be his, right? "Like that. That's exactly what I'm talking about." Flick looks around anxiously and a squeak escapes her as a few of the bikers turn to look. "Get off it," she begs in a desperate whisper.

"Hey, sweetheart. Get off there," yells one of the men moving towards me.

He's almost reached me when that deep voice comes from somewhere behind me and commands him to stop. He does, turning back to look at Solo as he emerges from the shop. There's a smirk on his face as he makes his way over. "Are you determined to get yourself hurt, Firecracker?" he drawls.

"I was in the area and couldn't resist a picture with this beast," I say, winking.

"Not you again," groans another biker from behind Solo.

I grin. "Lara," I introduce.

"Suicidal Lara," says Solo, arching a brow. "Get off the bike."

"Make me," I challenge.

He takes an impatient breath before plucking me from the bike like I weigh nothing more than air. Then, he slides me down his muscled chest and places me on the ground. "Now, stop trying to play with the big boys and stick to what you know," he whispers close to my ear. I shudder. He doesn't realise how his words only intrigue me more. "Run along, Suicide." I smile at his nickname for me. "I've always been attracted to danger," I whisper back.

"There's danger and then there's me. You don't want to be on my radar, so stop putting yourself there." Solo throws his leg over the bike. It's the sexiest move I've ever seen, and as he kick-starts it, I take a step back to appreciate the full image of perfection before me. I have no choice . . . I have to know him.

"What is it with you and dangerous men?" asks Robyn as she pays the bartender for our drinks.

I shrug. "I love danger."

"It's like you stand in a room of a hundred gorgeous guys, but there's that one fucked-up, nasty bastard and you're there, he's the one you always want."

"Even when he doesn't want you," Flick points out.

"Not always true," I argue.

"Name one," Robyn challenges. "Name one badass guy who worked out for you."

I pretend to think, but we both know there isn't one. My mind plays a movie reel of the aftermath I've endured after every fucked-up man I've ever tried to love. I shake my head to clear the images. "Can't you just try and fall for a decent guy?" Robyn asks.

Making our way to a table, I argue, "I have tried. There was boring Bill."

"His name was Ben, and he was actually really lovely," snaps Robyn. "If you'd have given him a chance, you'd be married now with a child." Ben was one of Robyn's friends who she set me up with. I made two dates before deleting his number.

"And tiresome Tim," I add.

"He was rich, Lara. He could have given you anything." Another of Robyn's matchmaking ideas.

"I like what I like, what can I say?"

"So, you're gonna keep following this guy until he gives in?" asks Flick. "Then what? Because we already know how it ends."

"Maybe it won't end that way," I mutter.

"Yes, of course, Lara. You'll be the one woman who comes into his life and changes him from a cage fighting, aggressive, violent, sadistic arsehole to a sweet, loving husband who wants to marry you and give you three little babies," says Robyn dreamily.

"Cage fighting?" I repeat, sitting straighter.

"Oh god," she groans, dropping her head onto the table and pretending to bang it. "That's all you heard!"

I grin. "He's a cage fighter?"

"The point is, he won't love you like you deserve, so just stop trying to get his attention. Because even if you do manage to get into his bed, it's a one-night deal. Why do you think he's called Solo?"

"Adam said it's because he likes to kill alone."

"And still, you want him?" she cries. "He's Solo because he always rides solo. Men like him usually take a woman, and she becomes respected amongst the club and is known as the President's ol' lady. But he hasn't ever had a woman on the back of his bike. It's meaningful to them, and the fact he's still solo, screams bad news."

"How do you know all this?" asks Flick.

"I did my research so I could convince this bunny boiler he isn't worth it."

"I think you've made it worse," Flick surmises.

I rush back to the table where the girls are sitting. "Okay, I know where we need to go," I say, smiling like a crazy woman. It took me five minutes to locate an underground ring used for cage fighting. The doormen were happy to help once I flirted a little.

"No!" snaps Flick firmly after I reveal my idea.

"Double no!" adds Robyn.

"I'm going with or without you," I point out, giving Derrick, the doorman, a little wave through the window. He winks.

"Who the hell is that?" asks Flick.

"He works here as security. He's taking me on a date to the fight club when he finishes here."

"What is wrong with you?" Robyn cries. "Why can't you be normal?"

"Normal is so overrated. And Derrick is bringing his sexy single friends," I say, pointing out the window to the other doormen. They can't deny the men are hot. Robyn resolves with a nod, and I squeal in delight.

"Fine, I'm in, but I'm not happy about it," says Flick.

SOLO

Siren sits on my lap, running her fingers through my hair. I can feel the way Kiki's eyes are burning into us, but I don't give a fuck. I need to relax, and she stresses me out with her complaining and nagging. Bringing Siren in for a kiss, I bite her lower lip as she pulls away. She smirks, running kisses up my neck and nipping along my jawline. She grinds her arse against my erection, and I hiss. There's a warm-up fight in the ring, and the crowds are going wild as Rock beats the crap out of his opponent. Boss leans close to me. "Two more, then it's your turn," he tells me. He's the fight organiser and also part of the MC. He's good at what he does and makes us a lot of money.

"Hear that," I tell Siren. "I've got a bit of time." She bites her lower lip and tries to hide the uncertainty in her eyes. I have a reputation amongst the club's whores—I like it rough.

One of the doormen from this area, who I know well, passes, catching my eye. He smiles and holds his fist out to me, which I knock with my own. "Derrick, you betting tonight?" I ask, and he nods.

"Of course. The other guy to win," he jokes, and I laugh. Derrick not only works the doors locally but also heads up a large security firm, and he's known for placing large bets on me to win. "I'll catch you after the fight," he adds, continuing on to his table. I watch as he grabs the hand of a woman . . . a woman I know far better than I should. Suicide is right behind him, and she doesn't give me a second glance as she takes a seat.

"Pres, ain't that—" begins Duke, and I nod. What the fuck is her game? And if she and Derrick are a thing, why the fuck is she hanging around me like a bad smell?

The first fight is easy. My opponent doesn't even make the second round before he's out cold. I roll my eyes at Boss, who shrugs with a grin. "I didn't get in here for a dance," I tell him. "Get me a fighter."

"He was the warm-up," says Boss, moving close to my ear. "Take this next guy to round three." I nod in response. Most of the fights are fixed, it's how we make money.

I drag the next fight to round three, and we're seconds in when I pound my opponent's face until he stumbles to his knees and crashes face down. I catch Suicide's eye, and she looks away, turning to Derrick to say something.

She's playing a game. One minute, she's in my face, and the next, I'm getting the cold shoulder. I crack my neck from side to side. Why do I even care? One fuck and she'd be history anyway. Siren enters the ring and throws herself at me. I let her, keeping my eyes on Suicide as I carry her from the ring.

CHAPTER FOUR

LARA

My plan's working. Solo hasn't been able to stop himself from looking over at me since I arrived. "What are you up to?" asks Flick suspiciously.

"You told me to stay clear of Solo, so I am."

She narrows her eyes. "Liar!"

"Well, stop pretending to be interested just so you can nag me. I'm going after him whether you like it or not. Now, if you'll excuse me, I need a drink." I've already spotted Solo at the bar with a group of his friends.

Pushing my way through until I'm beside him, I wave a twenty at the bartender. He winks, heading my way and ignoring the men who are already waiting to be served. There're a few groans from the crowd as I ask for a shot of tequila.

"I'm starting to think you're stalking me," Solo drawls in my ear. I keep a straight face as I pay for my drink.

"Says the guy who broke into my house. Don't flatter yourself. I'm here with someone."

"Yes, I saw. Derrick the dick."

"Please tell me he's called that because he has a huge—"

"No," he cuts in before I can finish. "It's because he is an actual dickhead."

"Weird you run in the same circles," I point out, smirking.

"First, you steal from me, and now, you insult me?"

"I know, I'm waiting for your reaction, and to be honest, I'm disappointed. I've been told all these stories about how I shouldn't cross you, and yet, I have, more than once, and nothing."

The way his eyes burn ignites something in me, and I can't help the flush that covers my cheeks. His tattooed hand shoots out so quickly, I don't have time to react, and when he wraps it around my throat for the second time, I smile. His nostrils flare and he pushes me against the bar until his body is almost crushing mine. "I don't know whether to kill you or fuck you," he growls. I stare at his lips, willing him to go with the second option. "There's a party back at the club. Be there."

He releases my throat and steps away. "Can I bring Derrick?" I ask innocently.

"Only if he likes to watch. I don't share unless it's with a brother."

My stomach does a flip and I grab my shot, knocking it back as he walks away.

Half an hour later, I slip my jacket on. "This is a terrible idea," says Flick as I wave down a cab.

"No one said you had to come. I'll be fine on my own."

"Hey, I'm coming. I want to see inside the place," says Robyn excitedly. She's naturally nosy.

"See, I'll be fine with Robyn if you want us to drop you home." Flick shakes her head, and I roll my eyes. She hates being left out of anything.

As the cab stops outside the tall gates of the clubhouse, my nerves set in. I'm never nervous, but there's something about this place that gives me the creeps. For starters, it looks like an abandoned warehouse. Situated on an industrial estate that was emptied of all business years ago, it's eerily quiet apart from the beat of the music that carries out from the clubhouse. I pay the driver, and we get out. There're voices and laughing in the distance, so it's a definite party.

"How do I look?" I ask, turning to the girls.

Robyn teases my long curls. "Gorgeous," she says, smacking me on the arse.

I take a breath and lead the way through the large gate, which is propped open. "No big dogs," I point out, but as if they heard, three huge black dogs run towards us. We all scream, grabbing onto each other and closing our eyes, waiting for the bite of sharp teeth. The clang of chains can be heard, and the dogs are ripped back. I laugh nervously, realising they're on a long chain. "Fuck," I whisper, keeping my hold on both women as we approach the doors to the club.

I try the handle, but it's locked, so I bang hard. When it opens, a large man sticks his head out and looks us up and down. "Yeah?"

"We're here for the party," I say.

"There's no party," he replies, beginning to close the door.

I put my hand against it, and he sighs. "Clearly, there is, cos I can hear the music. Solo invited me. We were at the fight."

"Name?"

"Lara."

He looks at a piece of paper. "No one here by that name." He tries to close the door for a second time, but again I stop him.

"Erm, try, Firecracker," I suggest, but he shakes his head. "Oh," I yell, grinning, "Suicide." He doesn't look happy as he opens the door wider for us to go inside, and I do a small happy dance.

The place is packed wall to wall with men in the same leather jacket as Solo, with women dotted around in next to nothing. A woman without a top passes us, and I stare wide-eyed at her perky breasts. "I don't know if this is our sort of thing," mutters Robyn.

"It's just a party," I say with uncertainty. "Look, there's a bar." I pull them over to it, and an older man fixes me with a hard stare. "Can we have three proseccos?"

He turns his back, grabbing three pint glasses which he proceeds to fill with beer. I exchange a look with Robyn that tells her not to argue. I try to hand over my bank card, but he moves on to serve the next person.

"I'm not sure we should sit down," Flick mutters, nodding to a bunch of couches spread down the centre of the long room. Most are occupied by men and women getting down to business.

"Just relax," I hiss. "We'll go sit and enjoy our drink," I add, holding up the pint of beer and wincing. None of us like beer, but at least it was free.

"Now, he has a hot body," says Robyn when we find an empty couch. The guy opposite us is on his phone with a cap pulled low over his eyes. When he looks up, it's the man Solo referred to as his VP.

He narrows his eyes. "Christ, Suicide, does Solo know you're here?"

"He told me to come," I say.

He grins. "Course he did. I might rename you 'stalker'." He looks around, then nods towards a couch along the row. "He's there. Go say hello."

The woman he was with earlier in the ring is on Solo's lap, and she's grinding her arse so hard, I'm surprised he hasn't impaled her through his jeans. "I'm good here," I say, forcing a smile.

"Pres," he shouts, waving his hand.

"No," I hiss, sinking down in my seat. "Don't shout him over."

"Suicide squad has arrived," he adds, laughing at his own joke.

"Excuse me, I'm not on her mission to death, so don't put us in a squad," says Robyn. He laughs hard, and she blushes.

Solo comes over with the hot chick a step behind, and they're holding hands. "You came," he says, sounding surprised.

"Just for one," I mutter, taking a sip of the warm beer and trying hard not to gag.

"One beer or one fuck?" he asks, and I almost choke on the drink. He releases the woman's hand, but she doesn't seem to mind. Instead, she totters off to the bar.

"What a guy," mutters Robyn sarcastically. "You should go for it."

A laugh escapes me as I nudge her in the ribs. "Stop."

"Well, ya know, I can totally see why you want to. Dick moves, vile mouth, no respect. You should totally fuck him."

I laugh harder. "I need to pee." I stand, pulling Solo's attention from his VP and back to me. "Pee?" I repeat, and he points to a door on the other side of the room.

I finish using the bathroom, and as I'm heading back out, an arm cuts in front of me. Solo looks me up and down. "You wanted to know how I was gonna make you pay?"

"Look, I'm not into cheating, and your girlfriend deserves better."

"I don't have girlfriends."

"Even more appealing," I say, rolling my eyes. "Maybe I should have stuck with Derrick."

My comment has the desired effect because Solo grabs me by the wrist and tugs me into an office, slamming the door behind us. "If you want two-point-four kids, Derrick is your man. But if you want a hard fuck, then you're in the right place."

I smirk. "I never did like kids."

He pushes me against the door, and I stare longingly at his lips. "Why are following me, Suicide?"

"I'm mentally ill."

"Aren't we all?" he whispers, gripping my chin between his fingers. "I don't think you can handle me."

I grin. "Is that right? Then let the games begin."

SOLO

She doesn't give me a chance to process her words because she slams her mouth against mine. I don't kiss, not when it's a one-night thing with a stranger, but I find myself running my fingers through her long hair and gripping a handful at the base of her neck. I sweep my tongue into her mouth, and she groans, catching my lower lip in her teeth and biting gently. She takes the lead, something else that's never happened to me before, but I'm curious to see how it plays out, so I let her shove me hard until I fall back onto my chair.

She stands before me, her legs slightly apart and her lips swollen from our kiss. She's fucking hot. I watch as she slowly pulls her dress up over her head and drops it to the floor. She gives me a minute to appreciate her curves encased in black lace, then she pulls a condom from her bra and places it on the desk.

Her hands run up my thighs and she reaches for my belt, kissing me while she opens it. Then she's on her knees, tugging my jeans down my legs. Taking the condom, she rips it open before pulling my shorts down and letting my erection spring free. She grins, gripping it in her small hand and rubbing her thumb over the head to wipe away the droplet of cum.

I close my eyes as she rolls the condom over my cock. "I like rough," she whispers. She pushes my cock into her mouth until it hits the back of her throat, and I hiss, gripping the chair as she fucks me with her mouth. She's so forward and in control, and it's all moving so fast, my head is spinning.

The noises she makes spur me on, but I can't embarrass myself. She's the kind of girl to bring it up in front of people, so I grip her throat and pull her to stand. "How rough?" I growl, towering over her. She doesn't look intimidated.

"As rough as you can give it."

I smirk, forcing her to bend over my desk and holding the back of her neck so she stays in place. I pull my belt from the loops, gripping it tightly, and lightly tap her thigh. She doesn't even wince, so I try a little harder. "How rough?" I repeat.

"I want to bleed," she whispers, and I suck in a breath. "My safe word is 'stalker'."

My cock strains as I bring the leather belt across her arse harder, and she moans in pleasure. I release her neck, because she clearly isn't going anywhere. I bring the belt down again, and she grips the edge of the desk. Her pale skin is now red, the raised edges of the stripe marks evident. I bring it down a fourth and fifth time, then run my finger over her knickers. She's dripping wet, and I bring the belt down harder until I see beads of blood on her skin. Suicide doesn't move from the desk as I rip her knickers from her body. I bend down, pushing my face between her legs and lapping her juices. She moans each time my tongue brushes her swollen clit.

I stand and place my arm across her lower back to hold her steady. Using my free hand to play with her wet pussy, I insert my thumb into her opening as my fingers circle her clit. It's minutes before she's wriggling in pleasure and crying out. I pin her to the desk, moving my fingers faster until she's shaking through her orgasm.

I don't give her a chance to recover. I push my cock into her and groan at the way her pussy grips me tight, sucking me in. "Fuck," I pant, digging my fingers into her red arse cheeks.

She reaches back and grabs my hand, guiding it to her throat. If she wants me to throttle her, I need to see her expression. Turning her over, I slam straight back into her, shoving her up the desk. I place both hands on her throat and squeeze with just enough pressure to slow her breathing. Watching her gasp is hot, and it isn't long before I feel the build-up of an orgasm. She gasps harder, gripping my wrists, and I move faster, chasing that feeling. Seconds later, she cries out a second time, shuddering and forcing me to follow her over the edge. I growl and my legs go weak as I empty into the condom. I've never come so fucking hard.

CHAPTER FIVE

LARA

My head spins as I stand. Solo pulls his jeans into place but doesn't bother to fasten them. Spinning me away from him, he runs a hand over my arse, and it stings. "Wait there," he orders, heading out the office. He returns minutes later with a bowl. He pushes me to bend over the desk again, and I bite my lower lip, thinking of what just happened. I clench my legs together, and he swipes a finger through my wetness.

"Fuck, you want it again?" he asks, laughing. He slaps his hand against my arse, and I clench harder, closing my eyes. "Too bad, it was a one-time deal, Suicide." He dabs a wet piece of cloth against my buttocks, and it instantly soothes the sting. When he's finished, he rubs ointment into the welts and then replaces my knickers.

"You can't turn up where I am again, Suicide," he mutters, grabbing my dress from the ground and handing it to me. I pull it on as he watches intently. He waits until I'm clothed before grabbing my neck again and pushing his face into mine. "Is that clear?"

"Crystal," I say, smiling.

He kisses me. It's soft and takes my breath away. I'm tempted to grip his shirt and try for round two, but instead, I pull away and glare at him. "Don't do that again," I snap, wiping my mouth, then I head for the door. "See you around."

I find the girls chatting to Duke and another biker. "Let's go," I say breezily. They all stare at me, and Robyn arches her carefully plucked brow at me. "I'll call a cab," I add.

When I feel him behind me, Robyn runs her eyes over him, then me. "You get what you came for?"

"Yeah," I say. "Lucas is blowing up my phone asking where I am. We really need to go now."

"You're still alive," says Adam the next day when I arrive for my shift.

"Try not to look too disappointed."

"You've not seen anything of him then?" asks Betsy. "Adam was convinced he'd come for you."

I smirk, grabbing my apron and tying it around my waist. "I didn't say that, did I? He happened to be at an underground fight I went to last night."

"Since when do you attend cage fights?" Adam laughs.

"Since I wanted to pick up tips to kick your arse."

"So, what happened?" Betsy cuts in excitedly.

I shrug. "Not much. I was there with another guy."

"Whore," mutters Adam, and I give him the middle finger.

"We got invited back to his clubhouse, where there was a huge party. I've never seen so many hot guys in one place."

Betsy fans her face dreamily. "Next time, take me! I need to find myself a hot guy."

"We're going out at the weekend. I'll find you a man," says Adam.

"I need a straight man, Adam. No offence, but all the places we go to are gay bars."

"Who said he'd see her again anyway? I bet she gave him what he wanted and now she won't hear from him. We'll have to watch her mope around for the next few weeks," says Adam.

"Rude," I mutter, hating how accurate he is. "I'll have you know I'm the one who walked out of there like a boss and didn't bother to look back."

He rolls his eyes. "But you had sex?" I look away and busy myself emptying the dishwasher. "When will you learn, Lara?"

"I wanted it. Why do you assume he was using me? Maybe I used him!"

A customer comes in, and I rush to serve him. Damn Adam and his annoying comments.

At six exactly, Liam hobbles in. "Ouch," mutters Adam. "What happened to your brother?"

"A run-in with some guy over a girl."

"You get off, I don't want him hanging around and scaring my customers away."

I laugh, grabbing my bag. "Thanks."

I hook my arm into Liam's. "I just gotta meet someone outside," he says, surprised Adam let me off half an hour early. "Wait in the car." He hands me his keys, and I let myself into his shiny BMW.

I'm busy checking my phone when, five minutes later, Liam shakes hands with a couple of guys. Narrowing my eyes, I sink back into the seat so Solo and his VP don't recognise me. I lower the window an inch so I can hear better.

"Is it all there?" asks Duke, taking a package from Liam.

"Yeah. I wouldn't rip you off."

"But you'd fuck our women."

"Man, I swear I didn't know. She didn't say she was with you guys."

Solo slaps Liam on the back, and he winces because he's still recovering from his beating. "It's forgotten. This makes up for it," he says, tapping the package Duke is holding. "Same time tomorrow?"

"Yeah, but not here. My sister works here, and I don't want her asking questions."

Solo looks at the coffee shop. "Sure. Text me a place and time."

They shake hands again, and Liam waits until they've walked away before getting in the car. "Who were they?" I ask innocently.

"Guys you don't want to know about."

"Why?"

"You ask too many questions."

"I'll ask Lucas instead then," I say, arching a brow.

He sighs. "I'm doing them a favour. No big deal. But Lucas can't know. He'll stress."

"Because they're bad news?"

"Because he stresses too much over small shit. Look, Lara, stay out of my business."

"Was it them who beat you up?"

"A misunderstanding with the guy's girlfriend. I didn't know she was his."

I spend the journey home in silence, wondering what crap Liam is involved in and if it'll have an impact on me and Lucas. He was always the wheeler dealer of the family, getting into bother. Lucas is forever bailing out his arse.

When we get home, I wait for Liam to go upstairs before sitting on the couch beside Lucas. "Night off?" I ask. Since purchasing the bar, he's spent every waking moment there.

"Yeah. I'm so tired. Callie offered to do an extra shift for me."

"I was wondering," I begin, and he gives me a wary look. "When The Depraved Devils came by the other night and you got all stressed, why was that?"

He shrugs. "They're just not good guys. You don't need to be on their radar."

"The girls were telling me all kinds of rumours. Do they carry guns?"

"Why are you asking? You returned the jacket, right?"

I nod, and he looks relieved, then he turns back to the television. "I just never heard of them before, so I'm curious."

Lucas sighs, pausing the television programme and looking back at me. "Lara, they sell drugs and fuck knows what else. They're a violent criminal gang. The guy whose jacket you stole, he's the leader, and he went to prison for murder when he was just a kid. His VP, Duke, is a nasty piece of work. He'd kill you rather than talk. Stay away from them and stop asking questions. Forget you ever saw him."

I nod. "Okay. I'm gonna take a shower and go for a walk."

"A walk?" he repeats.

"Too much energy," I say, heading upstairs. He doesn't bother to question me, knowing how I get sometimes.

SOLO

Tonight's fights were a little tougher, and I have the busted face to prove it. Splashing some cold water against my bruised cheek, I examine the cut above my eyebrow in the broken mirror. I've had worse, but I'm pissed that the last guy got in two clear shots. My mind isn't in the ring tonight—it's full of her. Fucking Lara. When Boss told me it was a free night, I couldn't resist, but free nights mean anyone can enter the ring without knowing each other's backgrounds. It's a risk you take, but the financial pay-out is worth it if you win.

I grab my bag of cash and head out. I'm crossing the dimly lit carpark when I spot someone hanging near my bike. Their hood is up, so I press a hand on my gun. "Can I help you?"

Lara stops pacing and glares at me. "Stay away from my brother!" she spits out.

I grin. "Suicide, you're back." I should be mad this bitch keeps turning up, but I'm excited, not knowing what she'll do next.

"What is the deal with you and Liam?"

"Now, that would be telling." I stuff the money in my saddlebag.

"Please, just stay away from him. For me."

I laugh. "For you? Why, what are you to me?"

Irritation passes over her face, and she balls her fists in a move that makes it clear she wants to punch me. "Be a decent human and leave him alone. He's a recovering addict, and I don't need him slipping back down that road." Her eyes plead, and I ignore the flicker in my chest that wants to ease her worry.

"I never said I was decent, Suicide. Besides, you already got off lightly, and now, you're here pleading for your brother? I can't keep giving."

"I got off lightly?" she snaps. "I didn't fucking do anything wrong!"

I grip her face between my fingers, pinching hard. "Careful, Lara, you're pushing your luck," I growl angrily.

She smirks. "You don't scare me, Solo."

I release her. "That's because you haven't seen my scary side."

"Just tell me," she almost whispers. "Is it drugs?" I hesitate before shaking my head. Relief floods her face. "Thank you."

She turns to walk away. "Wait," I say, and she freezes. I'm not ready for her to leave just yet, so I take her hand and pull her back to me. "We're not done here. I gave you some information, but it's not free."

She scoffs. "I'm not paying for that small piece of information. I don't even know what he's involved in."

"But you know it's not drugs."

"I'm not paying you," she snaps.

I spin her so her back is to my front and tug her hard against me. Pushing my hand into her jeans, I feel her damp knickers. I grin, pressing my mouth to her ear. "You're ready for me."

"That's not for you," she growls.

"No?" I circle her clit, and she hisses. "Feels like it is, Suicide."

She grips my wrist, and her breathing deepens. "Someone might see," she whispers.

"It's my payment, and I'll take it where and when I like." I pull my hand free and push my fingers into her mouth. She licks them, and I slap my other hand against her arse. "Part payment will do for now. I have somewhere to be, so I'll be in touch about the rest."

She watches me open-mouthed as I climb on my bike. "Go home, Lara. Wait for my collection."

CHAPTER SIX

LARA

Days pass, and I'm so busy working and helping Lucas out at his bar that I haven't had time to track down Solo and demand to know why he hasn't come to claim his debt. It's messed up that I even want him to. But when I hear the front door open and close and I head downstairs, I'm equally shocked and excited to see him standing in my hall. Both my brothers are out, and I know I locked the front door. "How did you get in?"

"Nice to see you too," he says, then he nods up the stairs. "Back that way," he orders. My stomach does a little flip, but I remain rooted to the spot. "I've had a bad day, Suicide. Don't make me ask twice."

"My brothers might be home any minute."

"Lucas is working at Maine's until closing, and Liam, well, let's just say I know where Liam is and he won't be home for a while." That nagging feeling returns when I think about my brother and what he's up to. "Don't think about it, Suicide, it'll only drive you crazy." He's right. Liam's a big boy who can take care of himself. I turn and head back upstairs to my room, followed by Solo.

"Face down on the bed," he mutters, kicking off his heavy boots. He shrugs out of his leather jacket and places it carefully on the chair.

"Why the jacket?" I ask.

"Bed, Lara."

"And why does everyone have the same one?" I get on the bed face down and turn my head to one side to watch him unfasten his belt. He rips it from the loops, and I bite my lip, remembering how good it felt burning my skin. "Do you ever get it mixed up with your mates?"

"Brothers," he mutters, lifting my T-shirt to reveal my comfortable knickers. He grins. "Different."

"It's Sunday. Women don't wear lace every night of the week. We need to give our bits a break."

"The women I'm around do," he says.

"They must also have shares in thrush cream."

He laughs, bringing his hand down hard on my arse. It shocks me and I cry out, gripping my pillow and burying my face into it. His fingers hook into the soft cotton of my knickers, and he sweeps them through my wetness. "This isn't about you, Suicide," he says, removing his hand. I squeeze my legs together to ease the ache, and he slaps my arse again. "You owe me, remember?"

He moves around the bed and stands before me with his erection in his hand. I watch as he pulls a condom on. "Hands behind your back," he orders, pressing the head of his cock to my lips. I cross my hands behind my back, and he tugs my head back by my hair. I open my mouth for him to push his cock inside. He fucks my mouth slowly, taking his time and watching through hooded eyes. It doesn't take him long to come. He crams his cock to the back of my throat and grunts, releasing into the condom.

The ache between my legs is unbearable, and I watch in disbelief as he wraps the condom in a tissue, stuffing it in his pocket before fastening his jeans and putting his boots back on. "It's called a kutte, and all club members have one."

I smile, happy he gave me a snippet of information. It feels like a victory, like he's warming to me. "Is my debt paid?"

"Yep," he grabs his kutte. "Forget about me after tonight," he adds.

"You came here," I remind him. "And you said that before."

"We're even. Let's call it quits before you get hurt."

"I don't hurt easily," I say, smirking.

"We both know that ain't true, Suicide. You pretend you don't give a crap, but you'll see me fucking some whore and you'll cry and get all mad and shit. I'm not the guy for you."

I laugh. "Listen to you thinking I want you for anything other than a good fuck. Why do men assume all women want to settle down and trap them? I'm single because I choose to be."

"Either way, it's best we go our separate ways. I don't want you turning up where I am."

"What if it's by accident?"

"It won't be. You see me, go the opposite way." He heads for the door. "See you around."

SOLO

See you around. It's becoming our line. I let myself out of Lara's place and lock the door with the master key I use to get entry to any place I want.

I'm meeting Liam at the docks. It was handy beating the crap out of him because we got talking and I discovered he worked security there. It's always helpful to know people in these places because now I can use it as a drop-off point as well as get supplies by boat.

I arrive, and he's already unloading. He passes me the packs of heroin from a fishing boat I had come in from Ireland. I hand him some cash for his trouble, and we shake hands. "Did you explain shit to your sister?" I ask.

He frowns. "My sister?"

"Yeah, you mentioned she was asking questions."

He rolls his eyes. "Yeah, she just worries. All's good."

"I'm glad I don't have sisters," I say. It's my way of getting him to talk about her. Why the hell do I want to talk about her?

"She's a pain in my arse, but she means well."

"Do you get along?"

He nods. "Yeah, it's been just us and my older brother for years. The three amigos."

"Parents are overrated," I say.

"Between Lucas and Lara, I feel like I have parents," he jokes.

When I get back to the club, there's another party, and I'm so fucking sick of partying, so I head straight for the office. Duke follows me minutes later. "You okay?" he asks, watching as I put the packages in the safe. "How come you collected them?" he asks.

"I was that way, so I thought I'd save the prospect a job."

"We send the prospect because we can't risk you getting pulled by the cops. Why were you that way?"

"Christ, Duke, are we playing twenty questions? You wanna put a tracker on my phone too?"

"I just wanna know what the fuck's going on. You're distracted, and now you're picking up the packages."

"If I knew it would cause this much drama, I wouldn't have bothered."

"You were with the girl?" He eyes me suspiciously.

I shrug. "She's a good fuck."

"She's dangerous is what she is."

"She's harmless, Duke. I fancied fresh pussy."

"Then bring in new girls, Pres. You get involved with outsiders and you end up with kids and a mortgage."

I laugh at his disgusted expression. "Man, she ain't the devil."

"See, you're not horrified at that thought! She's already working her magic."

I throw a balled-up piece of paper at him. "Don't be ridiculous."

CHAPTER SEVEN

LARA

"Liam's working a lot of extra shifts," I say to Lucas as he chops vegetables.

"Isn't he allowed?"

"Yeah, just strange. He hates that place." I know Lucas is listening to me. He'll get Liam on his own to question him, I'm just planting the seed.

"Where are you going tonight?" he asks, and I shrug. He wouldn't understand if I told him I was going to another fight night. I have the perfect excuse too, in case I bump into Solo. Robyn met a guy the last time we were there, and she wants to see if he's there again. "The dress is a little," he pauses, looking me up and down, "risky."

I laugh. "Good. That was the exact look I wanted." I bought the short, sleeveless black dress especially for tonight.

We go for a few drinks to calm our nerves before we head to the rundown building hosting the fights. It's crowded and hot, and there's no sign of Solo as we find a seat near the ring. Disappointment fills me. Robyn kicks my leg and whispers, "Look." She nods at a man taking people's money. He's wearing one of Solo's club kuttes.

"That's the guy?" I ask, and she nods.

Then, I spot Solo with a group of men from his club and a few women. They hang off him and I'm instantly jealous. I need to quash it in case he talks to me, cos he reads me well and he'll know I'm pissed.

Robyn's guy spots her and heads over. "I hoped you'd come back here to see me," he says, and she grins. His friend joins him, looking me up and down. He's good-looking, and I take full advantage of his interest because if Solo was to spot me, I want to give off the impression I haven't come here to stalk him.

"I'm Boss, and this is my brother, Thor."

I laugh. "Thor?" I repeat.

"Tricks with a hammer," he explains, shrugging. "Don't ask."

I think he means in a violent way and not in a DIY kind of way. He places a full bottle of vodka on the table and drags a chair to sit beside me. Boss says something about collecting payments and tells us he'll be back.

Thor pours us each a drink. "What brings you to this shithole?" he asks.

"Violence turns me on," I respond, and he grins at my flirting.

"Damn, we were made for each other."

I know the second Solo spots me. He's got a woman wrapped around him like a snake, kissing his neck and rubbing her thigh up his leg, and he looks up and catches my eye. I'm laughing at whatever Thor has just said, and Solo's eyes narrow at my choice in company. I smile and wave in his direction, like I would to a friend, and he frowns further. "You know the Pres?" asks Thor.

I nod. "Sort of."

"Small world. I should go and see him," he adds, looking worried.

"Solo doesn't look happy to see you here," whispers Robyn.

I shrug. "He doesn't get to tell me where I can go. I'm free."

Solo is talking in Thor's ear, and I wonder if he's warning him that I'm some kind of crazy stalker. Clarity hits me and I take a drink of vodka from the bottle. Maybe this is fucked up. "Perhaps we should go," I tell Robyn.

"No way. I come on all your mental ideas, so now, you have to repay the favour."

"But I think Solo's got the wrong idea. He looks mad as hell."

"Less than a minute ago, you gave me sass about him not owning you. Go fucking kiss Thor, then he'll see you've moved on."

When Thor returns, he smiles awkwardly and focuses on the men in the ring. Great, he thinks I'm a nutter. We watch a few warm-up fights before Solo gets in the ring and everyone cheers. He's popular and, suddenly, everyone is thrusting money at Boss, wanting a chance to make more cash. When he gets to our table, Robyn places a bet on Solo to win. "On the other guy," I say smugly, pulling out a twenty. Boss arches a brow but takes the cash anyway.

The fight is fast. The first round is mainly Solo battering his poor opponent until he's a ball on the floor. To my relief, the referee finally steps in, and some other guy gets in with a first aid kit to deal with him.

Solo heads our way, looking proud. He wipes blood from his lower lip, caused by the one punch the opponent got in. He grins at Thor. "You ask her yet?" Thor shakes his head, avoiding my eyes. Solo looks me up and down. "You bet against me, Suicide?"

"Aren't I allowed?"

"Your loss," he says, shrugging.

I stand, wanting to suddenly run and hide in the bathroom. His smouldering look and the way his eyes call to me makes me think stupid thoughts, but as I go to pass Solo, he grabs my wrist. "Not so fast," he mumbles in that sexy, deep growl. "I've got a question."

"Make it quick, I'm bored."

He sniggers. "Thor likes you," he says, "but he can't have you without my permission."

I laugh, trying to pull my wrist free. "You're not the boss of me!"

"But I am of him so . . ." He shrugs. "Do you want to fuck him, Suicide?"

I don't, but there's no way I'm telling this jackass. "I haven't decided. I've only just met him, but like I said, it's my decision."

His eyes linger on my breasts, and I regret the risky dress. "Not entirely true. But I've told him he can have my blessing if . . ." He pauses, biting on his lower lip. "If I'm there too."

I gasp, finally breaking free from his grip, and I slap him. I've never slapped a man in my life. I've never been offended enough to lash out, but this man brings out the worst in me. "How fucking dare you," I hiss.

He grins, rubbing his cheek. "Shit, that was hot," he mutters.

"You're such an arse!" I yell.

He grins wider, tugging me hard against him and kissing me. I'm too stunned to pull away as he thrusts his tongue in my mouth. It's hot and wrong all at the same time. He pulls back and whispers, "Imagine us both."

I shudder. "Fuck you," I whisper back before stomping off to the bathroom.

Robyn rushes in behind me. "Shit, Lara, that kiss was fucking hot. What the hell's going on between you guys?"

Bracing my hands on the sink unit, I stare at my reflection in the mirror. "Don't get me started. He's a dick."

"A hot dick who totally looks like he knows how to use his dick!"

"A little too much."

"He definitely brings out the bitch in you. I can't believe you slapped him!"

I lift my hand slightly to show her how it's shaking. "I can't believe it either. He wants a threesome."

She glares at me like I've lost my mind. "So, you hit him?"

"He's a pig."

"Lara, you've seen the guys he hangs with, they're all hot as fuck. Why the hell would you be offended by that?"

"I'm not a whore," I snap.

"So, people who love to explore their sexual desires are whores?" She looks pissed, and I rush to correct my reply.

"Of course not. I didn't mean it like that. He just made me feel like that."

"Two guys who both want you? It's a compliment, Lara. Get a grip. And go apologise before he realises you actually hit him and loses his mind."

I find Solo at his table with the girl on his lap. He looks me up and down. "I'd just like to apologise for slapping you," I mumble.

"I can't hear you," he says smugly.

I narrow my eyes. He can totally hear me. "I'm sorry I slapped you," I say louder. "Even though you deserved it," I add more quietly.

"That's not an apology."

"What do you want, a marching band?" I snap sarcastically.

"I'll think it over."

"Think what over? I've said sorry, it's done."

He stands quickly, almost tipping the poor girl from his lap, and pushes his face in mine. "It's done when I say it's done, Lara. Go home."

"I'm not going home," I argue. "I don't know why you think you're the boss of me."

He waves a hand over my head, and suddenly, I'm flanked by two large men. "Get rid of her," Solo orders.

I glare, wide-eyed. "Are you joking?"

"I told you already, stop showing up where I am. Next time, I won't be so patient." The men each take one of my arms and begin to lead me out. "Oh, and Suicide, wait for your punishment," he adds.

I look back over my shoulder. "For what?"

"You don't think the slap was for free, do you?"

CHAPTER EIGHT

SOLO

"Are you gonna tell me what it is about this stalker you like so much?" asks Duke, sitting down beside me and watching the two men in the ring dance about like fucking pussies.

"Just fucking hit him!" I yell at them. "Who said I like her?"

"Cos she keeps following you around, and you ain't killed her yet."

I clap as punches finally begin to land. "Don't mean I like her. She's a good fuck, I told you. Besides, her brother is Liam Maine."

"Are you shitting me?"

"Nope. So, consider her as collateral. If he's screwing us like we think, little sis is gonna feel my wrath."

Duke relaxes, smiling. "I should have known you had a plan."

"That's why I'm the President, brother."

Breaker hands the collections he made from Liam. I place the packages on the scales, one by one, and as predicted, they're all lighter than they should be. I shake my head, unlocking the safe and adding them to the pile. As Duke joins us, I mutter, "It's light," before he has the chance to ask.

"Again?" he growls. "That fucker has balls of steel."

"And a brain of mush," Breaker adds.

"Are we bringing him in?" asks Duke.

I shake my head. "Nah, let the fucker think he's winning. I wanna know what he's doing with it. It's too much for him to stick up his nose, but he ain't dripping in gold, so maybe it's for someone else, in which case, I wanna know who."

It's been a week since I promised Suicide a visit, and knowing her brother is cutting into my drugs pisses me off enough to make me climb through her bedroom window and wait for her. It's Saturday night. I didn't expect her to be home, since she's a party animal, so I take a seat by the window and wait.

She arrives home an hour later and turns on the bedroom light, jumping back in fright when she spots me waiting. "You're here." She almost sounds relieved, but I'm irritated, mainly at myself for waiting around like some bitch.

"You keep putting yourself in my debt."

"I don't mean to," she says innocently.

I stand, smirking. "I think you do, Suicide. Should I make you pay with your pussy or your mouth?"

She puts on a steely expression, like she isn't turned-on at my words. "Actually, I'm tired. I've been out on a date."

Moving closer, I back her up against the wall. "Is that right?" She nods, looking smug. "Am I supposed to get jealous now?"

"Maybe we can settle the debt another time? Or better still, not at all, seeing as you totally deserved the slap."

I grin, unfastening my belt, then my jeans. Her eyes flick down to my hands, and she presses her lips together in a fine line. "How about I let you choose . . . mouth or pussy?" She slowly lifts her skirt while turning away from me and bracing her hands against the wall. I pull out a condom. "Good choice."

The following day, I'm in my office when Viking calls to give me news on Liam. I sent him to watch him for the last couple of days. "Pres, I followed Liam to a warehouse owned by Charlie Reed," explains Viking, and I let out a growl. That little piece of shit is mixing with my enemy. "He's been in there for an hour. Should I wait around?"

"No, you'll get spotted. That's all I needed to know." I disconnect the call and relay the information back to Duke. "Didn't Breaker get anything back on Liam's checks?"

"Nothing. Petty crime, and he was an addict in his teenage years, but nothing since. We have to bring him in, Pres." I nod in agreement. "I got Breaker to run another check on the sister too," he adds.

I try to hide my surprised reaction. If Duke gets a hint of my interest in Suicide, I'll never hear the end of it. "Anything?" I ask.

"She's got history, alright." He smirks, and I arch an annoyed brow. "She's got real issues. Two restraining orders against her. Apparently, she loves to stalk her lovers."

Again, I force myself to show nothing. "But no drug history?"

"No, unless you count the sleeping pills, antidepressants, and that sort of shit."

"So, we can rule out big brother robbing us for his family."

"Aren't you slightly worried?" he asks.

"Why would I be?"

"She's shown up at fights, she's been here . . . I mean, she does have a habit of popping up when you're around. Maybe you're her next target."

I shrug. "She's unpredictable, I'll give her that, but I'm not worried, brother. What kind of man worries about that shit?" I grab my bike keys. "Go bring in Liam and put him in the lock-up for a few days. Give him some thinking time."

The new information I've learned about Suicide has me on edge. The last thing I need is issues, so when I spot her later, hanging around outside the clubhouse gates, anger fills me. I grab Viper and hiss, "Go find out what the fuck she wants." There are other brothers out here with me, all wondering who the fuck this chick is, and I don't need it getting back to Duke.

LARA

I really am here by coincidence this time, so when one of the grizzly-looking men marches my way, I smile nervously. "I'm waiting here for my friend," I explain.

"Who?"

"Ro . . . I mean, Robyn. She called and asked me to pick her up." I point to my car parked across the street.

Seconds later, Solo is in my face looking less than pleased to see me. "I told you to stay the fuck away from my club."

I'm taken aback. "I'm waiting for my friend."

"Sure you are. I know about your history, Lara. The last thing I need is some psycho following me around. Now, get the fuck away from here before I find a way to make you disappear."

At that exact moment, Robyn appears. She kisses Boss on the cheek and heads my way with a huge grin on her just-fucked face. Solo spots her, then lowers his eyes slightly. I

don't respond to his words, because what's the point? Instead,
I head back to my car with Robyn right behind me and an ache
in my chest. How the hell does he know about me?

"Good time?" I ask Robyn brightly, forcing a smile.

"Yeah, amazing. My god, Lara, he's an animal."

My mind conjures images of Solo, and I shake my head to
clear them. "An animal you want to see again?"

She grins. "Of course. However, he's not that sort of guy, so
I need to play it carefully. What did Solo say at the gate?"

I scoff bitterly. "He was being a dick. Don't worry about it,
I'm well and truly over him. He's not worth it."

"Aww, sorry, I know you liked him." She pauses before
adding, "To be honest, I'm kind of glad. I was getting worried
about you . . . yah know . . . what with everything before and—"

I cut in. "There's no need. I'm fine. Honestly."

"And the pills, are they still helping?"

I groan, gripping the steering wheel tighter. "Don't do that,
Ro. Please don't do that. I'm fine. Everything is fine. Pills and
all."

By the time I get home, Lucas is blowing up my phone. I
answer, and he begins yelling about Liam. "Hold on, I don't
understand," I say calmly. He always loses his head over something Liam's done.

"Have you seen him? He didn't show up for his lunchtime
shift, and he won't answer my calls."

"I'll check his room," I say, running up the stairs to find his
room empty. "No sign. Maybe he just forgot?"

"Or maybe he binned off his shift because he's irresponsible
and a liability. If you see him, tell him I'm mad as hell. We're
rushed off our feet here, and I can't let him off the hook

again!" He disconnects, and I roll my eyes. The pair of them are always fighting about something.

I shower and change into pyjamas before settling down in front of the television. Solo's words haunt me. How the hell did he find out stuff about me?

Flick lets herself in and joins me on the couch. "You look serious," she points out, grabbing the television remote and flipping through the channels.

"I went to pick up Robyn earlier from the biker club. Solo said something and it pissed me off."

"What?"

"He mentioned that he knew about my past."

"Oh," she winces. "And?"

I shrug. "I dunno, he just made me feel like a nutter. Did you tell him?"

"No way, Lara, I wouldn't do that. Look, there's always a chance your past will come back to haunt you, but you weren't well then and you're better now."

"Am I, though?"

She stares at me for a minute. "Yes."

"I still turned up where he was on purpose."

She takes my hand. "That's normal behaviour. You're attracted to him. How you are now to how you were back then is very different. If you start rummaging through his trash bins, I'll get worried." I smile, not mentioning the thought has crossed my mind. "Do you crave him?" I shake my head. "Then there you go. You just fancy the guy, and showing up where he is, is normal. Didn't Robyn do the same to put herself on Boss's radar?" I nod, feeling reassured.

I wake suddenly, a feeling of unease washing over me. Glancing around, I notice it's only six in the morning. I grab my dressing gown and decide to head down for coffee, and as I pass Liam's room, I pop my head in. His bed hasn't been slept in. It's not unusual.

I get downstairs and find Lucas is already up. "Did Liam show up for work in the end? His bed hasn't been slept in."

Lucas stares out the window with a faraway look on his face. "I'm worried because he hasn't answered my calls."

Liam had a bad drug addiction when he was nineteen years old, and it took a good year for us to get him to rehab. It put Lucas's dream of opening the bar back further because he used his savings to fund the recovery. "He'll have spent the last twenty-four hours with some girl. Don't worry, I'll go and look for him today. It's my day off."

He gives a sad smile. "We've been here before, Lara."

I kiss him on the cheek. "He's fine, don't worry."

SOLO

"Bag him," I mutter. I'm tired and irritable. Liam isn't giving up anything, and I'm getting bored with every passing second. He's lost both little fingers and his blood loss is making him drowsy. He fights against Viking's hands as they pull the plastic bag tightly around his neck, cutting off his oxygen. I wait until he's almost given up before nodding. Viking removes the bag, and Liam gasps air into his lungs. "Again," I order, and it's placed back as he takes a deep breath, sucking the plastic to his mouth and instantly making it hard for himself to breathe. He kicks his legs around and then sags in the chair. "Take it off." I slap his cheek to wake him up. "I'm getting bored. Why are you skimming my drugs?"

"I'm a user," he murmurs sleepily.

I grab his arm but find no track marks for the heroin, and he's showing no signs of withdrawal. Viking checked his pockets, and there wasn't so much as a credit card to cut the crack. "You're lying to me, Liam." He shrugs. "Fuck this shit. Shoot him up," I snap, and his eyes widen in panic.

Viper begins heating up the heroin using a spoon. "No, please, I don't use that," he begs.

I pull a tourniquet tight around his arm. "You just told me you skimmed my drugs to use for yourself," I yell. "So, enjoy your hit." He's held still while the heroin is injected into his arm, then his entire body relaxes within minutes. "Dump him somewhere. I want Charlie Reed to find him fucked. It'll make him think twice about getting involved with druggies."

CHAPTER NINE

LARA

I call a couple of Liam's friends, but no one has seen him. As I stop my car outside the Devils clubhouse, I take a deep breath. I pray Solo isn't around as I buzz the intercom at the gates. "Yeah?" comes a crackly response.

"Hi, I'm looking for my brother, Liam Maine." There's a long pause, and I press the intercom again. This time, the door opens, and I see Solo marching across the yard. "Fuck," I mutter to myself.

"Why are you here, Suicide?" he barks, stopping on the other side of the gate with his feet a shoulder width apart and his strong arms folded across his chest.

"I can't find my brother."

"And that's my problem because?"

"Because he told me he got caught with one of the girls from here. That's why he got beat up. I need to know if she's seen him."

"She hasn't," he snaps coldly.

"It's important, Solo. I need to find him."

"Then stop wasting your time at my club and go look for him."

"Wow, what a dick," I mutter, turning away and heading for my car.

"What did you say?"

I turn back to face him while walking backwards to my car. "I said, you're a dick."

"I've killed people for less," he warns.

I roll my eyes. "Makes you a bigger dick."

I drive around the streets, hoping I might spot him stumbling from a random bar. Then I decide to head to his workplace. When he's not at Maine's, he works down by the docks as a security guard, He hates it, but he gets regular shifts there.

The gates are open when I arrive, and there's nobody in the small gatehouse, so I wander through. It's busy with trucks getting loaded and people rushing about. I head to the shed where the security guys usually take their breaks, but it's locked. Stepping around to the side to look through the window, I gasp in horror at the sight of Liam propped up against the shed with a needle hanging from his arm.

SOLO

I briefly close my eyes as Suicide lets out a scream then begins yelling for help. Men run from all parts of the yard to where she's on her knees beside her brother, shaking him. I'd followed her from a distance while she combed the streets. I guess a part of me was hoping she didn't come here and find him herself. The other security guard was supposed to find him, but he called in sick to work today, so Liam's been lying here waiting to be discovered.

A man wraps his arms around Lara and comforts her while another calls an ambulance. Two dockworkers begin CPR in a bid to get his heart going again. It won't work—he's been sitting there dead for almost four hours now.

I call church and announce, "We need to find a new way to bring in the packages."

The men become unsettled. Using boats was a good earner and easy. Now, we'll have to go back to using trucks and risk them being searched. It's costly and a big risk. "Can't we just buy off another security guard?" asks Rock.

I shake my head. "Charlie Reed might know we bring it that way now, and he'll intercept or cause us disruption in some way. It's not worth the risk. We can go back to the old ways."

"That junkie has been plastered all over local news," Thor announces. "I didn't know he was related to the girl."

"What girl?" asks Viking.

"The girl stalking Pres."

"She was not stalking me," I say, rolling my eyes. "I fucked her, the end. Now, back to business."

"Does she know about our connection to her brother?" asks Breaker.

"She's a dumbass bitch who knows shit about her brother's dealings," says Duke. "As far as she's concerned, he's a junkie and he overdosed. Don't worry about her, and if she becomes a problem, I'll take care of it." I nod in agreement, even though his threat doesn't sit right with me.

LARA

I sit on a hardback chair wrapped in an itchy blanket the paramedic gave me while Lucas is pacing the small room. The door opens and a doctor enters with a grave look on his face. "I'm so sorry," he begins, but I don't hear the rest through my sobs. It was expected, they told me as much when we were in the ambulance and they were pumping on his chest and filling him with drugs to start his heart. They got a small pulse, but they weren't reassuring.

We arrive back home two hours after the death of my brother. Lucas is still pacing. He hasn't said a word, he hasn't let one tear escape . . . he just keeps pacing. Curling up in the itchy blanket, I stare at the picture of the three of us that sits on the shelf above the television. Flick rushes in without knocking and throws herself at Lucas. He wraps her in a stiff hug, and then she comes to me, sobbing into my neck. My tears have stopped. I just feel numb.

"I am so sorry," she whispers. "I can't believe it."

I'd called her from the hospital as we left. She had a right to know. She loved him just as much as we did.

"It was coming," says Lucas as Flick slides beside me on the couch. He's stopped pacing, and we both stare up at him. "This day was always coming. We were just waiting."

"Don't say that," I mutter. "He's been clean for years."

"He wasn't. We thought he was, but clearly, he's been going behind our backs and using. How didn't we see it? We both noticed him working late and disappearing. Why didn't we question him?" He begins to pace again. "I mean, I should have seen it right after he was beat up."

"No," I say, shaking my head. "That was a misunderstanding over a girl. Nothing to do with drugs."

"Don't be fucking naive, Lara," he snaps, and tears form in my eyes again. Flick gently squeezes my hand, giving me a sympathetic smile.

"I don't believe he was using," I mumble.

Lucas laughs angrily. "You found him with a needle hanging out his arm. There's no denying it."

I push to my feet, keeping the blanket wrapped around me tightly. "I need some air." Flick goes to follow, but I shake my head and she lowers onto the couch again. I need to be alone.

Stepping out, I look up to the grey sky. It's cold and rain drizzles miserably. Good, it matches my mood perfectly. The streets are busy, and as I move through the crowds, I let my tears flow. People must think I look crazy, but I don't care. I hardly notice their faces as I pass. Everything feels like a blur . . . a big empty blur.

SOLO

Gripping a handful of Kiki's hair, I watch as her mouth swallows my cock. I let my head fall back on the couch and close my eyes. It's exactly what I need after the day I've had. I block out the background noise around the club and I'm close to coming when a commotion interrupts my pleasure.

"What the fuck," shouts Viper. "Get back here!"

I look over in the direction of his voice and groan. Suicide is marching towards me, wrapped in a dripping wet, grey blanket. Her hair is sticking to her face and her eyes are red and swollen. I ignore the way my heart beats faster and shove Kiki from my cock, tucking it away. Suicide glances at the ground, her cheeks flushing.

"What are you doing here, Suicide?" I bark. Duke hovers in the background, ready to throw her out on my command.

"My brother's dead," she almost whispers.

I narrow my eyes. "What the fuck's that got to do with me?"

"He said he was beaten up because of a woman here," she begins. Her eyes fall to Kiki, who is still on her knees in front of me. "Was it you? Did he try it on with you?" Kiki looks to me for the answer. "Are you his girlfriend?" adds Lara angrily. "Did Solo beat up my brother because he hit on you?"

I roll my eyes impatiently. "Not this bullshit again."

"I need to know if it was because of her or if it was drugs. Was he lying to me?"

"Probably."

She begins to cry, wiping her face on the blanket. "He wasn't a junkie," she sobs.

There's a puddle of rainwater forming around her. I groan and get to my feet. "For fuck's sake," I hiss. Grabbing her upper arm, I lead her into my office and slam the door behind us. "What the fuck did I tell you about turning up in my life? I don't know anything about your brother, so you need to go home and do your crying there."

"He wasn't taking drugs," she sobs. "I know he wasn't."

"And like I keep telling you, I don't know about it, so fuck off."

"You said he wasn't involved in drugs," she says accusingly.

"I didn't know he was, Suicide. I can only tell you what I know."

"You can find whoever did this," she says, looking at me with hopeful eyes.

I laugh coldly. "What makes you think that?"

"Because you know people." She shrugs. "You found out all about me."

"Seriously, you should leave. My VP isn't keen on you and he's getting pissed with you stalking me."

She frowns. "I'm not."

"It sure looks like you are!"

"I saw you," she announces, and I keep my poker face in play, waiting for her big reveal. "You and your VP spoke with Liam one night after I finished work. He gave you something in a bag, and you asked if it was all there."

"I don't know what you're talking about," I say casually.

She reaches for the door. "Fine. I'll pass that onto the cops when I ask them to investigate Liam's death because I know he didn't fucking die from an overdose!"

I slam my hand over her head, keeping the door closed. Her back to me, I push my mouth closer to her ear. "Oh, Suicide, I really don't want this to get messy, but you're pushing me too far."

"What was he involved in?" she asks, her voice quiet and timid.

I spin her to face me and push her against the door. "I told you, I don't know anything!"

She stares into my eyes, squaring her shoulders and taking a deep breath. "I'll find out, Solo. I won't stop until I do."

CHAPTER TEN

LARA

It's been a week since Liam passed. A whole week. It's gone so fast, yet in the quietest moments, it's dragged. And now, as we stand by his graveside, I try to remember how we even got to this point. Everything seems to have passed in a blur.

Lucas grips my hand tightly in his, and it reminds me of when I was a small girl and he'd do the same. I tried to talk to him several times about my doubts on the cause of Liam's death, but he wouldn't hear it. As far as everyone is concerned, including the police, he overdosed on heroin. I feel like I've let Liam down, allowing it to be left, but Lucas practically begged me last night to drop it. He told me it hurts too much to keep going over it, so for his sake, I agreed.

After the burial, we head home for the wake. We paid caterers to come in while we were out and set up, and I'm glad we did because a lot of people have come back, even more than we expected. Robyn hooks her arm in mine and leads me out back. "How are you doing?" she asks and then rolls her eyes. "I know it's a shit question, but I mean it, how are you?"

I shrug. "Numb. I miss him so much and it doesn't feel real. I have to keep reminding myself."

"You did well today, standing up in church and reading that poem," she says, smiling. "I don't know how you did it without breaking down."

"I'm pretty sure all my tears have been cried."

"I have a bottle of vodka hidden in the kitchen. I'll go and grab it," she says, winking and heading back inside.

I lower and sit on the stone steps that lead to the patio. "Lara?" I look up and a man in a cheap suit stands there. He's bad news. I see it the second he lowers himself to join me on the step. His eyes scream danger, and the tattoos covering his neck and hands don't help ease my anxiety. Strange, because he'd usually be my type. "My name is Charlie," he says, holding out a hand for me to shake. "Charlie Reed."

"Hey. How did you know Liam?" I ask, shaking his offered hand.

He smiles fondly. "He was a friend. We sometimes worked together."

"At the docks?"

He nods, swishing the ice in his glass around before taking a sip. "It was a lovely service."

"Thanks."

"The trouble is, me and your brother had some unfinished business, Lara." My skin prickles. I don't like his cold expression as he stares out across the garden. "And now he's . . . well, dead, we have a problem."

"We do?" I glance around nervously for Robyn. Where the hell did she hide that vodka?

"We do. We'll need to discuss this further." He hands me a business card. "Tomorrow evening. Nine sharp." He stands and looks down at me. "And Lara, it would be wise to keep this to yourself. I'd hate for this to get messy. The less people involved, the better."

My heart sinks. Lucas is dealing with enough as it is, and even if I could tell him, I wouldn't want to add to his worries. I nod, and Charlie heads back inside.

"Found it," says Robyn, passing him as she stumbles out. "Lucas re-hid it. How does he always find our stash?"

I smile to myself. As teenagers, we could never sneak anything past him, he'd always find out. "We always said he should have been a detective."

After the wake, I slept. Which is good because I don't think I've slept a full hour since Liam died. So, when I wake at eight the following night, I panic. Charlie Reed didn't seem the type of man I can be late for.

I shower and dress quickly, grabbing my car keys and heading out without saying a word to Lucas, who's taken to his room too. Maybe he's slept a full sixteen hours.

The scrap metal yard is a twenty-minute drive. Parking outside, I stare at the stacked cars. It's dark out and there's no one about. Maybe I should have given Robyn and Flick the heads up in case this guy murders me. I get out of the car, and as I approach the gates, a burly man moves from the shadows, causing me to jump with fright. He stares at me, and I move a little closer, holding up the business card Charlie gave me. "I have to meet this guy here at nine."

He nods once and pulls open the large metal gate, which clangs noisily. He leads me to a metal container in the centre of the yard which has been adapted into an office. Inside is Charlie Reed and another man. They both look up as I enter, and Charlie smirks. "You made it on time."

The other guy looks me up and down with appraising eyes, and I shift uncomfortably. Everything about this place and these men feels off. "I don't have long."

Charlie smirks. "You'll have as long as I tell you, sweetheart. Because from this second on, I own you." His friend laughs. "So, sit down and listen." I lower onto a stool nervously. "Your brother owes me a lot of money, and now he's dead, you owe me a lot of money."

I shake my head in disbelief. "But I only work in a cafe."

"That's not my problem."

"How much did he owe?"

Charlie leans forward, bridging his hands under his chin. "Twenty—"

"Please don't say thousand," I mutter.

He winks. "You got it. Twenty large ones, and I know this is a shock, so I'm willing to be patient. I'll skip this week's payment and collect double next week. Friday work for you?"

"How much is the weekly payment?"

"A grand."

I gasp. "You want me to pay you a thousand pounds per week?"

He nods. "Now, I have lots to do, so if you don't mind." He nods at the door.

"I can't pay that, Mr. Reed. I don't earn that much a month, let alone a week." My heart beats hard in my chest and my mind is racing.

He gives me an annoyed glare. "Again, that isn't my problem."

I suddenly get the urge to vomit. "There must be something you can do, some kind of arrangement. Maybe a payment plan?"

He grins at his friend before smirking my way. "You do have an advantage over your brother," he says, glancing at my chest. I wrap my coat around me tighter. "There's plenty of work for a girl like you out there, just say the word."

Tears burn my eyes as I shake my head. "I'll sort something," I mumble.

"If you change your mind, call me. The number's on the card. We can have you sampled and out there in a day."

"Sampled?"

"I don't take on girls I haven't tried personally."

I shudder and make my way out the office. This can't be happening.

SOLO

I watched Liam's funeral from a distance, though I'm not sure why. I told myself it's because Lara's talk of involving cops got me twitching, and I wanted to make sure it all went smoothly with no last-minute hold-ups of post-mortems. It was obvious he'd taken a bad beating, and the missing fingers were a huge giveaway that he'd pissed someone off, but the cops probably couldn't give a fuck because to them, he was just another junkie.

But it's a day later and I still can't erase her from my mind. So, when she passes me in the street, my reaction is delayed, trying to work out if she's really there or I'm just thinking of her again. I spin back. "Lara?" She ignores me, so I rush after her and take her by the arm. She's sobbing so uncontrollably, I automatically pull her into my chest. "It's okay."

"Why is it so hard?" she cries. "It's all such a mess."

I hold her at arm's length. "What is?"

"My car broke down, I've had the worst few days, and . . ." She trails off. "Forget it." She pulls away and begins to walk off.

"I can fix the car," I say, and she slows again. "And if I can't, I know someone who can. Where is it?"

"Just up there," she mutters, nodding in the direction her car is.

"If you give me your registration, I'll send a truck to pick it up tomorrow. You look like you need a drink," I add.

"Why are you being nice? You were a dick the last time we spoke."

I shrug. "You look like you can't take much more that life has to throw, so what harm can a drink do?"

I point to an all-night café, and she nods, walking towards the entrance. Inside, I go to the counter and order two coffees as she takes a seat. When I place her coffee in front of her, she jumps like I'm interrupting her thoughts. "Sorry. I was miles away."

"Anywhere nice?"

She scoffs. "I was remembering what my life was like two weeks ago, before Liam died and I was left in this hell."

"It's shit. When my dad died, I was a mess. It gets easier. I know everyone says that, but it really does."

"Can you keep a secret?" she asks.

"No," I say bluntly.

"What about if I give you a name, will you tell me if you know it?"

"No," I repeat.

"Charlie Reed," she says, watching me closely for a reaction. She doesn't get it—I've been playing this game for years. She sighs heavily, shaking her head in frustration. "Everyone told me you were crazy. The panic in my friend's eyes when she saw me in your jacket made me think you were a monster. But you don't know real monsters, so I'm guessing you aren't as notorious as everyone seems to think."

I ignore her attempt to get me to confess to knowing Reed. "Why do you wanna know this guy anyway?"

"He was at Liam's funeral."

"So? Maybe Liam knew him."

"Oh, Liam knew him alright," she snaps. "Enough to get into debt with him."

"Why are you asking me about this man if you already know all this?" I ask.

"Because I met with him tonight after he demanded I be at his office at nine."

"He doesn't sound like a man you should be meeting, Suicide, no matter how daring you are." Reed would chew this little nutter up and spit her out.

"I didn't have a choice. But if you can't keep secrets and you don't know anything that can help me, I'm wasting my time." She pushes to stand. "Maybe you can turn up at my funeral in two weeks. Don't wear black . . . I hate black."

I arch a brow. "You've scheduled your own funeral?"

"When I can't pay this moron his money, he'll kill me. Or sell me. I'm not quite sure."

I frown, holding up my hand. "Hold on a minute. Start at the beginning."

She lowers back into her seat. "He said Liam owed him money and now I have to pay."

I groan. "How much?"

"Twenty grand. The first payment is due next Friday, and he wants a double payment of two grand."

"Go ask your older brother. Doesn't he own a bar?"

"Which he worked his arse off for. I can't take this to him. He's done enough for me and Liam, and I'm not screwing up his only dream."

"I think he'd rather help you out of this than lose his sister a week after losing his brother."

She shakes her head. "I'm going to ask my boss if he has the two grand and go from there." I watch her gather her belongings. "I should go."

"I'll call you about the car. Pass me your phone." She does as I ask, and I input my number and call my phone.

I watch her leave. Reed would have added ten grand on that debt easily, and if Lara doesn't pay, I suspect he'll convince her to join his girls on the streets, selling her body for cash. It's a debt he'll hold over her forever.

CHAPTER ELEVEN

LARA

My mobile shrills and I grab it. Lucas eyes me warily as I head out into the back garden. "Suicide," says Solo, and I find myself smiling. "I got your car. You ran out of petrol," he adds, and I detect a smirk in his tone.

"Oh shit, that's it? I'm so sorry. How much do I owe you?"

"Nothing. I'll drop it off to you."

"No, actually, I'll collect."

"Too late, I'm at your door." I groan, disconnecting. Lucas will lose his mind.

He's already answering the door as I go back inside the house. I walk up behind him and see Solo holding up my car keys. "Dropping Lara's car off."

"What was wrong with your car?" Lucas asks, turning to me.

"It ran out of petrol," I say, wincing.

"Are you kidding me?" he snaps. "What have I told you about keeping an eye on that, Lara? What if you break down in some shithole and get attacked?"

"I didn't. It's all sorted. Besides, I didn't know that was the problem."

Lucas sighs in frustration and turns back to Solo. "How much does she owe?"

"Nothing, it's on the house."

"No, she can pay for your time. It's the least she can do, and maybe then she'll learn her lesson."

"I did her a favour."

He throws the keys to me, and I catch them. "Thank you."

"No problem. Actually, do you have a minute?"

I nod and brush past Lucas, who's tense and glaring at me for an explanation. Ignoring him, I pull the door closed. "Sorry about that," I say. "He's overprotective."

"He should be. Have you come up with a plan yet?"

I shake my head. "No. Maybe I could just do what he says and sell myself . . ."

Solo laughs. "Not happening. I'm gonna take this to my guys and see if we can't come up with something."

"Like a loan?" I ask hopefully.

He shakes his head. "No, Suicide, not a loan because this man isn't bothered about the cash. You could pay him in full tomorrow, and he'd double the price. You'll never be able to pay him off."

"You mean I'll be stuck in this situation forever?" I wail.

"I'll call you."

SOLO

"This bitch isn't our problem," snaps Duke. The other brothers around the table nod in agreement.

"Don't be a dick," I grumble. "We killed her brother and it's fucked her over. I feel responsible."

"He screwed us over and deserved what he got. At least we know why he was skimming our drugs now—he must have been using that to pay his debts."

I shrug. "She doesn't deserve this."

"What are you proposing we do?" asks Viper.

"Take it to a vote." I shrug.

Viper frowns. "On what grounds? She isn't part of the club."

"Yet," I mutter, and his eyes widen.

"What's that supposed to mean?" Duke snaps.

"We could make her part of it. Charlie can't touch her then."

Duke laughs but it's cold and angry. "This is a joke, right? How the hell are you gonna make her part of the club, Solo?"

"I dunno," I lie. "Get someone to claim her?"

"And that someone is you, right?" Duke asks.

"Why don't you like her?" I snap.

"Why do you?" he counters.

"Because she's a good fuck."

Duke laughs again. "Bullshit. So is Kiki, but you haven't claimed her!"

I groan. "Something about this bitch haunts me, brother. I can't explain it, but I just know I don't want her out there selling her pussy for a debt that she can't pay. The alternative is I put a bullet in Charlie Reed and start a war."

Duke shakes his head angrily. "You wanna start a war for a woman you've fucked a few times? You've lost your damned mind."

I don't need him to tell me that. If someone had asked me a few weeks ago whether I wanted to claim this bitch and make her my ol' lady, I'd have laughed in their face. I don't settle down. In fact, it scares the shit out of me. But I have this overwhelming need to keep her safe. When I turned her away after Liam died, it tore me up inside, and I spent hours picturing her face. It tortured me. I can't do it again. I can't let her fight Charlie alone because she'll never win.

"Look," I say firmly, "maybe I grew a part of my heart back, I don't know. But this shit is a mess. She's a mess, and we're partly responsible for that."

"You wanna talk about responsibility?" snaps Duke. "What about your responsibility to this club?"

I rub my forehead. This conversation is stressing me out. "This bitch ain't gonna stop digging until she finds out what happened to her brother. If we leave her in Charlie's clutches, he's gonna tell her shit she doesn't need to know, and then she'll piece it together. What if she goes to the cops?"

"They'd have no proof, and you know it. If you want this chick, just be honest and tell us!" Duke demands.

I feel everyone's eyes on me. "Maybe I do," I mutter, taking a deep breath. "Maybe I do want her, but it's not permanent. It's only until I figure out what to do."

"So, you're claiming an ol' lady?" asks Duke doubtfully.

I nod. Thor stands, smiling, and holds out his hand for me to shake. "Congrats, Pres. It's about time." The other brothers follow. Duke keeps his eyes fixed on me but makes no move to congratulate me. I call an end to church and wait for the brothers to file out. Everyone except Duke.

"Say it," I snap.

"What?"

"Whatever it is that's got your balls in a twist."

"I just never thought I'd see the day," he utters.

"You're reading too much into it. I feel bad for her. She doesn't stand a fucking chance with Charlie on her back. He takes pleasure in picking on women, and why should we let him? Don't we own these streets too? Are you happy he's bullying women?"

"Why would I care what he's doing? As long as he stays off our patch!"

"She's on our patch, brother. You know he's got big houses full of women he keeps drugged, and he uses them for prostitution."

Duke shrugs. "It's a lucrative business."

"Well, it don't sit right with me. We're putting an end to his bullshit."

Duke sniggers, standing. He salutes me. "Yes, boss," he hisses before storming out.

LARA

It's my first day back at work since Liam. I felt ready . . . well, not exactly ready, but I needed to get out of the house and do something constructive to take my mind off Charlie Reed. Solo said he might be able to help, but I don't see how. If he hasn't even heard of Charlie, what kind of badass is he?

I step into the coffee shop, and the smell of roasted beans fills my nostrils, making me feel warm inside. This is normal. It's safe. It's something I know. Adam looks up from where he's got his head buried in a newspaper. "Lara," he says, sounding surprised.

"I texted Betsy to say I was coming in," I explain.

Shrugging out of my jacket, I try to avoid Adam's intense stare. "Are you sure you're ready?"

I want to scream. I am so sick of hearing the same questions, and I know he's being kind, which is unheard of for Adam, but still. "I wouldn't be here if I wasn't." He still looks unsure, and I sigh, dumping my things behind the counter. "Look, I need something to feel normal, and unfortunately, this job is all I have that cuts that. Let's talk work, be mean to each other, and just get me moving forward."

I see his mind working through my words. He folds the newspaper and dumps it on the shelf. "Those shoes are ugly," he mutters.

I bite my lip to stop my smile. "So is your face."

By lunch, I'm exhausted. I've spent days sleeping, so I don't know how that is even possible. Betsy bumps her hip against mine. "Isn't that your guy?"

I glance out of the window and, sure enough, Solo and his VP are heading towards the shop. My heart stutters in my chest. How does he have the ability to make me feel like this when he's such a dick to me? When I think of how he spoke to me that day I turned up at the club, it makes me sick. He's clearly got some kind of Jekyll and Hyde shit going on, and the

Lord knows I don't have any time for that complication right now. "He's not *my* guy."

"Your expression tells me something different. And who in Hades is his friend?"

"A bigger prick than him."

"When you look that good, you can be a prick. It's like a God-given right or something."

Solo pushes the door open. "We need to talk."

I glance behind me to see where Adam is, but he's nowhere to be seen. "I'm working."

"Now, Suicide," he orders. See, there it is again, that split personality.

"I have a break in ten minutes."

"Maybe you didn't hear me!" He glares at me, holding the door open and letting in the cool air.

"I'll cover," Betsy whispers.

"Where the fuck is that draft coming from?" Adam yells. He appears beside me, and I check his face for a reaction. His mouth hangs open as he stares at the two men standing outside his coffee shop with the door open. "Oh."

"Can I take my break now?" I ask, and he nods, not saying another word. I grab my jacket and head out.

The men walk ahead, and I follow them in the direction of a nearby bar. Inside, they lead me to a table at the back of the room. I look around the dimly lit place. It's a shithole. Duke goes to the bar, and I sit opposite Solo. "I have a plan," he says.

My heart lifts a little. "Great! What is it?"

He gives me a devilish grin, and I instantly feel on edge, like whatever he's about to say isn't good. "I make you mine."

I stare at his serious face and wait for him to laugh. When he doesn't, I lean a little closer. "Sorry, what?"

He nods as if to confirm what he just said. "Charlie can't touch you if you're club property."

"Club property?" I repeat

"Do you have a better idea?"

"Well, no, but . . . I mean, what exactly are you saying?"

Duke dumps a drink before Solo and lowers on the stool beside him. "What he's saying, sweetheart, is that you'll be tied to him forever, but at least Charlie won't force you into prostitution."

"Jesus, why the fuck did I let you come?" Solo snaps.

"I'm explaining it in dumb chick speak," Duke retorts, shrugging.

Solo rolls his eyes. "Don't be a dick."

"You gotta be dumb to go along with this bullshit idea," Duke continues.

"She isn't dumb. Fuck, man, you're making this stressful."

"You think this is stressful? You wait 'til she becomes your ol' lady and nags you or interferes with the club."

I'm so confused, my head spins. I slide the chair back and the legs make a godawful screeching sound on the tiled floor. Both men turn to look at me as I stand. "I have to get back," I mumble feebly.

"We just got here," says Duke.

"Thanks for the suggestion. I'll probably go with no, but it was nice of you to try and help." I head for the door and am about to step out when a hand slams it closed again. The voices around me lower to silent. I glance around nervously as all eyes turn to where Solo stands behind me holding the door closed.

"Sit back down, Suicide," he growls in my ear. "I'm not done."

"You're making a scene," I whisper.

"You ain't seen nothing. Try and leave."

I press my lips together in a tight line and work out my options. Technically, I'm all out, but making him wait gives me a little boost. I slowly turn to face him, and although my entire body is shaking, I force a smile. "You really need to work on your anger management." I slip back under his arm and sit at the table. Duke smirks.

"Why don't you like me?" I ask him, and his cocky grin falters. He's not used to being called out on his bad attitude.

Solo re-joins us and the conversations in the bar begin again. "It's not that he doesn't like you, Suicide. But he thinks you're crazy."

"I am."

He sniggers. "That's not true. You haven't been sectioned."

"Yet . . ." I take Solo's drink and knock it back, wincing when it burns in my chest. "It's not a good idea."

"Why?"

"Because I might slip back," I say, fixing my eyes on the now empty glass. "I can't do relationships without . . . well, without losing my mind really, so it's a no from me."

Solo sighs, then turns to Duke. "Give us ten." His VP doesn't look happy, but he heads to the bar anyway. "He's protective," explains Solo.

"Is that his role?"

"Yeah, but we're like brothers, and he's worried I'm making a mistake helping you."

"He's probably right. I'm beyond help."

"The thing is, I know Charlie Reed." He pauses, letting that information settle in. "We go way back and we're enemies. The hate between us runs deep, but we've lived side-by-side for a few years now and managed not to fuck each other off enough to start a war."

I frown. "War?"

"Yeah, a street war. Gangs, dealers, they all own parts of this city, and when shit goes down, it ends with a war between us all."

"So, why would you help me and risk the peace?"

Our eyes connect and I feel like he's looking into my soul. "Honestly, I don't know," he admits, and for a second, he looks vulnerable. "Duke thinks I've lost my mind." He looks away and gives an empty laugh. "Maybe I have. You're down on your luck and it doesn't sit right with me. Charlie will force you into a world that's so far from what you know. If I didn't know you, I wouldn't give a shit. He's done it for years, and I've never thought too much about it, but I know you." He frowns like this is all new information to him. "And I don't like the thought of him ruining something so . . ." He trails off. "I can't think of another way right now, so this is the quickest solution. Maybe it can give me enough time to think of something else, but right this minute, it's what I'm offering. And if it works, Reed will leave you alone for good. If it starts a war, I'll deal with it."

"How would it work?"

He shrugs. "That's just details. We can work that out."

"What would I tell people? What would I tell Lucas?"

"He knows we've met a few times, and I fixed your car, so just tell him we're dating."

"Wouldn't Charlie just go after him?"

Solo shakes his head. "My protection would reach anyone closely connected to you. Friends, brothers, parents."

My mum pops into my head and I rub the ring that used to belong to her. "So, I'd be safe . . . Lucas, Flick, and Robyn, they'd be safe?" He nods. "Right, well, let's do it then."

A look of relief passes over his face. "I'll pick you up after work. Five o' clock, right?"

He knows my schedule, weird. "Why are you picking me up?"

He stands. "You agreed, right, remember that. I'll be outside at five."

Adam gives a sheepish grin when I return. "You stole his jacket and now you're together?" He says, "I need to take some tips from you."

"It's complicated," I mutter.

"You've been single for so long," says Betsy excitedly. "And now you've bagged Mr. Hottie himself. You're so lucky."

I give an uneasy smile. Lucky or not, I can't shake this bad feeling I have in my stomach. I should feel relieved, this could solve my debt issues, but I feel sick and worried, more than before Solo's little plan. And thirty minutes later, when I spot a bike outside the shop with a biker leaning against it, the feeling grows.

CHAPTER TWELVE

SOLO

I open the text message from Lara and grin.

Lara: Why is there a biker outside the shop?

Me: Safety. You agreed.

Lara: So he's just gonna sit out there all day? It's weird and a little over the top, don't you think?

Me: Let me worry about that and you just go about your business.

Lara: Like the dumb woman I am?

I snigger. I knew she wouldn't let Duke's comments from earlier be forgotten.

Me: I never said that.

Lara: You didn't smack him in the face either, which practically means you agree.

Me: Do some work. See you at five.

Lara: Can't your biker friend just drop me home?

Me: You can't ride on someone else's bike. You belong to me.

The words feel better than I thought they would, and I smile to myself. I didn't expect her to agree to my offer right away, I thought I'd have to at least force her to accept, so I was pleasantly surprised. I'm expecting it to get complicated when she realises the extent to which I'm going to ensure she's mine, forever.

At four-forty-five, I stop my bike outside the coffee shop and greet the prospect. "All good?"

He nods. "Yeah, man, she hasn't left the shop."

"We're good now. See you back at the club."

I wait for him to leave before heading inside. The owner smiles and offers me a free coffee. I take it, and before long, Lara steps out from the back and freezes when she spots me. "You're early."

"I didn't want to risk you sneaking out of here before I arrived," I say, and she blushes, telling me that's exactly what she was thinking of doing.

At five, we all step out and I wait patiently while Adam locks up. I hand Lara the spare bike helmet. "You know, technically, Charlie isn't coming for his money until next week. Can we start this whole sham then?"

I grin, pushing the helmet onto her head. Truth is, I can't wait to start this whole sham, and we're beginning right now.

It feels good. Having Lara wrapped around me on the back of my bike, it's like some sense of pride has taken over and I feel a few inches taller. When I stop the bike, I feel her arms tighten. "Why have you stopped here?" she asks warily.

I untangle her arms from me and remove my helmet. She does the same before stepping from the bike. "You don't like tattoos?"

She looks up at the shop's blinking 'Closed' sign and shrugs. "Sure, but this place is closed."

"For a private booking," I reply, winking.

I grab her by the hand—another thing I've decided I like—and lead her inside. Arty stands and shakes my hand. His eyes flick to Lara appraisingly before he remembers who the fuck I am and pulls the curtain back. "Who's first?"

"First?" Lara repeats.

"In the chair?" Arty clarifies before frowning at me in confusion.

"You agreed, remember?" I say to her, and she narrows her eyes.

"You keep saying that like it explains everything, but it doesn't. First in the chair for what?" She looks around frantically, and I smile in amusement.

"It's part of it, Suicide . . . tattoos."

Lara shakes her head and takes a few steps back. "Oh, I . . . erm, no . . . that's not for me . . . no."

I tug her back to me, and she crashes against my chest. "Yes, Suicide, yes."

She swallows hard and looks up, her eyes begging me, and I grin. Why am I getting a kick from this?

"I . . . I don't like . . . erm . . ."

I give a reassuring wink. "You'll be fine. I'll go first."

"But I . . . oh god . . . I don't like . . ." Lara suddenly falls against me. She's like a dead weight, and I hook my arms under hers to hold her up.

"What the fuck?"

Arty peers closer. "Shit, man, has she just fainted?"

"Great. Yah know what, do it now while she's out."

I lift her into the chair, and Arty looks at me sceptically. "You want me to brand her without her consent? Cos I'll be honest with you, Pres, she didn't seem too keen."

"I sprung it on her, that's all. She'll be fine with it."

He raises his eyebrows and shrugs. "Whatever. You're the boss." He preps his kit, and I carefully lift Lara's jumper to expose her hip. My fingers brush her soft skin and I shiver. Even passed out, she's beautiful. "Ready?" asks Arty, bringing me from my daydream, and I nod. "You better stay by her in case she wakes up and loses her shit," he warns. I smirk cos the thought of pinning her down turns me the fuck on.

It doesn't take long for Arty to put my name on Lara's skin. He uses curvy writing, and I'm pretty sure she'll like it. It's girly enough yet clear who she belongs to. I stare at it for a few seconds and that sensation of pride grows in my chest again. She begins to wake, and I hold my breath, waiting for her to fully open her eyes before I smile down at her. She blinks. "You passed out," I say. "Right before you were about to tell me you hate needles?"

"Oh shit," she whispers, glancing around. "I really hate them. I can't have a tattoo, Solo. Sorry."

"No problem."

She smiles, relaxing. "Really?"

I nod. "Yeah, I sorted it."

She frowns. "How?"

I gently brush the area around her new tattoo, and she glances down. It takes a second for her to process before she sits up a little more and her eyes widen. "You gave me a tattoo?"

"Less drama if you're passed out," I explain.

"You gave me a tattoo?" she repeats, now glaring at Arty.

He shifts uncomfortably. "It wasn't my idea."

Lara jumps from the chair and moves to the mirror, lifting her jumper and staring at the black ink. "You put your fucking name on me!" she wails. "A tramp stamp!"

I laugh. It's hard not to when she comes out with that sort of bull. "A tramp stamp?"

"Lucas is gonna kill me. It's the one thing he made me swear I'd never do. Shit."

"He doesn't really get a say," I point out.

"I swear to God, if you say I agreed to it one more time, I'm gonna . . . I'm gonna . . ." I arch an eyebrow, waiting to hear her threat, but it doesn't come. Instead, she growls and stamps her foot. "I'm so fucking angry!"

"Well, you keep whining about it, Suicide, but it ain't gonna change." I move to the chair she's just vacated.

"I can't be around you right now," she mutters and then rushes for the door. I'm behind her in seconds, pulling her back into the room. She fights, trying hard to push my hands away.

I try to keep my cool, but she's pissing me off with her dramatics, so I give up the Mr. Nice Guy act and slam her against the wall. She freezes, her eyes boring into mine angrily. "Just calm the fuck down," I hiss. "This is part of it, Lara. I can't change tradition because you're having a hissy fit. It's done. Get over it. If I take you back to my club without that," I snap, pointing to her hip, "then you're fair game. My brothers can take turns on you, and I can't do shit about it."

Her chest heaves and her jaw's clenched. She's pissed alright, but she knows I'm right. She takes a deep breath and I back away, eyeing her suspiciously in case she makes a sudden run for it. "This is permanent," she whispers. I nod, taking a seat in the chair while Arty preps his equipment for a second time. "What if we solve the issues with Charlie?"

"You agreed to be mine," I say firmly, giving her a steely look.

LARA

I swallow the lump in my throat. I feel violated, and I don't care if he thinks I'm being dramatic. In my world, men don't force women to have their names tattooed on their skin. I have no problem with tattoos, but Lucas hates them, and he hates the whole name on skin thing. Solo looks relaxed as Arty begins work on his arm. "I agreed to you helping me out until we can come up with a better plan."

His blue eyes reach mine and he smirks. "This is the plan, Lara. The only plan."

I shake my head. "You said you'd come up with something else and we could do this until you come up with something."

"Did I? Well, I meant to also add that there is no other option, no other plan, this is it. You're mine, and now the name on your skin proves it." When I don't respond, he smiles, but it isn't friendly, though it never seems to be with him. "What's the problem? You've followed me for weeks but now I'm making it official, you don't want to?"

"We don't even know each other," I mumble feebly.

He grins. "How much more do you need to know when I've had my cock pressed against your tonsils?" Arty sniggers, and I feel my face burning. "Your trouble is, you're used to being in control. Following men, stalking, spying . . . you've never met your match."

"Huh?"

"Me, Lara. You think you're the only one who's a little crazy?"

I shrug. "I'm starting to see there's crazier out there."

He grins again. "Restraining orders were created for me, Suicide."

I stuff my hands in my pockets to stop the nervous fiddle of my fingers. The way he's laughing puts me on edge. I don't know him, not really, and I've accepted his help without knowing all the facts. This is what Lucas would refer to as a Lara-ism moment, jumping in without thinking things through. I take another calming breath before stepping closer to see Solo's tattoo. Arty wipes over the L in black ink hidden amongst the many other tattoos littering his skin. I frown.

"That's not my name." Solo goes to get up, but I hold my hand up. "No, that's not my fucking name. If I have to have this monstrosity on my skin, then the least you can do is have my full name."

"There's no room," Solo argues.

"Then find some," I hiss.

We have a staring standoff, and when he sees I'm not budging on this, he laughs. "Fine. I'll have your full name."

"Bigger," I push, arching a brow.

He closes his eyes briefly, shaking his head, and then he shrugs. He lifts his shirt up, removing it, and I gasp aloud. I've never really had time to appreciate his toned chest and abs and they're not to be scoffed at. The man is like a chiselled god. He eases back into the chair. "Where are we going with this?" asks Arty.

"Let the lady decide. She's got all the suggestions," says Solo, staring at me.

I point to a clear piece of skin on his chest. Solo grabs my hand and pulls me closer, causing me to yelp in surprise. "Show me," he whispers, placing my hand against his chest. I stare at where our skin meets, wondering why the hell I can feel an electric pulse between us but can't see the damn sparks. "Get her a pen," Solo murmurs, not taking his eyes off my own. Arty holds a pen out, and I take it in my free hand. "Write it," Solo orders.

"Oh, erm . . . I'm not an artist."

"Write your name, Suicide."

My mouth is dry, and my heart is pumping so fast, I think it might stop completely. I put the pen to my mouth, and Solo follows the movement. Taking the pen lid between my teeth, I pull it free and, with a shaky hand, hover over his skin, staring at the blank space. I got a good grade in art, so I know I can make this a great tattoo if I wasn't so damn nervous.

"Give us five," Solo tells Arty, who nods and goes back out front. Solo's hand brushes my jaw and cups the back of my head. He tugs my face closer to his. "Take your time," he whispers before placing a gentle kiss on my lips.

I bite my lower lip, concentrating as I use the pen to mark out the letters of my name on his skin. When I'm happy, I take a step back and tilt my head. Solo grins. "Arty, get back in here," he says, and Arty appears.

He looks closely at my work. "That ain't bad, Lara. You should do some designs for me to try out." I grin, happy under his praise. "Suicide by Lara," he reads, smirking. "I love it." 'Suicide by' is in smaller lettering while my name is large. It looks good, and as Arty makes it permanent, the anger over my own tattoo melts away.

CHAPTER THIRTEEN

SOLO

When I stop the bike outside the clubhouse, Lara jumps off and removes her helmet. She looks pissed again, and I groan. "What now?"

"Why are we here?"

I frown, confused. "It's where I live."

"I have to get home, Solo. I thought you were taking me home."

I roll my eyes. This really is taking a while for her to get her head around. I get off my bike and head towards the club, and I hear her running behind to keep up with my long strides. "Solo," she snaps, "answer me."

"I'm gonna eat, then we're gonna talk."

"What do I tell Lucas?" she wails.

"The truth? You've moved in with me."

There's silence, but I know she's still behind me because as I step inside the building, my brothers all turn to look. "Pres is back," yells Thor to no one in particular. I don't know why they always feel the need to announce my arrival like the fucking town crier.

I stomp through to the kitchen, where Kiki is cooking. She smiles wide when she spots me. I know without checking she's cooked something simple, burgers probably, but I'm too hungry to whine, so I take a seat at the table. Lara stands in the doorway.

"Sit," I tell her, but she remains in the same spot.

Kiki places a plate in front of me, not missing the chance to run a hand over my shoulder. "Enjoy," she whispers in my ear, remaining by my side as I tuck into the greasy burger. "What would you like for dessert?" purrs Kiki.

"Kiki, meet Lara. Lara, Kiki."

There's ice between the pair. "We've met," says Lara. "Only the last time we didn't get an introduction because she was choking on your cock."

I grin. "That right? I don't remember."

"Some things are hard to forget," Lara says bitterly, and I like the fact she's jealous.

"Kiki, get the good lady some food," I say.

Lara joins me at the table and screws her nose up at my plate. "No, thanks. I'm not hungry."

"Suit yourself," mutters Kiki. She places a chaste kiss on my cheek before leaving the kitchen.

"You don't wanna upset the club whores," I advise. "Kiki especially."

"Would it ruin your chances?" she asks sarcastically.

I laugh. "Nothing could ruin my chance, I'm the President. But it'll make your life easier if you get along and make an effort."

"Well, thanks for your advice, but it's not needed because I won't be staying here."

"No?" I ask, tilting my head to look at her. "So, where exactly will you be staying?"

"At home with Lucas."

I place the burger back on my plate and wipe my mouth on a tissue. "Interesting. You wanna claim to be my ol' lady but live separately?"

"Yes."

"No!"

"You can't possibly expect me to live here." She looks around the kitchen. "I mean, I wouldn't fit in."

"You'd better make an effort to. Start with Kiki."

She looks aghast. "I can't make friends with the woman that you fuck, Solo. It's weird."

"It's not like that. Kiki will be fine. All the girls will."

"All the girls?" she repeats. "How many girls are here that you sleep with?"

I shrug. "All of them."

Her eyes widen. "And they just let you bed hop like fucking Peter Rabbit?" she snaps, and I laugh. "Not only is it disgusting but dangerous. Are they checked regularly?"

"Late to be asking me that shit, Suicide."

"We used a condom. Thankfully."

"The girls get checked, so do the guys. I can show you my results."

She screws her face up. "No need. It's not like we'll be doing that again."

I push my empty plate away, grinning while shaking my head at her amusing statement. I head for the main room, still smiling and wondering when she'll actually get it. "We're together. You're mine."

"We've been through this," she says, following me.

I grab a beer from the bar and pop the cap off. "Exactly, so what don't you understand?"

"You seriously can't expect me to sleep with you when you've," she glances around before leaning closer and lowering her voice, "just told me you sleep with the club women . . . all of them."

"All the men do. It's how it works around here. But relax, now you're my ol' lady, I won't do that anymore."

She rolls her eyes. "Great, yay for me."

"Sarcasm doesn't suit you, Suicide." I take a seat at my usual table, and she sits beside me. "Rules," I say, taking a pull on my beer.

"I can't wait to hear this," she mutters.

"When you leave this club, even if it's just to go to the shops, you take a brother. I'll introduce you to the prospects later, they're usually on babysitting duty."

"That sounds appealing, thank you," she mutters, continuing to choose sarcasm.

"All socialising events should be run by me before you make arrangements, and definitely no nightclubs or girly nights."

Her mouth drops open. "Are you joking?"

"Do you want to die?" I snap. "Because Reed is just waiting to make that dream come true."

"I owe him money, not my life, and actually, I don't even owe him. It's not my debt."

I sigh. "When he finds out about us, he'll be pissed."

"What do you mean, Solo? You said this would solve my problems, not make them worse."

"Like all good plans, things take time to settle. But initially, I don't think he'll take the news well."

"You think he'll come after me?"

She sounds on the border of hysteria, so I shake my head. "Probably not, but just in case. Like I said, we have history." I take another drink. "We'll need to get your things from home."

Tears well in her eyes when she looks at me and I almost feel bad. "Lucas won't have anyone there, Solo. I can't leave him, not right after losing Liam. He's always looked after us and put us first."

"You're an adult, and it's time to fly the nest."

"I'll do anything else, but don't make me tell him I'm leaving. I can't do that to him."

I think it over, then nod. "Fine. We'll spend most of the time here but spend the odd night back there to keep him happy. For now. But it can't go on forever."

She nods eagerly. "Okay. That's fine."

"Which brings me to the next point. Sex."

She almost chokes and looks around to check no one has heard. Shit, if she knew the stuff we've done here, she'd turn red permanently. "I told you—"

"You just said you'd do anything," I point out.

Lara scowls. "You can't force me to have sex," she hisses.

I scoff. "I don't need to force anyone, Suicide, that's not my thing. But I have needs, and you're my ol' lady, so—"

"I don't give a shit," she snaps. "That wasn't mentioned as part of the deal."

"What's the problem? It's not like we haven't already, or do you just prefer it when you're in stalking mode?"

"I was not stalking you," she growls.

"Fine, have it your way, but I warn you, I can't go a day without it so . . ." I look around the room and nod at Siren, who rushes over. "If I can't get it with you, I'll have to go elsewhere."

Lara folds her arms over her chest stubbornly. "Whatever."

I tug Siren onto my lap, and she automatically kisses my neck. I close my eyes and let my head fall back. "Hadn't you better text your brother and explain where you are?" I ask in a bored tone.

"Are you just gonna . . . yah know, do it . . . here?" she hisses.

I open one eye, and she's glaring at me again. "I'm not embarrassed," I say, shrugging. Kiki joins us, and I grin. "Now the party's starting."

"Oh my god," mutters Lara.

"You sure you wanna be stubborn about this?" I ask.

She stands. "Even if I had changed my mind, this little show has put me right off," she snaps, stomping off towards the exit.

I groan. It feels wrong, so I push the women from me. "Fuck off," I mutter. "Thor, lock the gates down. Don't let her out of here."

"Got it, Pres," he says, heading to my office to secure the gates.

LARA

I explore the car park. Cos what else is there to do in a strange place where I don't know anyone? Solo doesn't run after me, which means the gates must be locked, or he's more interested in those women than me. The thought pisses me off and I groan out loud. Why am I so affected by him? And it's not the usual feelings I get for a guy. I don't feel crazy but maybe that's the meds. Either way, the urge to be glued to his side isn't there. In fact, he seems keener than me right now, which I've never experienced.

"What are you doing out here?" It's Duke, great, just what I need.

"He's busy," I mutter.

He peers through the club window. "Doesn't look busy to me. Does he know you're out here?"

"You never answered me before," I say, changing the subject. "Why don't you like me?"

"You're bad for each other," he states.

"You don't know me."

He scoffs. "I know enough."

"You read a file on me? Big deal. That's not who I am."

"Well, it looks as if you're sticking around, so you'll have lots of time to prove that to me."

"I don't have to prove myself to you," I snap, folding my arms over my chest. "Solo is helping me out, that's all."

He gives a sly grin and steps close, pushing his face into mine. "Let me tell you something, sweetheart. Solo doesn't do anything for anyone. If he's helping you, there's something in it for him."

"Aren't you supposed to be his closest friend?"

He laughs this time. "Darlin', we're more than that—we're brothers. He's my life, and that's exactly why I'm telling you the truth. If I was you, I'd run before it's too late."

"Are you like this with all his ol' ladies?"

"Solo doesn't have ol' ladies. He's not the kind of guy to settle down. The last woman he got with ended up—" Suddenly, the door opens and Solo fills the entryway. Duke falls silent and takes a step back.

"Everything okay out here?" he asks.

"Never better, Pres. Was just bringing her back inside."

"And you have to be so close to her for that?"

"Relax, man. She was giving me sass is all." Duke winks at me, then heads inside. Solo steps out, eyeing me suspiciously.

"Finished already?" I ask, arching a brow. "Not very impressive, I'll be honest."

"Suicide, you know I could go all night, so a five-second fuck ain't my thing. But I made a decision. I'm your ol' man, and out of respect, I'll stay away from the club whores."

I press my lips together to hide my smile. "You don't have to, I don't care."

He chuckles. "Now, we both know that ain't true."

SOLO

I show Lara around the club. She asks questions because she's so fucking inquisitive, but it doesn't annoy me like I expected it to. By the end of it, she knows more about club life and the important roles within it. "So, it's like a brotherhood," she surmises, and I nod. "It must be nice to have so many brothers."

"You have Lucas," I point out.

"Our little family is getting smaller by the day. If Charlie Reed has his way, Lucas will be the only Maine left."

"It won't come to that," I promise, pulling her to stop. "He won't hurt you while you're in my care." I stare at her lips. "You know, when we first had sex, you kissed me." She nods. "I'd never kissed a stranger before that. It always felt too intimate. But lately, that's all I think about."

She smiles and presses her lips against mine. Her fingers rake up the sides of my head and she takes the kiss deeper, sweeping her tongue against mine. I reach behind her and push the door to my bedroom open. I walk her backwards until we're inside, then I kick the door closed. My hands pull at her shirt, and she breaks the kiss so I can remove it. She's not wearing a bra, and I groan. She's hot. "I guess you're right. If we're stuck together for a while, we'll need an outlet for our frustrations," she pants, pushing her leggings down.

I nod in agreement, rushing to get out my own clothes. I daren't speak in case I break the spell, and fuck knows I need this right now, my cock's painfully hard. I don't give her a chance to think before I'm pushing her against the wall and guiding her leg around my waist. "Wait," she pants, pushing against my chest. I growl, resting my head against her shoulder. "Condom," she reminds me, and I feel a glimmer of hope because at least she isn't saying no. I grab a new condom from my bedside drawer and rip it open. She watches as I pull it down my length. "Stay there," she says, smirking, and I frown. She leans back against the wall and spreads her legs. Her fingers brush her folds, and she moans, closing her eyes and losing herself in the moment.

"Lara," I hiss, gripping the base of my cock. If I don't fuck her soon, I might explode. She opens one eye. "I hate to break up the party for one but . . ." I point to my erection, and she grins.

"Actually, Solo," she begins, dropping her hand to her side. Disappointment hits me hard as I watch her head for the bed. "I'm really tired. Maybe some other time." She throws the sheets back and slips under them, winking at me.

"Are you kidding me?" I grit out.

"Nope," she says, popping the P. "Night."

I pull the condom off and drop it in the waste bin and tug my jeans back into place, then I storm out of the room. I need to put distance between us.

LARA

Solo never returned to his bedroom after I played him last night. Why would he think I'd jump into bed with him after he threatened to sleep with other women? Like I should be grateful he changed his mind. Fuck that. If he wants me, he needs to work for me and convince me he isn't going to jump on the next woman the second he gets a chance.

"Earth to Lara." Adam waves a hand in front of my face. "Where did you go?"

"Sorry, it's been a long twenty-four hours."

"How's life with your new boyfriend?" he asks, smirking. "You go from nothing to him picking you up after work, dropping you off, and posting one of his men outside all day."

"It was all a little out of the blue, if I'm honest," I say, spotting the prospect getting off his bike to greet another club member.

"And what's all that about?" Betsy asks, nodding to where the bikers are talking.

"He's a little overprotective," I say, shrugging. It sounds stupid when I say it out loud. The girls will never believe all this bullshit, and they won't stand for us being followed around by prospects. And then there's Lucas to consider. I texted him earlier, promising I'd be home tonight to cook dinner for us. I left out the part about Solo.

"Actually, ladies, why don't you go on a break?" suggests Adam. "Have the full hour. I can manage here, it's dead."

I exchange a surprised look with Betsy. Adam never lets us take an early break and never together. "Well, go on, before I change my mind," he pushes. I grab my coat, and Betsy follows. He doesn't need to ask twice.

The prospect sees us, and Duke turns to face us. I groan. "I'm taking an hour for lunch," I say.

Duke nods to the prospect. "Off you go. Follow wherever she goes."

"Is that necessary?" I ask.

"Should I ask Solo?" he retorts, and I resist the urge to show him the middle finger. "Thought not. Enjoy your lunch."

Later, I get home just after five and find Lucas is in pyjamas and he's unshaven. "I went away for one night and you turned into a tramp?"

"Ha-ha. I was tired. I worked late at the bar and didn't crawl into bed until nine this morning."

"Go take a shower and I'll start dinner."

My phone buzzes and I pull it out, rolling my eyes when I see Solo's name on the screen. He was running late to pick me up this evening and told me to wait for him, but I went ahead and left by the back door. Charlie isn't looking for me right now, so I think Solo is being over the top.

Solo: Where the fuck are you, Lara?

Me: Home. I'll call you later. I'm having dinner with Lucas.

I wait for a reply, but it doesn't come, so I set about chopping the onions for Lucas's favourite spaghetti Bolognese.

Ten minutes later, the front door opens and Solo breezes in like he lives here. I almost drop the tin of tomatoes I was about to pour into the saucepan. "What the hell are you doing here?" I hiss, pulling him into the kitchen and closing the door so Lucas doesn't hear us.

"I've come to see my ol' lady," he says innocently.

"Lucas cannot see you here, Solo. I haven't told him about you."

"Then it's the perfect time. And for the record, there will be a consequence for you rushing off after work."

"You have to go," I snap.

Solo grips my chin and his eyes bore into mine. He's towering over me, but I'm not intimidated. Instead, I'm turned on, and I know he sees it because he smirks. "Oh, Suicide, this is gonna be so much fun." His lips crash against mine in a bruising kiss. I hear Lucas's footsteps as he comes downstairs, and a strangled plea leaves the back of my throat. Solo pulls away and takes a seat at the kitchen table just as my big brother enters the kitchen. He stops dead and looks between us both in surprise.

"Oh, sorry, I forgot to mention I'd invited Solo to thank him for fixing my car."

Lucas nods and then, remembering his manners, holds out his hand for Solo to shake, which he does. "We've met a couple of times, but there always seems to be something going off."

"Yeah, the first time, your sister stole from me," Solo reminds us, and I roll my eyes.

"Hardly stealing when you got it back."

"And then I rescued you," he adds.

"You put petrol in my car."

"Still counts."

Lucas takes a seat. "So, you two have stayed in touch even after she stole your jacket?"

"I've become her guardian angel," says Solo dryly, and I give him a warning glare.

"Lucas, tell Solo about your bar." It'll keep them distracted from talk of claiming ol' ladies while I finish making the dinner. Lucas is proud of his achievement and never misses a chance to talk about it.

Twenty minutes later, I place the dish in the centre of the table just as Solo's mobile rings. He glances at the screen. "Sorry, I gotta take this," he mutters, heading out the kitchen.

Lucas leans closer to me. "Why the fuck is he here, Lara?"

"I told you," I whisper-hiss, "to thank him."

"Bullshit. You're hanging around with criminals now?" he practically wails.

"No. He's not so bad," I mutter.

His eyes bug out of his head. "Oh Christ, tell me you're not, yah now, following him and shit."

I bite my tongue to stop the harsh words wanting to escape. "No, of course not."

"And you're on your meds?"

"Yes!"

He looks mildly calmer. "So, he's a friend? An acquaintance? Your mechanic?"

"Lucas, please don't make a big deal. It's just dinner."

"With a violent criminal," he hisses.

"With a man who helped me out of a tight spot. Why are you acting like this? It's not a bad thing to know a man like him, is it? Especially after whatever Liam was up to."

Lucas pauses. "What does that mean?"

I place the plates out on the table. "Nothing."

"Lara, what are you talking about? Has something happened?"

"No," I say, scoffing. "Garlic bread?" I ask, chopping it into pieces.

Solo returns. "Get the pills," says Lucas, completely ignoring the fact Solo has come back.

"What?" I ask, confused.

"Get me your pills so I can check."

I feel my cheeks burning with embarrassment. "I don't need to get them, Lucas. I'm taking them."

"I wanna see."

I hesitate, glancing at Solo, who stares at his empty plate. The whole situation is awkward, and the atmosphere is thick with tension. Shaking my head in annoyance, I grab my bag, tip it upside down, and empty the contents onto the table.

Pens, screwed-up pieces of paper, coins, and tampons spill out. I grab the pill bottle and drop it in front of Lucas on the table. He opens it, looking inside. "Have you taken today's?" he asks, and I want to punch him.

"I take it with dinner every evening," I say through gritted teeth. He pops the pill out and holds it out to me. I take it and swallow without water.

Scooping the mess back into my bag, I begin to fill the plates with spaghetti and then the sauce. We eat in silence, and after a few mouthfuls, I drop my fork onto my plate and stand. "I'm not hungry."

"Eat," Lucas and Solo say at the same time. They look at each other in shock.

"You're sleeping with him?" Lucas gasps.

"No," I deny.

"Yes," says Solo, shovelling food into his mouth like this is all normal.

"Oh god," murmurs Lucas, covering his face with his hands. "You said this was nothing."

"Ouch," says Solo.

"It's . . . complicated," I add.

CHAPTER FOURTEEN

SOLO

"It's because I didn't lay down enough rules," Lucas mutters, pacing back and forth.

"No, it's not," says Lara desperately. "You were a great parent to me and Liam."

"Clearly not, cos he's dead and you're . . . well you're screwing him." He glances at me. "No offence."

"Some taken," I mutter, "but she's right, this ain't on you."

"Since she took that jacket of yours, things have gone from bad to worse," he rants.

"That's true," I say, nodding, "but this is down to Liam."

Lucas stops pacing to look at me. "No, it's not," Lara cuts in, glaring at me again. She doesn't seem to get that I don't care about her pointed looks or warning glances. This guy needs the truth or he's gonna cause me problems.

"He got in with the wrong crowd and they came for Lara."

"What?" he yells.

"It's really not so bad," she explains.

"She's got another week to come up with two grand."

"Why didn't you come to me? I can get that together," he snaps.

I roll my eyes at his naivety. This is exactly why I couldn't leave them to deal with Charlie. "It's not just that two grand. He wanted a thousand a week for God knows how long."

"We'll go to the police," says Lucas.

"And you'd be dead before he was arrested," I say.

"So, why are you here?" asks Lucas.

"To help," I say, shrugging.

He shakes his head. "No, men like you don't help for free."

"I never said it was for free." I grin. "Lara agreed to be mine."

"What does that mean?" He looks horrified.

"Why aren't you explaining it better?" wails Lara. "You're making it sound terrible."

"There's a good way to say he owns you?" yells Lucas.

Lara looks ready to cry again. "I was trying to keep you out of it, you've got enough on." She sniffles, and Lucas melts. *Pussy.*

"I'm your big brother, it's what I'm here for." He wraps his arms around her, and a stab of jealousy hits my chest. Ridiculous, he's her brother for God's sake, but I hate to see anyone else comforting what's mine.

"Solo is helping. He's protecting me from Charlie Reed, the man Liam owes money to. Apparently, if he thinks I'm with Solo, he can't hurt me."

"What about in a few months when he realises you're not a real thing?"

I stand and lift her top enough to expose her tattoo. "It's a little more permanent than that."

Lucas's eyes bug out for a second time as he peers closer. "You got a tattoo?"

"It's not forever, but I had to make it believable. I can get it covered eventually," Lara explains in a rush.

Lucas grabs his jacket. "I need to get some air. Don't wait up," he mutters before storming out.

"Why did you do that?" Lara screams at me as I lower into the chair. "I wanted to tell him my way, in my own time," she continues. "How dare you?" I've heard enough, so I pull her over my knee and slap my hand over her arse. She yelps, and I do it again, this time harder.

"First, you leave work without an escort. Then, you yell at me for turning up here. Then, you make excuses about why you agreed to be with me, though let's not pretend you hate the idea. And then, you tell him the tattoo isn't permanent?" Another slap rings out. "We're in for a long night."

I stare at Lara's red, freshly spanked arse and stroke my cock. She's bent over the end of her bed with her backside in the air and her legs tied to each bed post. Fuck, she's never looked so beautiful. The fact she's gagged helps because now she can't sass me. I pull her hands behind her back and bind them together with pull-ties. With her tits pushed forward like that, she's even better. I pull her head back by her hair. "Now, Suicide, tell me again how bad you want my cock." She makes a groaning sound, and I smile. "That's what I thought."

I snap the belt in my hand, and she jerks, tensing. Her body was crying out for this. I run a finger through her wet pussy, and she moans, her head falling forward. "Maybe I should repay you for leading me on last night?" I whisper next to her ear, and she groans in protest, shaking her head. "Or maybe I should take all the pleasure and leave you frustrated?"

I climb onto the bed so I'm in front of her, and she stares hungrily at my erection. "I'm gonna take the gag off, but I don't wanna hear your voice. You speak, I leave you frustrated." She nods obediently, and I smile smugly. I remove the cloth from her mouth and replace it with my cock before she gets a chance to ruin the silence. My head falls back as she sucks me into her mouth, the stress of the last few days beginning to melt away, and then I thrust up, hitting the back of her throat.

It kills me to pull away, but I'm close to blowing in her mouth and I need to be inside her. It's all I've thought about for days. Her eyes widen when I replace my cock with the gag. I position myself behind her, rubbing the red welts on her arse.

There's a bang downstairs and I pause. "It's just me," yells Lucas, and I grin. Lara begins to fidget, and I place my hand on her back, stilling her.

"Baby, I don't give a fuck if he walks in here, I ain't stopping. You made me wait too long for this." I thrust inside her, and she buries her face into the bed, groaning. "You think you can be quiet, Suicide?" She nods, and I grin. Challenge accepted.

Gripping her hips, I withdraw slowly before slamming inside her hard. She cries into the gag and her muffled sounds turn me on enough to repeat the move. I grab a handful of her sore backside, and she sucks in a sharp breath. I pull from her, then rub my hand over her pussy, and she bucks against me as I drag the wetness up to rub my thumb over her puckered, tight arsehole. She tries to stop me with her bound hands, but they don't quite reach me, and I grin at her failed attempts as I insert my thumb into her arse while rubbing her pussy. She hisses but stops resisting. I take some of her juices and coat my erection.

"Let's see how quiet you can be, Suicide," I whisper, lining myself up where my thumb was just exploring. I continue to rub her pussy fast, paying close attention to her clit while I force my cock into her arse. It's so tight, I struggle to hold it together, and with each gentle push forward, she makes small mewling sounds. I'm halfway in before I start to withdraw, and she almost sags in relief. "Oh, I'm not done, baby." I smirk, easing back in.

We repeat it a few more times before I feel her body begin to subtly tremor. I circle her clit with my fingers, sending her over the edge. She cries into her gag and as I slip my fingers inside her, she clenches against them, her body shaking more violently. Her pussy is dripping when I slam back into her to chase my own orgasm. She's still not over her release, and as I fuck her hard, she continues to shake and moan. I feel the build-up rushing to the surface and I freeze, pushing deeper until I'm fully inside her. I come so hard, squeezing handfuls of her sore arse cheeks and growling uncontrollably. I ease my cock out an inch, and slowly push back in, draining every last drop from my satisfied body. I'm panting so fast that I get lightheaded, so I flop down on the bed, and she stares at me. "You look good with your mouth full," I say, grinning. She narrows her eyes, and I'm about to pull the gag off when Lucas taps on the bedroom door.

"I'm sorry, okay. Let's talk." I bite my lower lip to stop me laughing out loud at Lara's panicked expression. "We're close, La. I love you and I hate it when we fight," he continues. I pull the gag free and kiss her, thrusting my tongue into her mouth. She pulls away, glaring at me angrily.

"I'll be out shortly," she says to Lucas. "I fell asleep. Give me a minute to wake up," she adds.

"Okay. I'll be downstairs." His footsteps retreat.

"Get me free right now," she snaps.

"Relax, he clearly didn't hear us."

"You need to be gone."

I move behind her and rub my hand over her arse, admiring the redness. She tries to shake me off. "I ain't going anywhere. I told you, I'm staying here with you when you're not at the club."

"Solo, this is my life. What the fuck is your real name?" She wails, "I can't call you Solo when we're arguing."

I snap the cable ties and then move to free her ankles. "This isn't an argument," I say calmly. "I don't argue, and no one ever tries to argue with me. It's a stupid move."

She spins to face me, rubbing her wrists. "You didn't use a condom," she states.

I shrug. "I was in the moment. Besides, I know you're on contraception, I saw the packet in your bag."

"That's not the fucking point," she hisses. "I don't know where the hell that's been." She nods towards my semi-hard cock.

I bite my tongue and breathe deep to keep calm. She gets away with far more than anyone else in my life. "I'm clean. I told you, I get checked."

"You're missing the point. I didn't give permission for you to come inside me."

"I didn't hear you complaining when you were coming over my cock," I point out.

Her hand connects with my cheek, and I twitch angrily. "Get out," she growls.

I rub my cheek and smile. "Twice you've hit me, Lara. Twice." I swallow the rage burning my throat. "You need to leave the room."

"Like hell I do," she yells.

I have her by the throat and against the wall in a second. She stiffens, her eyes glaring at me defiantly. "Get dressed and go and see your brother. I need a minute," I whisper coldly.

LARA

I stand outside my bedroom and rub my neck where Solo had just grabbed me. I wasn't scared. Despite the anger pouring from him, he didn't even grip me hard. He doesn't want to hurt me, but he's conflicted with how much shit he should take from me before he puts his foot down. I hear him pacing on the other side of the door. I don't like this ache in my chest when we're mad at each other, and a part of me wants to rush back in there and throw my arms around him.

Downstairs, I find Lucas nursing a coffee in the kitchen. I take a seat and offer a weak smile. "I'm sorry I stormed out," he says, and my heart melts. He always apologises, even when he did nothing wrong.

"I've piled all this shit on your plate," I begin. "I should be saying sorry."

"I'm your big brother, I can handle it all, Lara, but why didn't you come to me first? You went to a complete stranger over me."

My eyes prickle with tears. "I didn't know what to do. Charlie Reed was at the funeral, and he approached me when I wasn't really in the right frame of mind. He said Liam owed him a twenty-grand debt and now that debt belonged to me. How does that even work?"

"Men like him don't care how they get money. He has no morals."

"I didn't run to Solo and tell him. It just sort of came out when I bumped into him, and he said he'd think of something."

"You've jumped out of the frying pan and into the fire," says Lucas, rubbing his forehead. He looks tired and stressed, and it hurts my heart. "Charlie Reed is a dick, but Solo, he's dangerous, Lara."

I clasp my hands and bite my lower lip. "He's not so bad, Lucas. Not with me." Images of Solo's cold eyes as he pinned me against the wall just now filter through into my mind and I look away.

"That's the side he's showing you now, but what about when he wants more from you? What if he decides he wants money or something we can't give?"

"He won't. He hates Charlie and sees this as a way to piss him off. It's a win-win."

Lucas groans in frustration. "No, it's not a win-win. Not for us. We're stuck in the middle of Liam's mess and he's not even here to help sort it. I think we should leave."

"Leave?"

"Leave London. I can sell the bar and get the money wired to wherever we are."

"You've spent your whole life wanting your own business. That bar is your dream."

"I can open a bar anywhere. I can't get a new sister."

I smile sadly and grab his hand. "Why should we run? We haven't done anything wrong. I think Solo really does want to help me. I trust him."

Lucas snatches his hand back and buries his face. "Lara, you're so fucking naïve. This is a terrible idea. One of your worst. Are you obsessed with him, honestly?"

I shake my head. "No. It feels different. At first, I liked annoying him." I give a small laugh. "It was fun to piss him off. And when he sent me away, I didn't get the urge to check up on him or follow him or even stalk the girl I knew he was sleeping with. I walked away. But then Liam happened, and somehow, I found my way back to him . . . or maybe he came to me, I don't know. But I do know he was put in my path for a reason, and if that's to stop Charlie Reed ruining us, then I'm taking the chance."

"And who will come along to stop Solo ruining you?"

"I'll handle that. Let's get through this first."

Lucas stands. "I can't let you do this, Lara. I've spent my life looking out for you and my gut is telling me this is wrong. I've set the wheels in motion to sell the bar and I've got us tickets out of here." He holds up his mobile phone showing flight times. "You're coming even if I have to drag you."

I wince when Solo appears in the doorway. "Lara," he says sternly, holding out his hand.

Lucas shakes his head angrily. "She's not going with you, man. She's my sister, and I'll look after her."

Solo smiles and continues to hold his hand out to me. "Now, Suicide."

I stand, but Lucas blocks my path. "Lara, I will get us out of this. Don't listen to him," he pleads. "He's a criminal. He'll break you or get you killed."

"Lucas, he won't."

He grabs my wrist. "You're not leaving with him."

The click rings out, causing me to jump in fright. Solo's gun is pointing at Lucas's head, and I scream. "The trouble is, Lucas, your sister is mine. She agreed. So, you have to let her go because nothing can stand in the way of me and my ol' lady, including her brother. I don't want to start off our family connection in this way, but you're leaving me no choice."

Lucas's eyes are fixed on mine. "Do you see?" he asks quietly. "This is who he is."

I'm shaking so hard as I turn to Solo. "Please," I whisper, "he's just looking out for me. Put that away."

Solo holds his hand out, and I look back one last time at Lucas before taking it. A strangled sound leaves Lucas's throat and tears finally fall down my cheeks. I didn't see him cry when we lost Liam—he held it together for me, I suspect—but watching him break now is killing me. Solo tucks his gun away. I didn't even know he carried a weapon, and it's the first time I've ever knowingly been in the same room as one.

"I'll look after her. I always protect what's mine," says Solo.

"She's not property," spits Lucas.

"Why can't you see I'm the good guy here?"

Lucas laughs coldly. "There are no good guys in your world, only bad. She's innocent, and you'll crush that. She can't shine in your shadow, Solo. And who will protect her from you?"

"She's stronger than you give her credit for."

We step outside, and I shiver against the cold. Solo places an arm around my shoulder, but I shrug him off. He gives up, shaking his head and pulling me towards his bike.

CHAPTER FIFTEEN

SOLO

Lara has been quiet since things with her brother exploded two days ago. She's hardly eaten or spoken, and I hate to admit it, but I miss her sassy mouth. I'd even let her slap me a third time if it would make her smile.

I bang the gavel on the table to get the guys' attention. Once it's quiet, I sit down in my chair. "We make our first move tonight," I announce. "Boss signed me up for an underground fight where Charlie Reed will be. It's not our usual stomping grounds, so we need to be alert."

"By move, you mean what?" asks Viking.

"I mean it's the first time I'll be making it clear I've claimed Lara. By the end of the night, Reed will know she belongs to me, and he'll realise he can't come for her without bringing himself a war."

"And what if it's a war he's after?" asks Viper.

"Then a war is what he'll get. He's got a lot to lose, including the docks."

"What's the end plan?" asks Duke. "Cos the docks will triple our workload, and if anyone else steps in, they might be more hassle than Reed."

He's right, I don't want the docks, but I can't let another gang step up and run it for that reason. Reed might be a dick, but he stays out of my way and that suits me. "Let's just hope seeing me and Lara together is enough to shut him the fuck up. He can carry on in his lane, and we'll continue in ours." I take a deep breath. "Anymore business?" No one speaks so I slam the gavel on the table, ending church.

The men clear out, but Duke hangs back. "You missed the part where you've fallen for the junkie's sister."

"I told you, there's something about her, but once she's out of my system and Reed is off her back, we'll go back to normal. I need the men to stay focussed tonight in case this goes wrong, and he does something stupid."

"I don't think he'll want Lara that badly," he says dryly.

I roll my eyes. His hatred for her is annoying. "But he might still want his money and we're removing his free meal ticket. At the fight, when I'm in the ring, you'll need to leave Lara alone for a few minutes. We need an opportunity for him to speak to her so she can relay the information I feed her."

"Are you telling her the plan?"

I shake my head. "No, she'll only panic. Don't leave her long enough to get hurt or worse, taken."

LARA

I'm half asleep when the bed dips and Solo presses himself against me. "I'm tired," I mutter, shifting away. He hooks an arm around my waist and tugs me back into position, pushing his erection at my entrance.

"It's the middle of the day," he says, groaning in pleasure as he enters me. "You're in my bed naked, so you're giving me mixed signals."

He's ignored my blatant mood at the way he treated Lucas and fucked me more times than I've ever been fucked in a short space of time. But it doesn't matter how mad I am with him, I still can't turn him away, and that worries me. What is it about him that has me hooked, hoping he comes to my bed every night and doesn't turn to Kiki or one of the others? I crave his hands on me in any way I can get them, and it doesn't matter that he spoke to me like crap or that he grabbed me up. I even made excuses to myself about deserving it after I hit him. That alone tells me how toxic this is. But I can't stop it—I want him more than I don't.

Solo chases his release like an animal, holding me down and fucking me until his throat is hoarse from groaning. I've never met anyone like him. He's insatiable, never quite satisfied until he's fucked me three or four times a day. And because I don't come before him, he then turns me onto my back and buries his face between my legs, not giving up until I'm crying through my own release. That just makes him hard again, and I have to stop him from fucking me a second time. My body really can't take anymore right now.

I push him away and head for the walk-in shower. He lies on his back, placing his arms behind his head to watch me. "We're going out this evening," he announces.

It's the last thing I want to do. "I'm not in the mood."

"Then get in the mood."

"Take someone else. Kiki maybe."

He sighs, irritated by my suggestion. "I'm taking you. I want my ol' lady beside me when I fight."

I look over to him. "You're fighting?"

"I haven't been in the ring for a week, at least. I need to get rid of this energy before I exhaust your body completely."

I arch a brow. "I was wondering if you're always like this."

He laughs. "Fighting helps."

Later, once my hair is curled and my makeup is in place, I pull on a short black midi dress and my heeled boots. Solo steps into the room, stopping to take in the sight of me up and dressed, and relief floods his face. Maybe he was expecting another argument, but I'm eager to tire him out, and if fighting works, I'm there.

"You're missing something," he says, holding up something leather and moving towards me. He runs a finger over my bare arm before placing a cropped leather jacket over my shoulders. "Much better." ·

I slip my arms in. "I like it," I say, turning sideways and staring in the mirror. I catch a glimpse of the club emblem on the back and stop. 'The Depraved Devils MC' is in big, bold letters around the skull motif, and across the top it says 'Property of Solo'. I'm surprised and my face shows it.

"Part of the package," he says, shrugging.

"It makes quite the statement. Do all ol' ladies wear these?"

"Usually, although there aren't any here at the moment."

"Why?"

"The guys haven't settled. It's a big deal taking an ol' lady."

He turns me to face him, and for a second, his eyes look full of something . . . pride, maybe? But he kisses me on the head and then turns away, taking my hand and leading me downstairs to the club bar.

A few of the men whistle, and Solo holds my hand above my head and spins me around so they can see the jacket. A few more whistles and cheers assault my ears, and Solo grins, hooking an arm over my shoulders and pulling me into his side. It's only Duke who looks pissed.

I hear the clicking of heels behind me and inwardly groan. The club girls must have a full view of the jacket, so I brace myself for a catty comment, but nothing comes. Instead, they pass me like I'm not even there, which suits me just fine.

We go to a different underground place, not the one where I used to watch Solo fight. The atmosphere feels different here. There are less women and lots more men, and when we arrive, everyone seems to pay attention to us. Solo knows a lot of them, and they either shake hands or bump fists, but I get the impression it's all a show and none of these men actually like each other. We're shown to a back room where Solo can warm up and get changed. Duke sticks with us, and although I'd rather not be around him, I feel safer in here than out there.

"So," says Solo, taking my hands and looking at me. "Surprise, Charlie Reed is here tonight."

My blood runs cold. "Huh?"

"You don't have to do anything. You just have to keep the jacket on and stick to my side."

"What about when you're fighting?" I almost screech in panic.

"Duke will be with you."

I glance at Duke, who looks equally as unhappy about that news. "I'll just stay in here," I decide.

"Nuh-uh. He needs to know who you belong to."

I cross my arms and shudder. "Please stop saying that."

"You're safe with us, so just act normal. If he does manage to speak to you—"

"Oh my god," I mutter.

"Then you'll need to be clear that we've been a thing since before your brother died. I want you to lie and tell him we've been together for a couple of months. Say Liam didn't know because you kept it a secret, and you didn't mention it to him when he came for his debt because you didn't think it was important. I need him to think you're blind to the darker side of our world."

"But he won't get to talk to me, will he, because you won't leave me."

He kisses me on the lips. "Just in case is all."

CHAPTER SIXTEEN

LARA

The fights pass in a blur, mainly because I can't relax. I find myself constantly looking around for Charlie Reed. It doesn't matter how many times Solo growls in my ear to chill out, I just can't steady my pounding heart, so when he gets up to head in the ring, I practically cling to him like he's my lifeline. He glares at me and begins to peel my fingers from his arm. "Lara, stop. Nothing bad will happen. Stay with the guys."

I watch him stomp away and lower back into my seat. Glancing around, I notice most of the guys have gone off to the bar. Duke is busy on his mobile when he suddenly looks up and smiles awkwardly. "I have to get this."

"But you can't leave me," I say, standing with him.

"Lara, I haven't even seen Reed, I doubt he's here. I'll be right outside. Don't move from this spot."

I nod nervously, swallowing down the huge lump in my throat. The fight begins, and I try my hardest to focus on Solo. The other guy is getting a few hits, which is strange considering Solo usually pounds his opponents straight away.

I feel a presence at my back and stiffen. "Get up without a fuss," hisses Reed. I look around frantically, trying to get the attention of Rock, who's not too far away, but he's laughing at something Kiki is saying. I stand on shaky legs. "Good girl. This way." Reed leads me to the passage that connects the change rooms, slamming me hard against the wall, and one of his men sneers while blocking the doorway back to the ring. "You wanna tell me what the fuck's going on?"

I smile awkwardly. "I still have a couple of days to pay, right?"

"I mean about your boyfriend," he hisses.

"Oh, Solo? Do you guys know each other?" I ask, innocently.

"Are you taking the piss?" he growls, then looks at his friend. "Is she taking the piss?" he asks him, but the guy shrugs. Reed grabs my throat, though it's not in the same way Solo does it. His fingers dig into my skin, and I try to pull them from the death grip they have on me. "Your little boyfriend and I go way back."

I cough and try to answer, but when it's clear I can't, he releases me and I gasp. "I've only been seeing him a few months."

"Funny because Liam never mentioned it."

"He didn't know. My brothers are protective."

"I'm not buying it," he snaps, slamming his hand against the wall right above my head. I flinch. "If you're his ol' lady, where's your tattoo?" I point to my hip. "Show me."

The thought of exposing my underwear to this creep makes me shudder, but I don't want him to hurt me, so I lift the dress and show him the tattoo. "Fuck," he growls. "Have you told him about the money you owe me?" I shake my head. "Good. Don't tell him about this little meeting either or I'll cut you in two. Is that clear? He should be more careful with his property." He storms off, and I sag with relief, rubbing my throat.

The door opens and Duke rushes towards me. "What the hell are you doing here? I thought I told you to stay put."

"And I thought you weren't supposed to leave my side," I snap, pushing past him and going back to my seat.

Solo is stepping out of the ring, watching me closely as he approaches. "You okay?"

"I want to go."

"Not yet, we have to be seen."

"He's seen us. Your work here is done. I want to go."

He smirks, leaning close. "I don't know why you think you're the boss of me, Suicide. Keep up with your smart mouth and I'll take it outside for a fuck."

I lean back and give him my best defiant glare. "I showed Reed my underwear."

Solo's face darkens. "What?"

He heard me, but he's daring me to repeat it. I smirk. "He wanted to see my tattoo and there was no other way." Solo grabs my upper arm and hauls me to my feet. I smile. "Now, can we go?"

I'm marched out the building and shoved towards Solo's bike. I'm not convinced the fight worked in tiring him out and his erratic driving proves as much. I cling for dear life as he weaves in and out of traffic. Once we're back at the clubhouse, we barely make it through the door before he's picking me up and pushing me against the wall. "You won't like that side of me, Suicide," he hisses, tearing my knickers in two and stuffing them in his pocket. He pushes into me, and I cry out, gripping his shoulders as jealousy rips through him and he takes it out on me. He comes in minutes, burying his head in the crook of my neck and breathing heavily.

"You said I was safe," I mutter.

"Where was Duke?" He runs a finger over the marks on my neck left by Reed.

"Taking a call."

"And the others?"

"Busy, I don't know, Solo. You said you'd keep me safe and you didn't. What if he comes after me? He wasn't happy when I told him we were a thing."

Solo smiles. "Good."

"Not good. I think I'm in more danger now than ever. You've painted a fucking target on my back."

Solo pulls from me and tucks himself away. "Nothing happens without me wanting it to, Suicide. Remember that."

"What's that mean?"

"It means, Reed only got to you because I let it happen."

Realisation hits me and I stare open-mouthed. Solo goes behind the bar and pours himself a drink. He does that a lot, gets himself something but not me. "You set me up?"

"I needed him to know we were a thing."

"And the big fucking letters on my back weren't enough?" I scream, ripping the jacket off and throwing it at him. He catches it and places it on the bar.

"Careful, Suicide, let's not repeat past mistakes."

"He's gonna come for me, isn't he?" Solo shakes his head. "I don't believe you. How can I trust you after tonight?"

"What choice do you have?" he asks.

"I need air," I mutter, stepping back outside.

I wait a few minutes. The gates don't close and he doesn't come after me, so I edge towards the gate. When I'm almost there, I look back. He's nowhere to be seen. He must trust me to stay here after my little run-in with Reed. I make a run for it, getting halfway down the road before kicking off my heels and continuing until a cab passes. I wave frantically, and he stops. Once in the car, I call Robyn. Solo knows Flick lives next door to me, so he'll look there, but he doesn't know where Robyn lives and she's got a posh apartment with security at the entrance.

"Stranger," says Robyn when she answers.

"Can I crash with you?" I ask.

"Like you need to ask."

"Don't tell anyone, not even Flick."

SOLO

I give Lara time to cool off before heading out after her. Glancing around, the car park is empty. I take a walk round the back but she isn't there either. I start to panic when I realise the gates are still wide open. I was so desperate to fuck away the jealousy, I didn't push the button for the gates. Fuck.

I call her, but she cancels it. I try again and the same thing happens. At least she's seeing my calls, which means Reed hasn't got her . . . yet. I text her.

Me: Come back, Lara. It's not safe.

Lara: I'm not safe with you either.

Me: You are. I wouldn't have let anything bad happen. I was in control. I head back inside, gripping my phone tightly in my hand while I wait for her reply.

Lara: He saw my knickers. He grabbed my throat and not in the kinky fuckery way.

Me: I don't want to have to hunt you down, Lara. It's not going to end well.

She doesn't reply and now I'm left with thoughts of Reed staring at her underwear and squeezing her throat. I growl, hitting the wall and busting my hand. Duke comes in followed by the others. "We were looking for you," he says, glancing at my hand. Kiki grabs it to take a closer look. "Get the Pres a drink," Duke shouts. "Kiki, go get the kit to clean him up," he adds, and she rushes off. "What's going on with you?" he asks more quietly.

"Lara made a run for it," I mutter.

"Right, well, maybe that's for the best, Pres. It ain't exactly a match made in heaven."

"What's that supposed to mean?" I snap.

"She ain't used to this life. Find a woman who is, it's less hassle. Besides, if your plan's worked, Reed will stay well away from her and we can all live happily ever after."

He stomps off as Kiki returns and pulls me to sit on a bar stool. She leans closer than necessary to clean the cut below my eye. I had to drag my fight out earlier to give Reed time to make his move. "If your ol' lady isn't around, I could keep you busy," she whispers, pushing her tits against me.

"I'm not in the mood, Ki," I mutter.

She pouts. "I've never seen you like this before. Duke said it was nothing, just part of a plan."

I stand abruptly. "Well, he shouldn't be shooting his mouth off."

"Breaker," I yell, and he appears. "Find Lara. Track her phone, get me the names of every person she's ever fucked . . . I don't care how, just do it." He nods and rushes off to the office.

"You really like this girl, don't yah?" asks Viper in a low voice.

"Something about her, Vipe," I mutter, scrubbing my hands over my tired face.

He slaps me on the back. "Ain't it about time you started listening to this," he says, tapping my chest over my heart, "instead of the VP?"

"Duke knows me," I say, sighing. "He knows what's best for me and the club."

Viper shrugs. "Does he? All I see is you pushing the one thing away that could make you happy, and he's the driving force behind that. Lara ain't so bad. I reckon we could use a good woman around here to help out. If she can look after our Pres too, that's a bonus."

"I'm different when she's around. Like I can breathe a little easier," I admit. "I don't like the thought of her being with anyone but me. I wanna tear the world apart right now just to find her."

Viper grins. "Sounds like you need her, Pres. Keeping her is the hard part. You gotta tell her how you feel instead of making her feel like a transaction or a piece of property. And set the VP straight—he needs to know she's here for good."

I nod but hesitate before asking, "What if she doesn't want to stay?"

"She does. You just gotta treat her better."

LARA

I made it a whole night without Solo turning up, but it made no difference because I didn't sleep a wink, expecting him to appear unannounced. I borrow some of Robyn's clothes for work and turn up on time. Adam almost chokes on his coffee. "Did you shit the bed?"

"Don't mess with me today, Adam. I have a headache and I didn't sleep."

"Everything alright?" His kindness is too much and a stray tear rolls down my cheek. "Take that as a no."

"I've just had a lot going on."

"Sit, let's have a coffee before we open up."

"I'm starting to worry about you," I say, sitting down. "You've let me leave early, take long lunches, have a coffee and chat . . . what's wrong with you?"

He places a coffee in front of me and joins me. "Maybe I'm getting kind in my old age." I smile because he's thirty, hardly old. "Is this to do with the biker?"

"Solo is so intense. Duke hates me, the club girls are bitches, and it's clear I'm not welcome at their stupid club."

"Hunny, you realise you outrank those bitches?"

"I don't think so. I'm like the new girlfriend that everyone hates."

"And Duke's giving you a hard time?"

I nod, wiping my nose on a napkin. "He's had a problem with me from the start. Last night, he was supposed to watch over me and he didn't. I got caught up in stuff that I shouldn't have," I try to explain without giving too much away.

"It sounds to me like you need a helping hand," states Adam. "I might be mean to you, but it doesn't mean anyone else can be. Those club girls need putting in their place. Choose a time when Solo is around and let them know he's your man, and that if they don't back the fuck off, you're kicking them out. You're above them in the club, you can do that. And you need something to hold over Duke. I'm going to tell you to take a long lunch at twelve. I want you to pop back in at ten past and come into the back room. I'll have something for you to shut Duke up."

I smile. "Thanks, Adam."

"What are bitches for?" he asks, winking. "Now, get some work done. This place doesn't open itself."

Despite our fight, Solo still sends a prospect to shadow me. It makes me feel safer, and as we open the door to the sandwich shop at lunchtime, I pause and Betsy looks back at me. "Shit, I forgot my bag. Give me a minute," I say.

"I can pay," she offers.

"No, I need my phone anyway. Order for me and I'll be five minutes." I hear the prospect groan as I head back to work which is just up the road. As I enter, I notice the 'Closed' sign is on. I check my watch. It's ten past, but I have no idea why Adam was so specific and why he couldn't just tell me what he has on Duke.

The prospect waits outside as I make my way through the shop to the back room. I push the door open and freeze. My mouth falls open and I must make some kind of sound because both men stop what they're doing. Adam smirks as Duke withdraws his erection from Adam's backside. I don't know why I continue to stare in shock because it's not something I want to see, but it's like I'm glued to the spot. Duke hurriedly fastens his jeans, and Adam does the same. "Lara, it's not what it seems," Duke explains.

I stare at his panic-stricken face. He's desperate for me to fall for his bullshit. "Was it him?" I ask Adam. "Was he the Depraved Devil you were screwin'?"

Adam nods. "It stopped for a while, but we saw each other again when Solo came here for you."

"Bullshit," growls Duke. "Lara, that's not true. This is the only time. It's never happened before."

"Adam, could you give us a minute?" I ask, and he leaves the room. "That's why you hate me?" I ask, and Duke avoids my eyes. "You love him. You love Solo."

"Don't talk shit. He's my President."

"It makes sense now."

"You two would never work," he snaps. "He's like you, gets obsessed. He tracked you down within half an hour of you leaving last night and sat outside your friend's house the entire night."

My heart swells. He kept me safe even though we were fighting. Not only that, but he gave me space. He didn't charge in and fuck sense into me, maybe he's learning. "There's been others?" I ask.

"Just one," he mumbles.

"Where is she now?"

He hesitates, and I arch a brow, reminding him I have all the power here. "Fine, but you didn't get any of this from me. She's dead. She got caught up between Reed and Solo."

"What?" I screech.

"Chas was Charlie's girl, and Solo took her. He ended up falling for her but then she went back to Charlie. It tore Solo up. He followed her, took his eye off the ball with the club. It nearly ruined us all, but he was obsessed."

"How did she die?"

"A hit and run."

"Accident?" I push.

"Honestly, I don't know. Still to this day, I don't know. It could have been Charlie, but it also could have been Solo. Neither wanted the other to have her."

"Solo wouldn't," I mutter.

"You don't know him," snaps Duke. "He's not the type of guy to buy you flowers and give you kids. If you wanna stay with him, you need to realise he's not a good guy."

"You're meant to be his VP," I snap.

"I want what's best for him and that's not you."

"Well, you're wrong. I'm gonna prove to you how wrong, but you're gonna back the fuck off because if you don't start being nice, I'm gonna share your little secret."

"You think Solo would believe you over me?" He scoffs.

I grin. "I don't know, but are you willing to find out?"

SOLO

I listened to Viper. I respected Lara's need for space and I gave it to her. It was the hardest thing ever, to sit outside that fucking apartment all night knowing she was inside. I watched her go to work, then sent a prospect to stand over her, but now, as she makes her way back to that posh apartment after she finished her shift, I decide I'm done being patient.

I wait for a couple to pass before pouncing, wrapping my arm around her waist and covering her mouth with the other. "Did you miss me, Suicide?" I growl in her ear. She stops struggling, and I release her.

"Christ, why can't you be normal and just call me to meet you?" she cries.

"Doesn't sound like fun."

"Try it sometime, you'll be surprised. Why are you following me?"

"Because—"

She holds a hand up. "Do not say I belong to you or I might scream."

"I miss you."

We stare at each other and a small smile tugs on her lips. I'm relieved I've said the right thing because I really didn't want to throw her over my shoulder and make a scene. "I thought you might have spent the night getting reacquainted with Kiki."

I shake my head and grab her hand, placing it over my semi hard cock. "It's been in this state since you left," I tell her, and she grins. "I need you to come home."

"I quite liked the peace." She smirks. "Nobody prodded me in the early hours."

I kiss her, really kiss her, stealing her breath. "I know because I was right out here making sure no booty call came to your rescue," I whisper against her mouth. "Please come home. I'm sorry."

She sucks in a surprised breath. "Did you just apologise?"

"I'll deny it if anyone asks."

I can't wait to get her into bed, but first, there's someone she needs to see, and as I lead her into the kitchen, I shake hands with Lucas. He doesn't look happy to see me but beams when he sets eyes on his sister. She throws her arms around him, and he spins her. "I missed you so much," she cries.

"I'm sorry, Lara. So sorry for upsetting you like that."

"I'm just glad to see you," she says as he sets her back on the ground.

Lucas looks at me. "Thanks for calling me to arrange this."

"You did this?" asks Lara, grinning wider.

"You were miserable without him. I want you to be happy."

I leave them to catch up and go back through to the bar. It's lively, despite it being only six o' clock. Duke's at our usual table with his back to everyone, staring down at his empty glass. I sit down, and he jumps like he didn't hear me coming.

"Good job I wasn't coming to slit your throat," I joke, but it doesn't raise a smile. "You okay?"

"Why wouldn't I be?"

Kiki places a drink in front of me and gives a sexy smile before joining the rest of the club girls who are dancing to whatever shit they have blaring out from the jukebox. "You don't look in the party mood," I point out.

He glances around like it's the first time he's realised he's in a room full of people. "It's fucking six o' clock," he snaps. "What the hell is everyone celebrating?"

"Does this lot need a reason?" I ask, laughing.

"Yeah, actually, they do, cos I'm sick of this," he growls, standing. He marches over to the jukebox and rips the power line out. The room falls silent, all eyes on Duke. "If you're bored, I can find everyone a fucking job to do," he warns. "Clear out and look busy or you'll all be on runs for the rest of the week." Some of the guys begin to clear out, muttering to each other.

I arch a brow as he re-joins me. "Since when did you hate a good party?"

"Since I realised we do that more than we pull in the money. These fuckers need to focus more on work and less on pussy. Skank pussy at that," he utters, giving the women the side-eye.

"Jesus, what hit you in the balls?"

"Don't you get sick of it?" he asks. "The constant drinking, the shit music, the hangovers?"

I shrug. "Never really thought about it, but when I'm not in the mood, I sit in my office and block it out."

"I guess it's why you're falling for Lara, right?"

It's the first time he's said something without a bitchy comment. "Maybe. She certainly makes me look at life differently."

He looks me in the eye. "How?"

I shift uncomfortably. We don't often have heart-to-hearts, and never about women. "I have to think of her. I didn't know I was doing it, but it sort of snuck in naturally." I check his expression to make sure he ain't laughing at me. He looks interested, so I continue. "It's little changes, like I don't get wasted when I'm around Kiki in case I make a stupid decision. Lara is always at the back of my mind, and when she's not here, I have to fight the urge to go find her, even if it's just so I can see with my own eyes that she's okay."

"Like last night?" he asks. I nod, not realising he knew I was gone.

"I know you think we're not right for one another," I begin, "but we get each other. She'll get used to this life. She already is. All I know is, right now, I can't let her go."

"Like Chas?" he asks cautiously.

I look away, shaking my head. "No, nothing like her," I say bitterly.

Kiki comes back and tops up our drinks. "Pres, can I have a word?" I'm about to say no, mainly because I feel like I'm getting Duke on side with the whole me and Lara situation, but he stands.

"I'm gonna head out on the road for a bit," he says, shaking my hand. "I'm happy for you, Pres. Honest." It's a relief to hear.

Kiki drags a stool so she's right beside me, our knees touching. "What is, Ki?" I ask warily.

"I miss you," she whispers, and I roll my eyes. "Please just hear me out," she begs, and I glance at the kitchen door. Lara is still in there, so I nod. If I don't hear it now, she'll just keep pushing. "I gave my everything. Whenever you clicked your fingers, I came, literally." She giggles. "And now she's here, you don't even look in my direction. Don't you miss us?" She runs a hand along my thigh.

"Us?" I ask, laughing. "There is no us, Kiki. You were hot pussy."

"I spent months in your bed."

"Until you became clingy," I point out.

"I know this club. I know your brothers—"

"Some a little too well," I cut in.

"And she doesn't. She'll hate this life, especially when she sees the dark side. Have you crawled into bed covered in blood yet, or had her pull a bullet from your leg?"

"It's nice you're worried about her, Kiki, but there's no need. Lara will cope just fine."

"What about when she finds out the truth?" she asks, arching a brow. I wait for her to continue. "When she finds out what you did to her brother?"

I move fast, grabbing her hair and pulling her to stand. She grins, probably turned on. "You bring that up again and I'll make sure I remove your fucking tongue," I hiss.

"Does she like this side of it, Pres?" she purrs, running her tongue over her plump lower lip.

"She takes everything I give her." I smirk, and her smile fades. "Now, stay away from Lara and keep your mouth shut." I shove her away just as the kitchen door opens and Lara emerges with Lucas. She walks him to the door and they embrace before he leaves. Lara rushes to me and throws herself at me, wrapping her legs around my waist and kissing me like I'm everything she's ever needed. I feel Kiki's eyes burning into us.

"Thank you for knowing exactly what I need," she whispers.

I cup her arse, pulling her against my strained cock. "If I knew this would be the reaction, I'd have done it days ago."

She runs her hands through my hair. "Is it too early for bed?"

I grin, carrying her towards the stairs. "Never too early when there's a long night ahead."

CHAPTER SEVENTEEN

LARA

I wake in the middle of the night with Solo wrapped around me. I slide from his hold, pull his T-shirt on, and head downstairs. We skipped dinner in favour of some alone time and now my stomach is growling. There's no way I can fall back to sleep when I'm this hungry. I'm relieved when I get downstairs and the place is in darkness and quiet. These men often party into the early hours.

Kiki is in the kitchen nursing a bottle of wine. She spots me, so there's no way I can back out and pretend I was never here. Adam's words haunt me, and I know I have to lay claim or these women will always think they can treat me like crap.

I peer inside the fridge. There're a lot of leftovers but nothing remotely appealing. These guys must have shares in burgers and other greasy foods. Spotting a packet of cookies, I take a couple along with the milk. I'm pouring myself a glass when Kiki clears her throat. "Milk and cookies, Christ, you really are Nancy fucking Drew."

"Cold burgers don't appeal to me at this time of the morning," I say, placing the milk bottle back in the fridge.

"Of course, they don't. You're too good for the food I cook."

"That's not true," I mutter, grabbing my glass and heading for the door. Kiki rushes to get in front, blocking my escape.

"You know you'll never give him what he needs."

I arch a brow. "My arse disagrees." The soreness where his belt came down hard earlier stings at the mention.

"You might be able to keep up with him in the bedroom, but what about when he really needs you?"

"I don't want to have this conversation with you." I try to move around her, but she blocks me again.

"There are times when his world is so dark, he struggles to find a way out. I'm that way out for him. It's me he runs to when he needs light."

I scoff. "A real saviour. Should I bow at your feet?"

"Laugh it up, bitch, but time will tell. Those nights when he doesn't return to your bed, you'll know he's with me. I'll clean him up and show him real love, the type a man like him needs."

"That's what you have with him?" I ask, smirking. "Real love? Because he gave me the impression you were just a club whore, here to keep the men happy."

"If I was, I'd be in someone's bed tonight," she snaps. "Solo kept me for himself, and he hasn't given the other men permission to touch me, so I guess it means he's keeping me here for when he's done with you. I mean, God, do you honestly think you can handle a man like him? You're here with your perfect hair and innocent smile, but how will you cope when he's covered head to toe in someone else's blood? When he's so tired because he's wiped out an entire family all because one guy crossed him? Will you still give him your cute smiles knowing he raped their wife? Will you giggle while he makes you wash their blood from his skin and then fucks you because he's buzzing from the energy?"

That's not Solo, not the man I know. I force my expression to remain neutral as she continues. "I didn't think so. It's me who handles him when he's like that. It's me who Duke sends to distract him. He's kept me in his bed days at a time just to help him through. Can you look at him the same knowing he's taken lives? Knowing he's put drugs out on the streets and ruined families?"

"Solo is helping me. He's not a bad person," I mutter.

Kiki laughs. "Wow, you really believe that, don't you? You think he's so kind and innocent. He once killed a woman just like you. She wasn't as dreary and *Brady Bunch*-like, but he loved her, or at least claimed to. She crossed him, and he made her pay."

"How?" Duke's conversation lingers in my mind. Even he doesn't know who killed Solo's ex, so how would she know?

"She was pregnant with Solo's kid but told Charlie Reed it was his. Solo couldn't let her get away with making him look weak, so he arranged for her to be killed."

"Bullshit. You don't know the truth. It's common knowledge she died."

Kiki grins. "Oh, I know the truth. He told me when we laid in his bed talking the night away once. Because it wasn't all just sex—we spent hours getting to know each other. I know him better than anyone. He paid someone to kill her. It was a hit and run, and they never caught the guy responsible."

I shake my head in annoyance. "I don't care, Kiki. I don't care about his past because I'm his future, so don't waste your time trying to come between us. It won't work."

The door swings open and Solo stands there completely naked and looking tired. "What are you doing?" he asks, yawning. His eyes fall to Kiki and he suddenly looks more awake. "What the hell's going on?"

I force a smile. "Nothing, I was getting a snack."

He eyes Kiki suspiciously before holding his hand out for me to take. "Then you should have woken me to get it for you.

I don't like waking up and finding you gone." He pulls me from the room.

"Why are you naked?"

"It's the middle of the night."

"Kiki saw you," I point out, and he grins, reminding me yet again that she's seen him a million times before. "Don't do that again. Or maybe I'll walk around naked and let your brothers see me." His eyes darken. "Exactly."

"What was she talking to you about anyway?"

"Nothing important, why?"

He shrugs. "I just didn't think you were friends."

"If I'm sticking around, I need to make an effort, right?"

We get into bed, and he snuggles up behind me. I know his intentions, but after my chat with Kiki, I'm really not in the mood, so I move away, mumbling about being too tired.

The following morning, Solo drops me at work and leaves the prospect to watch from outside the shop. Adam is eagerly waiting, and I laugh as he follows me into the back room. "Did you put Duke in his place?"

"How come you kept it a secret?" I demand to know.

"I wasn't gonna give up the chance to connect with him again. You should see the size of his—"

"Thanks, but TMI."

"He's alright, just scared to come out of the closet."

"Why? I don't think the guys would care," I tell him as I hang my coat up.

"Are you kidding? Of course, they would. How many of them are gay in that club, Lara? No one openly. They're all about crime, violence, and sex."

"So, gay men can't be any of the above?" I ask, laughing.

"I don't make the rules, your boyfriend does. Ask him."

"I don't think Solo would care. Duke's his closest brother, and he'd just want him to be happy."

The sarcastic look on Adam's face reminds me of the one on Kiki's last night. "Aww, listen to you in your little cute bubble where everyone loves everyone. It's hard enough for me as a gay man who's open about his sexuality, but for guys like Duke, there's a certain expectation, and he doesn't wanna risk losing that club. For some reason, he likes it there. It's his life."

"What's the point in that when he's not truly happy?"

"It works for us. I'm happy to be his dirty little secret with none of the relationship drama, and he's happy to get what he needs so he can go on living a lie."

Felicity comes in. "You are coming out tonight, no excuses," she snaps before I've even greeted her.

"Good morning to you too," says Adam.

"You move in with the guy and don't bother to tell me?" she hisses. "Then you ignore my calls." Not strictly true, I was just busy, but I let her rant. "You don't text. I went to see Lucas, and he was broken."

"We've sorted it out now."

"Not the point. You're supposed to be my best friend, and I swear, if you're not in Maine's by eight tonight, we're over."

I can't help the smile pulling at my lips. She's so dramatic, it's cute. "Okay."

"Now, get me a coffee. It's tiring being so bossy."

SOLO

"Pres, phone call," says Viper from behind the bar.

I frown. Who calls the landline these days? He hands me the receiver. "Yep?"

"Long time no speak, Solo."

"Well, if it isn't Charlie Reed," I say, my eyes connecting with Viper. "What can I do for you?"

"We need to talk."

"I'd say so."

"Tonight, eight, at the docks." He disconnects the call.

"What did he want?" asks Duke, appearing beside me.

"To meet tonight at the docks."

"Are we taking him out?" asks Viper.

I shake my head. "Not yet. Let's see what he wants first."

"Come on, Pres, ain't it time we ended this motherfucker? He's done enough to this club."

"I'll tell you when, Viper. Now, leave it."

I get Lara from work at five, and she heads straight upstairs. She's quiet and it reminds me to interrogate Kiki on their previous night's conversation. Lara's in the shower when I bury myself inside of her. She moans, pressing her hands against the tiles. "I'm meeting Flick tonight," she whispers. I wrap my hand in her hair and tug her head back, slamming into her roughly. "Just for a quick drink."

"Not a chance," I pant.

"I wasn't asking."

"Don't make me gag you, Suicide."

We come together, and although it's not enough and I need to go again, she pulls away and continues to wash her hair. "What's wrong with you?" I ask. It comes out sharper than I meant it to, and she looks annoyed. "You've been weird since I saw you with Kiki last night. Is it the whole naked thing? I wasn't thinking, I'm sorry."

"Before me, did you often walk around naked?"

I shrug, trying not to smirk because now isn't the time. "Not always."

She turns the shower off and steps out, wrapping a towel around herself. "So, before me, if that happened, would you have had sex with her in the kitchen?"

"Why are we talking about this? I'm with you."

"I want to know. I want to know more about you and your life, and how things were before me, and how they are when I'm not around."

"It's not important. What's important is this, right now. Us."

"What's your next move with Reed?" she asks.

I sigh heavily and head into the bedroom. "I can't discuss club business with you, Lara."

"Now you use my name. Speaking of names, what is yours again?"

"You know my name, Solo."

"I mean your real name. Your mother didn't call you Solo. Speaking of mothers, where is she?"

I turn around and Lara's right behind me. I grin, gripping her hips and walking her backwards to the bed. "You have so many questions, Suicide. Which do you want me to answer first?"

"Any of them . . . all of them? We know nothing about each other and yet I have your fake name permanently on my skin. Am I staying forever, or is this until you've had enough of me?"

I laugh, lowering her to the bed. I run my hand up her leg, but she slaps it away. "Do you want to stay forever?"

"I'm asking you," she snaps.

I slide the handcuffs out from under the pillow. She's too busy being mad to notice. "I'm gonna ask you again, Lara, what did you and Kiki talk about?"

"It doesn't matter. Tell me about your father. Was he in this club?" I kiss her hard, stealing her breath while moving her hand above her head. I snap the cuff around her wrist, and she looks up, breaking our kiss. "Solo, not now. I want to talk." I snap the other end of the cuff to the bed post. "Seriously, I'm not having sex with you."

I jump up from the bed and smile down at her. "We both know all I need to do is put my hand in your knickers and you'd be putty in my hands. But I don't want sex right now,

Suicide, because all your fucking questions turned me off." I head for the door. "I'm gonna go talk with your new bestie."

Kiki is naked when I burst into her room like a bear on a rampage. She doesn't bother to cover herself, instead rolling onto her back and smiling at me. "Pres, finally."

I grab her upper arm and haul her to her feet. She yelps but doesn't fight me, and I think she thinks this is gonna be a rough fuck. She couldn't be further from the truth. I march her back to my room and shove her inside. Lara glares at me. "Now, someone tell me what the fuck went on last night."

LARA

"I told you, nothing. Get this cuff off me now!"

"So, you both politely sat together and didn't talk?"

"Since when do you care about old woman drama?" snaps Kiki.

"Since she started bending my ear about getting to know each other. What did you say to her?" he hisses, moving closer. Kiki takes a step back, her confident posture shrinking. "I'm gonna ask one more time and then I'm kicking your arse out of here."

"I told her she couldn't keep you happy," Kiki admits. "I'm sorry, Pres. I'm jealous and I miss you."

"Don't forget the part about him murdering his ex," I add smugly. Kiki throws me a disgusted look.

Solo glares at her, arching a brow. She visibly cowers before blurting out, "I'm so sorry."

"Get out of my sight, Kiki," he growls, and she rushes out, slamming the door closed.

"Now, will you let me out of the cuffs?"

He grabs my ankles, pulling my legs apart and lying between them. "I have something important to do tonight. When I get back, we'll talk. You get to ask three questions, and I choose which ones I answer." He unlocks the cuff, freeing my hand. "Choose your questions wisely." He jumps up and I rub my wrist. He heads for the door and glances back, "No leaving the club, Lara. I have no men free to watch you. Rearrange your little get together." He doesn't give me time to reply before he's out the door.

"Mojitos all around," says Robyn excitedly.

"And add three shots, whatever you have on hand," I tell the barman.

We carry the drinks to a nearby table and Flick shrugs out of her jacket. "Start from the beginning."

"I don't even know where the beginning is," I complain. "One minute, Solo is telling me to stay away from him, and the next, he's offering to help."

"With?" asks Robyn, drinking her shot.

"Some guy who came after Liam," I say, keeping my voice low. They both gasp. "Anyway, next thing I know, I'm being tattooed, moved into the club, and claimed as his." Robyn's eyes bug out of her head. "What the fuck?"

"Right!" I exclaim. "He's completely over the top, and I swear, he'd tie me to him twenty-four-seven if he could."

"How did he feel about you meeting us?" asks Flick.

I lower my eyes. "He doesn't know."

"You snuck out?" asks Robyn, grinning. I nod, and she high fives me. "Go you. Don't let any man tell you what to do."

"But you're not in danger or anything, are you?" asks Flick. She groans when I hesitate. "Jesus, Lara, what if that guy comes for you?"

"In a busy bar?" I ask, looking around. "I doubt it. We're having a couple of drinks. How will he know where I am?"

CHAPTER EIGHTEEN

SOLO

I ignore the incoming call from Kiki. I've got six missed ones already, and I don't know why she doesn't take the hint. I check my watch. "He's late," I mutter. Reed hasn't shown at the docks, and something feels off.

"You wanna go?" asks Duke.

My phone buzzes again. "Fuck's sake," I growl, answering it. "What, Kiki?"

"Sorry, Pres. I thought you'd wanna know, Lara has gone out of the club."

I frown. "What do you mean?"

"I went to apologise to her, but she's not in your room. We've checked everywhere, and she isn't here."

I disconnect. "Fuck! Lara's gone AWOL."

"You think that's why Reed hasn't shown up?"

I try calling her while we rush back to the bikes, but it goes straight to voicemail. I call Lucas. "Lara's left the club, have you seen her?" I bark down the phone when he answers.

"I haven't seen her, but she was meeting Robyn and Flick for drinks."

"Where would she be?" I snap, my blood boiling. He reels off a list of places she might go, and we head off in the direction of the first one.

By the fourth bar on the list, I'm giving up hope. Scenarios of Reed putting a bullet in her head haunt me. But then, I hear her, and my eyes search desperately until they land on her sitting at a table with her friends laughing. Fucking laughing. I've been tearing the town apart while she's having the time of her life.

"Word of warning," hisses Duke, holding me back by my arm. "You wade in there yelling, and it'll end with her leaving your arse."

"Since when do you care?" I growl, shrugging him off.

He holds his hands up. "Don't say I didn't warn you."

Her friends spot me first. Flick pales and stops talking mid-sentence. Robyn sits a little straighter and nods in my direction, causing Lara to turn to see what could possibly have caught their attention. She almost looks amused when her eyes land on me. "Two hours. I had bets on within the first hour at least," she jokes.

"Breathe," Duke advises me from behind.

"I told you to stay home," I growl. My eyes wander over her half naked body. She's practically out in her underwear. The bra-style top literally covers her tits and that's it. The skirt is so short that it rides up her thighs because she's sitting down. I suck in a breath, my nostrils flaring.

"It was supposed to be a couple of drinks but then the cocktails were half-price and there were new ones on the menu—"

"Let's go," I snap, cutting her off.

"No. You're not my dad."

"Thank fucking god," I murmur, and her eyes narrow. "It's not safe. You know it isn't."

"I don't know shit because you don't tell me anything. And how the hell would Charlie Reed know where to find me?"

I glance around, suddenly remembering he could be lurking. "Trust me, he'll know if he wants to hurt you badly enough."

She stands, holding her arms out to her sides and wobbling slightly. "Well, I'm alive, so I guess he doesn't give a fuck."

Flick also stands, gently resting her hand on my arm. "Actually, can I have a quick word?"

Robyn is talking in Lara's ear, so I agree and she pulls me to one side. "Robyn and I are worried about her. Has she taken her meds?"

I shrug. "I don't know. I assume so, she's an adult."

"It's just she's acting erratic, a bit like when she's not medicated. We haven't seen her so up and down in a long time."

"She doesn't tell me anything about her medication or why she takes it. Have you asked her?"

"I mentioned it, but she got angry. Said she's sick of everyone checking up on her."

"Then there's your answer. It's up to her, and if she's stopped, that's her choice."

Flick's eyes widen. "She's in your home, a place you tricked her into going. The least you could do is keep an eye on her."

"What do you think I'm doing?" I snap, and Flick looks away nervously. "But she's a typical fucking woman, doing exactly as she pleases. Do you know how much danger she put herself in tonight?"

"No," she hisses, straightening her shoulders, "because I don't get to see her anymore. Since you took her, we hardly speak."

"That's not my fault!"

"Well, it sure as shit isn't mine. Lara needs her friends and family. She needs routine and normality, and she needs to take her meds. If you really want to help her, sort this Reed guy out so she can get back to her life."

I grin. "I *am* her life now. She agreed to be mine, and I intend to hold her to that."

"Even if she's unhappy?" Flick hisses, going back to the table. I follow.

"Lara, we have to go," I say firmly.

"I told you, no."

I sigh as Flick's words float around my head. "Look, maybe you can arrange for the girls to come over to the club some-time. Drink in our bar, where you're safe." I take her arm and pull her to stand. "But right now, I have to get you out of here. Reed didn't show up for a meeting tonight, and there's every chance he could turn up here." Lara opens her mouth to protest, but I'm done playing the nice guy. I tip her over my shoulder and carry her out kicking and screaming.

By the time we get back to the clubhouse, she's in no mood to talk, so I let her go off to bed and take a seat at the bar with Duke. "Get me something strong," I say to Kiki.

"You found her then?" she asks, not looking happy. I was surprised she bothered to call me in the first place, since she's the first person wanting rid of Lara.

"I still haven't decided if you're sticking around here," I snap, and she lowers her eyes. "Just get the drinks and get out of my sight."

"What are we gonna do about Reed?"

I cover my face with my hands. "Him arranging that meeting makes me wonder if he was playing to see if we'd turn up. He's made us look like idiots, and I'm sick of it. I'm gonna tell him I know about his threat to Lara. It's a reason to end him."

"Whatever you say, Pres."

Once Reed's out the picture, I'm worried that Lara might wanna leave the club and I can't let her go. But I can't let Reed think he's in charge, and I can't let him think Lara hasn't told me her secrets because he'll think he can get away with more shit. It's a fucking mess.

"Get the guys together. We'll roll out in an hour."

LARA

Stepping from the shower, I find Solo waiting on the bed. He's pissed, I can tell by his expression. "What you did tonight was stupid."

I roll my eyes. "What I did was act like a young woman wanting to see her friends."

"What do you take these for?" he asks, shaking my pill bottle.

I snatch it from him. "Suddenly you wanna get to know each other?"

"I wanna know why you take them."

"They help stabilise my moods." I'm not ashamed of my bi-polar but standing here in front of Solo like this, makes me feel vulnerable, like he'll laugh at me.

"Do they help?" he asks, and I nod. "I never see you take them."

"I'm not off my meds, if that's what you're getting at," I snap. I've been worried myself, maybe that's why I'm so touchy. I have been taking them, one a day, exactly like the doctor said. But lately, I've been feeling more anxious. At first, I put it down to the situation with Reed, but I feel safe with Solo and yet still my mind constantly races and I'm not sleeping as well as usual. They're all signs from before, when I wasn't well, when I'd been struggling silently for too long.

He shrugs. "I don't care if you're on or off them. You're responsible for you and you know what's best for you." I like that he trusts me instead of treating me like I'm crazy, but maybe it's because he hasn't seen that side of me. I open the bottle and pop one of the pills into my mouth, swallowing it. "I drove myself nuts a couple of years back," he says. "My ex was troubled, but I was fucking crazy about her. She was fiery and knew exactly what she wanted in life, apart from when it came to men. She flitted back and forth between me and

Reed, playing us off against each other. And then, none of it mattered because she died in the hit and run."

I lower onto the bed. "And she was pregnant?"

"She said she was. First, she said it was my baby, then it was his. I don't think she knew. Anyway, it's old news." He runs a finger over my bare knee. "It's not important now."

"Was it an accident?" I ask, cautiously.

"Yes, Lara. I loved her, and I didn't kill her despite her fucking with my head. I don't even think Reed did it. It was just an accident."

"Kiki thinks you'll get bored of me eventually and go back to her."

"If I wanted her, I'd have made her my ol' lady. I need to ask you something, and I want an honest answer." He pauses before adding, "Once Reed is sorted, will you leave the club?"

I don't know what he wants to hear. "Do you want me to?"

He shakes his head and relief floods me. "I'd like to see how things work out between us," I admit, and relief smooths out the worried lines on his forehead.

"Good cos I was kinda getting used to having you around." He winks, and I smile. "I have to sort some business. Can I trust you to stay here?" I nod. "We'll have that talk. I promise."

SOLO

The screams of ecstasy are bordering on ridiculous, and I exchange an eye roll with Viper as we move into Reed's compound. The place is a shithole, with dirty used needles and empty beer bottles scattered around. There're a few people passed out on a mattress but no signs of security. He really thinks he's gotten away with crossing me. I open the door to the office, where I've been once before to retrieve my ex from Reed. I should have killed him then, but I didn't wanna be that guy who lost his head over a woman. Otherwise, enemies would always target my women.

Reed is balls deep in some skank-looking woman. She's almost corpse-like with straggly blonde hair and dirty, bruised skin. The track marks up her arms are recent.

He grins as I lean in the doorway and take it all in. There's a video camera recording the sordid scene. "Jesus, who the fuck's gonna wanna see this?" asks Viper from behind me.

I snigger. "Is this your next moneymaking scheme?"

"Banging crackheads?" adds Duke.

"Well, I was hoping to have the lovely Lara bent over my desk by the end of the month, but you came to her rescue," he says, tucking his junk away and pushing the girl from him. "She would have made me some good money."

"It's sick, really," says Duke, heading over to the camera and turning it off, "picking on grieving women knowing full well they owe you nothing and can't pay."

He stiffens slightly at the knowledge that we know the truth. "That was kind of the idea. The end game was always gonna be this," he says, grinning.

"I was disappointed you didn't show up to our meeting earlier. We need to talk," I say, taking a seat.

"Are you tired of her already? I can take her off your hands."

He's trying to get under my skin, but it won't work. "I like having her around. She's got a mouth like a vacuum and she's willing to do anything," I say, winking. "Anything."

"If you're worried about the cash, I'll give her longer to pay," says Reed, looking amused. "Unless you're here to settle the debt."

I laugh, Viper and Duke joining me. "You think I'm gonna pay a penny for a debt I know Liam didn't owe?"

"You didn't know shit about Liam. He was running for me."

"And for me." He looks annoyed now, so I smirk. "Where do you think he was getting the drugs from, Charlie? You think he stumbled across that powder?"

Reed narrows his eyes. "He got it from you?"

"He was skimming me," I snap. "So, I think you'll find that you owe me."

He shakes his head, suddenly understanding the reason for my visit. "Nah, I don't. I knew nothing about any of that." I glance at Duke, who looks convinced. Maybe he didn't know, but he can't prove it either. "I don't care. As you pointed out, he was running for you, so you should have kept a closer eye on him."

"You can't come after me for money for something he did."

"You tried to with Lara," points out Viper.

"But once I knew she was yours, I backed off. She was due to pay last week, and I never called it in."

"If I'm honest, Charlie, I'm tired of you. I should have put a bullet in you years ago, but I liked the competition. You kept me amused. And now, I'm bored. What with Liam dying and my poor ol' lady grieving, then you turning up and making dick moves, I just want some peace."

"You killed him." Reed gasps. "He wasn't using again, I knew he wasn't. You did that to send me a message."

"You clearly were delayed in getting it," says Duke dryly.

"Because I told you already, I didn't fucking know about the skimming."

"Either way, this little thing we have," I say, pointing at the space between us, "has to end."

He backs away until he falls into his chair. Duke points the gun at his head and pulls the trigger without a further warning. The pop from the silencer makes the woman jump and she screams. I grab her, tugging her to my lap and covering her mouth. "Shh," I whisper in her ear. Her eyes are wild, frantically looking for a way out.

Her hand slaps my face, and she scrapes her nails down my cheek, drawing blood. I hiss before snapping her neck. "Fucking bitch," I mutter, pushing her to the floor. She slumps, her wide, lifeless eyes staring up at me. "Let's get out of here, this place gives me the heebie-jeebies."

Viper pours petrol over the office as we leave and then flicks a match to light it. Hopefully, it'll burn well before the fire brigade get here.

LARA

I can feel Kiki's eyes burning into me while I stir my coffee. "Why did you tell Solo I'd gone if you want me out of here so badly?" I eventually ask.

"He would have killed me if I hadn't."

"Bullshit. All you had to say was you thought I was in my room."

"Maybe I thought he'd realise he's better off without you. If he saw how much trouble you were, he'd give up."

I grin. "Wow, that must have hurt like a bitch when he dropped what he was doing to come looking for me. I think you wanted to get me into trouble."

"I'm playing the long game," she announces. "He'll get bored."

"He asked if I wanted to stay, actually." She narrows her eyes. "And I said yes, of course."

She shakes her head angrily. "If you knew him, knew what he'd done."

"He didn't kill his ex. He told me all about her." I can't hide the smugness in my voice.

"Argh!" she cries. "You're so fucking stupid. Your brother wasn't using again," she hisses in a low voice, and I still at the mention of Liam. "Solo put that needle in his arm. He killed your brother." It takes a moment for her words to make sense. I stare, my mouth opening and closing. My head feels like a whirlwind, a jumble of thoughts whizzing around, so I grip it and close my eyes in the hope something will make sense. "Liam was skimming drugs to pay off Reed. The club found out and Liam paid the price. So, when you lie in bed next to your ol' man, remember, you don't know him, not really, not like I do."

I back away towards the door, not able to breathe because the pain in my chest is too much. "You're lying," I whisper.

"Think what you want. Liam died here and they took him to the docks for Reed to find."

I rub the ache over my heart. "You win," I mutter. "You win."

SOLO

We pull into the parking lot and dismount. Duke removes his helmet and stares up at the building. "How would you feel about me hitting the road for a while?" he asks.

I frown. "What brought this on?"

"I need some time out, brother, to get my head straight."

Siren comes out and rushes towards me. "Pres, I need a word," she says in a hushed tone.

Duke winks, moving towards the clubhouse. "We'll talk about this later," I shout after him.

"Kiki did something really bad," Siren whispers.

"Okay, what?"

"She's been emptying the powder out of Lara's pills and putting the empty capsules back in her pill jar."

Anger boils my blood. "How do you know?"

"I saw her in your room earlier, and she admitted it to me. I swore I wouldn't tell, but I like Lara, and Kiki's lost her mind."

I kiss her on the cheek and head inside. The place is unusually quiet as I head straight upstairs. I open the bedroom door, and Lara rushes at me screaming. I manage to grab her wrists in time to halt her attack. "Jesus," I yell. "What the fuck are you doing?"

"Tell me the truth!" she shouts, her arms and legs flailing around, making it hard for me to keep hold of her and dodge the hits at the same time.

"Can I get a hint?"

"Liam," she growls.

"What about him?"

"You killed him!"

I keep my face neutral. "Not true. Next question."

"Liar! You're lying! I knew he wasn't using again. I knew it. Was he stealing drugs from the club?"

It's clear Kiki's been messing with way more than Lara's pills. "You need to calm down if you wanna talk, baby."

"Baby!" she screeches, unleashing another attempt at an attack. "Now, I know you're guilty. You never call me that."

"Fuck, Lara, calm down or I'm gonna tie you up."

CHAPTER NINETEEN

SOLO

"Start talking, or I swear to God, I'll make you," she growls.

I smile, which sends her over the edge, and she pulls away, ripping my gun from my waistband and pointing it at me. It's a smooth move, and if she didn't have it aimed at my face, I'd probably be impressed. "Suicide, have you ever fired a gun before?" I ask, keeping my tone light and amused. I'm assuming not, seeing as she's made no move to remove the safety. "It's not how it is in the movies."

"Talk," she screams.

I stroke my chin, trying not to lose my shit. "You know, if any of my brothers walk in here, Suicide, they'll kill you."

"Then talk faster!"

"What's this gonna solve? You're pointing a fucking gun at my head because Kiki fed you some bullshit," I snap.

"She wasn't lying. I knew he didn't kill himself. He wasn't using drugs," she spits angrily. "And you knew the fucking truth. All along, you knew, and you kept it from me. You're sick in the head."

I shrug. "I never pretended I wasn't, Suicide. You came after me, remember? You were so fucking desperate to put yourself on my radar. I told you to stay away, but you kept on coming back."

"Well, I'm done now. You were right, this world is not for me."

I smirk. "Bit late now, though."

"I'm walking out of here today with the truth and then I'm gone. You'll never see me again."

"Not that simple and you know it."

"Tell me about my brother," she repeats as tears fill her eyes and make slow trails down her cheeks.

"You know already. Liam died from a drug overdose. Damn it, Lara, you saw the needle in his arm."

She swipes angrily at the tears, keeping one hand on the gun, which shakes under its weight. "Who put the needle there?"

I sigh impatiently. "You know how many people have pointed a gun at my head and lived to tell the tale?"

"If I'm gonna die, let me die knowing the truth."

"The truth is your brother was a fucking junkie. Yes, he stole drugs from my club and shot them into his vein until his body gave up."

"He was beat up," she yells. "He had bruises and missing fingers."

"That was my fault," drawls Duke, appearing in the doorway. He leans against the frame casually, and Lara backs up more so she can point the gun at either of us should we make a move. "I caught him out, and he paid for it."

"With his life?" she screams, pointing the gun at him.

I discreetly shake my head at Duke, biting down the anger coursing through my body at the sight of her waving the gun around. "You told me you'd prove you could stick this place," Duke says, arching a brow. "You're failing at the first hurdle, and trust me, there will be plenty more whores who come along to take your man, plenty more to fill your crazy head with bullshit. Are you gonna wave a gun around every time?"

"I'm done with this club and with your president," she hisses. "You can fucking keep him and his bullshit lies."

"He isn't lying, Lara. He didn't put that needle in Liam's arm."

"You would say that, it's your job to protect him."

"True, but I'm not protecting him this time. I beat Liam senseless, and he probably went off to lick his wounds and turned to old habits. It's the life we're in. Liam knew the game and he knew the price he'd pay if he got caught."

"No!" Lara cries, sobbing hard and shaking the gun in Duke's direction. "He didn't deserve that." She presses her finger on the trigger, squeezing her eyes shut and holding her breath. When nothing happens, Duke smirks.

I stand, snatching the gun from her and putting it back in my waistband, hardly believing she pulled the fucking trigger on my VP. She rushes at Duke, shoving him, but he doesn't budge. Instead, he grabs her wrists and twists her arm up her back. She cries harder. "Who the fuck do you think you are?" he hisses in her ear. "I should slit your throat right here."

"Do it," she yells. "I'd rather be dead than in this room with you murderers."

"Let her go," I mutter. Duke shoves her hard, and she crashes into my chest. "Pack your shit up," I add, stepping back from her. She looks up at me, her cheeks wet, and heartbreak is written all over her face.

"You're letting her go?" Duke snaps. I step out of the room, pulling the door closed and leaving Lara to pack. "What are you doing?" he hisses.

"Find Kiki, bring her to me."

"And what about her? What if she goes to the police? She knows deep down I put that needle in his arm."

"She won't," I say. "And if she does, what proof does she have? The cops didn't care before, and they won't care now."

"Look, I ain't her biggest fan, but you love her, Pres. Take out all the hysteria and maybe she ain't so bad. You could work this out."

I shake my head. Too much has been said. She'll know deep down I ordered Liam's death. Nothing happens in this club without my say so. "Aside from the fact she just pointed my own gun at my head, she also pointed it at my VP. Brothers first, right? She's lucky to walk out of here alive."

"You can forgive that. Besides, I'm going anyway. Tell her you kicked me out for going behind your back, she'll never know."

"You're set on leaving?"

He nods. "Viper is dying for a shot at VP. Not permanent, mind, just until I clear my head."

LARA

My heart hurts. It's almost as bad as finding Liam slumped against that gatehouse with a needle in his arm. I feel like a fool for trusting men I knew were bad. Lowering myself onto the bed, I take a few deep breaths. The way Solo just looked at me, like he was done, was the final nail in the coffin. I'm torn. Confused. I want to hate him so bad, and I should after what they've done, but deep down my heart aches because I love him so much. How did I fall for a man who I know must've ordered my brother's death? Another sob leaves my aching chest.

The door opens and Duke steps inside. Hatred fills me and I shake uncontrollably with the urge to hurt him like he's hurt me. "I know you hate me," he mutters. "I don't blame you cos I have a hard time liking myself, to be honest."

"Get out."

"You need to hear me out first. I'm leaving. I made the decision a few days ago and I'm all packed, ready to hit the road." The news surprises me. Duke is a big part of this club and his leaving will hurt Solo. "I confessed to Pres that I was responsible for hurting Liam after I made the decision, so it would make it easier on him. I knew he'd choose you when it came down to it."

"You expect me to believe he didn't know? That he didn't order you to kill him?" I ask, laughing coldly. "Nothing happens in this club without him knowing."

"Not strictly true. He thinks that, but so much happens he's not aware of. Take me, for instance—he doesn't have a hint of the fact I'm bisexual. He doesn't know that one of the brothers drove that car into Chas to end her life." I gasp, and Duke shrugs. "We protect him at all costs, Lara. Chas was a liability, and he couldn't see it. I'm telling you this because Solo wants to be good deep down, and you help him with that. He loves you. If you leave him, it'll kill him."

"He told me to pack my shit," I point out.

"Because he thinks you blame him, and he doesn't think you'll believe the truth. Just give him a chance. Before this all came out, you were happy, right?"

I nod. "Really happy."

"Then make it right. I'm not gonna be a problem."

"I should go to the cops and hand you in," I whisper.

Duke laughs. "You could," he says, nodding, "but you won't. And they wouldn't be interested. Liam fucked up and would have known what was coming. You don't rip off The Depraved Devils and get away with it." He turns to leave. "For what it's worth, I'm sorry you got caught up in all this."

SOLO

Kiki screams as I drag her up the stairs. I open my bedroom door where Lara is still sitting on the bed looking lost and heartbroken. I shut my feelings down and push Kiki into the room. "Tell her what you did," I yell.

"Pres, please," Kiki cries.

I grab Lara's pills and unscrew the cap. "You're fucking messed up," I yell, tipping the pills onto the bed. I pick one up and pull the capsule apart, showing there's nothing inside. Lara stares blankly. "She messed with your meds," I snap.

"She loves you," whispers Lara, her eyes watering again. "She was desperate."

"So, I get a gun to my head, and she gets sympathy?" I glare at Kiki, and she wilts. "Get out. I'll find you when I'm ready to deal with you." She scrambles from the room.

"It's your fault," Lara mumbles, not bothering to look at me.

"Please, enlighten me, what have I done now?"

"You were having sex, of course, she was gonna catch feelings. You kept her in your bed and warned the others off her, so what was she supposed to think?"

"That she was my personal whore?"

"Nice. What a charmer."

"Aren't you supposed to be packing?" I snap.

"Is it easier to push me away than face the mess?" she asks, slowly standing and looking around the room. I grab her bag from the top of the wardrobe and throw it on the bed. *Is that what I'm doing?* I've had too much drama for one night and I've come to the conclusion it's pointless fighting for a woman. I can get anyone I want. All this bullshit reminds me why the hell I avoid relationships.

"Life was just easier when you weren't around, Lara."

She stares for a moment, then opens the bag. "My mum was bipolar," she mutters, walking over to the drawers. "She wasn't on top of it. Never took her meds, and on the rare occasion she did, it only hurt me more because I'd get a glimpse of what we were missing out on. But when Lucas fought for us, I realised I didn't need her, that my brothers were enough. So, I get this setup, why you're happy here with your brothers, doing what you do. But one day, you'll wake up and realise you wanted more. You needed more."

"Like you?" I scoff, rolling my eyes.

"I thought I had all I needed in my life . . . Lucas, Liam, my girls." She smiles sadly. "When I saw you that first time, I knew

I was gonna make you mine, no matter what you did or said. I wanted you, and it wasn't in a crazy way. I didn't wanna stalk you into submission, even if it seemed like that's what I was doing." She smirks. "I wanted you to notice me, to want me too."

"This is all well and good, but I have shit to do, so make it quick," I say bluntly, heading for the door. My heart twists when she grabs my wrist. I stop but keep my back to her.

"I won't beg to stay," she whispers.

"And I won't beg you to." I force myself to walk out the door. She's gonna leave one day anyway, so why prolong it?

Kiki is at the bar when I move behind it to snatch a bottle from the shelf. "Won't help," she mutters. I spin, throwing it across the room. It shatters against a wall.

"You need to leave," I growl at her. "Get your stuff and get out of my club."

She nods, pointing to an already packed suitcase. "I guessed as much."

"You're getting off lightly. I could kill you for the shit you've caused." I don't add that it's only Lara's words that stopped me putting a bullet in her. "You messed with my ol' lady."

"I'm sorry, Solo. Jealousy got the better of me."

"I don't wanna see you around here again. Stay away from my club and the brothers. You're not welcome and be thankful you're walking out alive." She nods, grabbing her suitcase and dragging it out the door.

I call Viper over. "Give it a few days," I say, and he nods, understanding my order for another hit and run, only this time on Kiki.

"Duke said Lara's leaving," he says. "Is she really leaving . . . alive?"

"Yes, she hasn't crossed the club. It's just not working out. Call Arty and get me in to get this shit removed off my chest," I add, looking up in time to see Lara staring at me. I inwardly groan as a hurt expression passes over her face. "All packed?" I ask brightly, and she nods. "You need a taxi?"

"No. Robyn's on her way."

I grab a different bottle from the shelf to hide the overwhelming urge I have to beg her not to walk out that door. Instead, I grin in the direction of Siren and tip my head. She comes over, and I hook my arm around her shoulders and kiss her gently on the lips. "Let's go to bed, baby. It's been a stressful day."

She glances at Lara nervously, but I don't give her a chance to object before pulling her towards the stairs.

LARA

"That was for show," says Viper, winking at me. "He's not gonna fuck her."

I force a smile. "None of my business, he's a free man. Put that call in to Arty. I don't want my name on his skin." I throw my bag over my shoulder and head out.

The second I get into Robyn's car, I break. The sobs are out of my control, so I let them come, shaking my entire body until I'm too exhausted to think straight. She occasionally rubs my arm, waiting patiently for me to get it out of my system. "I called Lucas after I got your text. He's getting you some more pills. In a few days, once they're back in your system, you'll feel much better."

I rest my forehead on the window, closing my eyes as the cold cools me down. Even the tablets won't cure my broken heart. There's only one man who can do that.

The days blur into one. I tried to hide in my bed and sleep the days away, but Lucas only stood that for twenty-four hours and then he forced me to get up and dress. By the following day, he was dragging me into work and ordering Adam to keep me busy. In the evenings, he was making excuses as to why I needed to help him at Maine's. First, he was short staffed and then he was overwhelmed with paperwork. It was annoying, but as the days have moved on, I appreciate the effort he's gone to in order to keep me going. The pills are kicking back in and I feel normal again, if there is such a thing. My mind is calmer, and although I feel sad beyond anything I've felt since Liam was taken, I can think clearly.

CHAPTER TWENTY

SOLO

I cancelled the hit on Kiki. Lara was right—I messed with her heart, and she was hurting when she fucked up. We've all been guilty of that. Viper looked relieved when I told him, and I wondered how many times I've ordered my men to do something they didn't want to. It made me realise that all the decisions affecting the club should be made by the club, so I called church and told my brothers that from now on, we'd vote on every decision, and it would need full backing to go ahead.

The place is quiet without Duke, but he checks in every couple of days. I can't help wondering if he's running from telling me his truths because he thinks I'll change my opinion of him. That shit hurts cos I thought we were closer than that, and he couldn't be further from the truth. He's my brother no matter who he loves or doesn't. But I'll let him have a few months away before I pull him back. I'm hoping in that time he'll find the strength to tell me he's bisexual, I'd prefer him to do it in his own time.

By the time I've finished deep thinking, my opponent is flat out in the ring and the crowd is cheering. Stepping out, Boss hands me a bag of cash, patting me on the back. I give it to Viper for safe keeping. He's making a good VP while Duke is away. "I got somewhere to be," I say, patting him on the back. "I'll see you back at the club."

When I step outside, there's someone lingering by my bike. I keep a hand on my gun but relax when Lucas turns to face me. "Let's go for a drink," he says coldly.

"As much as I'd love to," I lie, "I have somewhere to be."

"Sitting outside my bar waiting to catch a glimpse of my little sister?" he asks, and I lower my eyes to the ground. "I see you there night after night, man. Let's go." I bite my tongue, deciding not to argue for once and listen to what he's got to say. I predict he wants to warn me off, but he doesn't need to. I won't hassle Lara, but a sick part of me can't stop watching her. It's torture, which is exactly what I deserve after everything I did.

We head back inside the fight club, get a whiskey, and sit. "How is she?" I ask.

"Messed up, like you by the looks of things. When did you last sleep, or shave, or fucking eat something?"

I smirk. "You worried about me?"

"Nah, I don't give a shit about you," he mutters, staring down at his drink. "But she does." We fall silent for a few and then he looks at me. "She told me everything . . . what your VP did to Liam."

"Well, my VP's gone so—"

"I'm not here to talk about Liam," he cuts in. "I knew he was messing in the wrong crowd and I couldn't stop him, so I left him to it. Maybe I'm partly to blame too. I don't buy that you had nothing to do with it, but we all had some part in his death, so I can't sit here and take the moral high ground. Yah know, he gave me cash towards the bar. I knew deep down it wasn't from legitimate gains, but I didn't question it cos I wanted that bar and I was so fucking close." He laughs bitterly. "So, we all have our guilty little secrets. But Lara doesn't deserve the pain she's feeling right now."

"I know," I admit. "I wish I could take it away for her but—"

"You can." He glares at me. "She's not eating properly, she's not sleeping. I'm pushing her to work every hour God sends because if I don't, I'm scared she'll never get out of bed . . . just like our mum."

"If you want me to stop following her—"

He cuts me off again, this time holding up a hand. "No, that's not why I'm here." He sighs. "I can't believe I'm saying this, but she loves you, Solo. And being away from you is killing her inside. I can't bear that she doesn't smile or laugh . . . fuck, I miss her annoying laugh." He shakes his head sadly. "She's missing you. Go and fix this mess and make her smile again."

"It's not that easy," I mutter. "She deserves better."

"I agree," he says, "one hundred percent, but she doesn't want better. She wants you."

LARA

Working twelve hours straight is a killer, and as I put my key in the front door of the house, I vow to tell Lucas I can't help at the bar anymore. I kick off my shoes and, using the last of my energy level, I take the stairs two at a time. Running a bath, I drop bubbles in and swirl them before turning on the radio. It's the one thing I've thought about all day, and as I sink into the warmth, I smile. Nothing beats this.

"You've lost weight." I sit up, yelping in surprise. The water sloshes over the edge of the bath and Solo looks down at his wet boots. "When did you last eat?"

"What are you doing here?" I gasp, wiping water from my face. My heart races as I assess him. He looks good, clean shaven, and apart from the dark circles under his eyes, you'd think he'd sailed through this break-up. "How did you get in?"

He crouches beside the bath and dips his hand in the water. "I've brought food downstairs. Why don't we go eat?" He runs his finger over my ribs, and I shudder. "You're too thin."

"What are you doing here, Solo?" I repeat, confused. I've heard nothing from him since I left, and now, he's here in my bathroom like nothing happened. The thought crosses my mind he's here to hurt me, to silence me.

Solo stands and grabs my towel, holding it open for me. I debate whether to send him away, but I can't deny my heart is happy to see him. I push to stand, and he wraps the towel around me. "Dress. I'll go and put the food out." He goes to walk away. "If I come back up here before you're dressed, don't let me in," he says, his eyes dark with need.

I rush to my room and lock the door, breathing fast. The way his eyes burned into me cause me to shudder again. I dress in record time, making it casual with joggers and a cropped top, before heading down to where he's piling Chinese onto plates. My stomach growls. I've hardly eaten since I came home. My appetite was on a full protest.

I slide into the seat, and he sits opposite me. "Eat," he orders, nodding to my plate.

I take a few bites before placing my fork down. "Solo, what's going on?"

"Can't a man see how his ol' lady's doing after he fucked up and broke her heart?" he asks, and my stomach does a summersault. "I've already worked out you're not eating, but are you at least sleeping?"

I shrug. "A couple of hours."

"Are you going to work?"

"Yes." I eat another mouthful, and Solo smiles encouragingly. "What about you?" I ask.

"Well, Kiki is gone, so we've been getting takeout a lot. We've just hired a cook. She's at least ninety, but she comes highly recommended."

I give a small smile. "Good." Maybe she'll be healthier than Kiki was.

"And sleep is hard when you feel like your heart wants to burst from your chest. I discovered after you left that you're the reason I sleep. Nothing beats lying next to you."

I push the noodles around my plate. "Why are you here?"

"Lucas came to see me." I look up in surprise. "He still doesn't like me, does he?" he asks, grinning. "But he's worried."

Guilt hits me hard. I've tried to act happy when he's around, but I must have failed to fool him. "I'll be fine. These things take time." The realisation that Solo only came to check on me for Lucas burns, and I stand abruptly, needing to put space between us. "Thanks for this, but honestly, I'm good."

"I'm not," he says quietly, and I pause to look at his sad eyes. "I fucked up, Suicide, big time. And it's not like I haven't messed up before . . . fuck, I must do it on repeat at least a hundred times a week. But with you, it cuts different." He stands and moves towards me. "I should have been honest from the start. I wanted you. I needed you. You put yourself in my life until I couldn't ignore you any longer and I gave in, making up some bullshit about protecting you when I could have killed Reed that day and made you safe. But I dragged it out because I needed to keep you for myself. I was a selfish prick, but I did it because I love you. I've never loved anyone like I love you, Lara. I want to be a better person when you're around. Please forgive me."

Tears balance on my lash line as he continues. "If you want me to leave, just say it. Say you don't love me, and I'll walk away and never bother you again. But if there's a small part that still feels something for me, please forgive me and give us a chance." He rubs his thumb over the tattoo on my hip, and I watch, mesmerised by the feel of him touching me.

I suck in a breath and look into his eyes. I place my hand over his heart where his tattoo was. Desperate to know if it's still there, I pull his top up, and he lets me remove it completely. I drop it to the floor and run my hand over my name. "I couldn't go through with it," he whispers, running his fingers through my hair. "I'll always belong to you, no matter what you choose. There's no one. Only you."

"No more lies," I whisper, looking into his eyes, and he nods. I cup his face in my hands and we stare at each other. "I mean it, Solo. No more."

He nods again. "No more lies," he repeats.

I smile, placing a kiss on his lips and resting my forehead against his. I close my eyes. "Did you give the order for Duke to kill Liam?" The words ring out in the silence as I wait for his reply.

When I open my eyes again, his are filled with regret and I know . . . even before he nods, I know the answer. Maybe I always did.

A stray tear rolls down my cheek and my smile hurts as I take a step back, letting my hands fall to my side. He makes a grab for my hand, but I step farther away, shaking my head. "No," I snap.

"My real name is Cade. Cade Walker," he says desperately. I continue to shake my head. "And I had parents who hated one another. My dad was in an MC, and my mum was a drug addict."

"Stop," I whisper. "It's too late."

"And I thought I only ever needed the club. The guys never let me down, and they're the one constant in my life. I never had that before, but then I met you and—"

"Stop!" I say it more firmly this time. "Just stop." I take a breath. "I thought if I heard the words, if you could be honest, then I'd feel better. That this aching ball in my chest," I hit the area over my heart, "would go. But it's worse. And even though everyone warned me about you, even when they told me you were dangerous, I wouldn't believe them."

"I can change. I *want* to change," he pleads.

"I couldn't imagine you being so cruel and cold as to take someone's life. I mean, that alone is fucked up, but you lied to me. You lied to my face. And you let me into your bed when you knew the truth. You watched me fall apart after Liam." I frown as that realisation hits me. "Was it some sort of sick power trip? Did you laugh at my pain?"

"No, Lara. Christ, no. I love you. I didn't do any of this to hurt you. It's just how my life is."

"Killing? Murder? Who the fuck made you judge and jury, Solo? Why do you think you have a right to decide who lives and who dies? My brother might have had his issues, but he was a good man. A good brother. He didn't deserve to die like that!" I picture Liam lifeless and a sob escapes me. I swipe my wet cheeks and dry my hands on my joggers. "You should leave now."

"No."

"We're over."

He grabs my wrists and holds me close. Staring into my eyes, he pleads. "We can work it out. Now it's all out in the open, there's nothing stopping us."

"I'm stopping us. It'll never work. Too much has happened, and I can't look at you without seeing Liam, my beautiful brother, dead with a needle in his arm. I can't get over that, Solo." There's pain in every word as my heart twists in my chest.

"I don't believe you. Look me in the eyes and tell me you don't love me."

I take another deep breath, ignoring the pain in my heart as I look right into his eyes. "I don't love you. I don't love you, Solo. We're done."

He drops my wrists, stepping back and shaking his head in denial. "You're wrong." He bends down to collect his shirt from the floor and pulls it over his head, then he grabs his kutte. "You're my ol' lady, Lara. That'll never change. So, take some time, get your head right, and I'll wait."

"Solo, there is no quick fix. We're not getting back together."

He grins, slipping his kutte on. "We never broke up, Suicide. So, fight it if you want, but it won't change the fact that I love you and you love me. This ain't over. Not until I say it is." I watch in disbelief as he presses a kiss to my forehead. "Eat something. You're gonna make yourself ill." And then he walks out.

CHAPTER TWENTY-ONE

LARA

One month later...

Lucas stares at me from across the breakfast table as I pick pieces of my burnt toast and drop it on my plate. "I hate it when you do that," he mutters. I brush my hands together, causing crumbs to fly in all directions. "What are your plans for the weekend?"

He has a habit of making conversation whenever I'm like this. I feel bad for him, I must be hard work, but there are some days when even getting my head off the pillow feels like too much. "I have to get my pills from the pharmacy," I mutter.

"I told you already, I'll collect them for you. Why don't you call the girls and get together for a night out? I don't remember the last time you let your hair down."

I scoff. The last time is clear in both our minds. It was the opening night of his bar, Maine's. The night I met Solo. I shudder at the memory. "I'm not in the mood."

Lucas sighs. "Lara, I'm tired," he mutters, and I raise my eyes until we're staring at each other. "I can't keep doing this. You have to pick yourself up or he's won."

"How do you do it?" I ask.

"Do what?"

"Pretend he didn't admit to killing our brother? We'll never get justice for Liam, and you're getting on with life like Solo didn't fuck us over."

"You think any of this is easy for me?" he snaps, standing and pushing back his chair. "Liam died, and all I keep thinking is, you brought Solo into our lives. You wouldn't leave him alone. If you hadn't have done that, we wouldn't know the truth. Liam would have died from an overdose, and we wouldn't know the fucked-up truth. But we do, and I can't change it. Just like I can't change the fact that you fell in love with the man responsible for his murder. So, tell me, Lara, which part of that sounds easy?"

The tears don't fall like they usually would when Lucas yells at me. Partly because I'm all cried out and partly because everything, he just said is true.

I push my plate away slowly. "I'm going to the gym," I say, standing.

"It wouldn't hurt to run a damn brush through your hair once in a while," he shouts after me.

I push myself hard in the gym. It helps take my mind off everything. And when I'm done, I call into the café to see Adam. He looks surprised. "I want to come back to work," I declare. He'd given me a few weeks off to sort myself out. "The sooner, the better."

"Does your brother know?" he asks.

"It's not up to him."

He exchanges a worried look with Betsy. "I don't know, Lara. You've been through—"

"Spare the bullshit, Adam. If you don't want me back, just say. I get it. I wouldn't want a crazy person working for me either."

"Jesus," he hisses, "that's not the reason. Get in the office."

I stomp through, and he follows, closing the door behind us. "Lucas has kept in touch these last few weeks. He's been worried about you. We've all been worried."

"Don't be nice," I almost whisper. "I can take everyone else creeping around me, but not you. Yell or say something mean and sarcastic. It's how we work."

He gives a sympathetic smile. "I do miss having you around to yell at. Betsy doesn't fuck up as much as you."

"I just need to get back to normal," I admit.

"How about we take it one day at a time, a small shift to start, and see how you feel. We can build it up gradually."

I nod. "Thanks, Adam."

"Tomorrow at ten sharp. Don't be late or I'll make you clean the urinals."

I find Lucas in his office at Maine's. I knock once and enter, and the second he lays eyes on me, his expression turns to guilt. He stands and makes his way towards me. "I am so sorry for what I said earlier," he begins.

I'm already shaking my head as his words tumble out. "Don't be. It was all true."

He places his hands on my shoulders and smiles sympathetically. "It isn't true. Everything happens for a reason. We might never understand what it is, but there's always a reason."

"I thought about it, and I've decided to go back to work." He begins to protest. "I need to get back into a routine. It'll help."

"You don't think it's too soon?" he asks.

I shake my head. "Nah, having Adam yell at me, what could be better?" We both smirk.

"Just as long as you take it at your own pace. No cramming in shifts." He pauses and then sighs. "Do you think Solo will make an appearance once he sees you back at work?"

It's something we're probably both dreading. Solo made it clear I was his, no matter what, and then he disappeared on me. A solid four weeks and I've heard nothing. "I doubt it. I think he's gotten the message." Lucas gives me a doubtful look. "Anyway, I'm going home to make myself beautiful. I've made arrangements to meet the girls for a few drinks."

"That's great, Lara. It'll be nice to see your hungover face at the breakfast table again. I've missed it."

Later, when I meet the girls at our favourite bar, Robyn and Flick are being over-cautious. It's annoying the hell out of me, and when Flick asks me for the hundredth time if I'm okay, I almost bite her head off. "Sorry, we're being too full on, aren't we?" she asks, wincing.

"A little," I agree. "I need a normal night out. If I wanted babysitting, I'd have called Lucas."

They laugh. "It's nice having you back out with us," admits Robyn. "Flick is so boring."

Flick fakes insult. "I am not. Just because I don't wanna take risks does not make me a bore. The last time we took a risk, look what happened." She slams her hand over her mouth as her eyes stare at me wide. "Oh god, I'm so sorry."

"Good one, Flick," hisses Robyn.

I laugh. "Girls, please, it's fine. Stop pretending like it didn't happen, or I might think it was all a bad dream."

They give me a sympathetic smile. "Have you heard from him?"

I shake my head. "Which is a good thing because I hate him. Like, really hate him."

"There's a fine line between love and hate," says Flick.

"Trust me, it's hate. He killed my brother. Liam's blood is on his hands. And I made a decision today," I say, grinning. "I'm going to find out exactly who Solo is." When they don't reply, I continue. "I mean it. I'm going to discover every damn secret about that man."

"Why?" asks Robyn. "Why would you want to know anything about him?"

"So I can bring him down, obviously."

They exchange a look. "Don't you think you should leave it well alone? He doesn't seem like he'd be very happy having you poke around in his life."

"He deserves it. I want him to suffer like I have. Like Liam did. I want him squirming until I'm ready to break him. And when he least expects it, I'm going to turn his world upside down."

Flick is already shaking her head. "It's a bad idea, Lara. A very bad idea. You saw what he did to Liam. What he's capable of. Just walk away. It's what we should have done in the first place."

"I'm meeting a woman here any minute who used to date him, or at least sleep with him."

"What?" snaps Robyn. "You've already been snooping?"

"Is that why you wanted to come out tonight?" asks Flick.

"Are you taking your meds?" Robyn hisses.

I glare at her, and she presses her lips into a tight line, clearly regretting her words but refusing to back down. "Yes," I snap angrily. "I never stopped, remember?"

"I know," she mutters. "It's just . . ."

"You're acting crazy," Flick finishes for her. "Messing with Solo and The Depraved Devils is a suicide mission."

I spot the woman entering the bar, recognising her from her social media page, and wave until she also sees me. "Maybe so, but I can't just let Liam's death be for nothing. I'm going to prove he's a bad person."

"Because you think we don't already know?" hisses Robyn desperately. "We know who he is. We know he's bad. But this is madness, Lara. You have to stop."

I rise to my feet and declare, "I will. When I've made him pay." Then, I make my way over to Cheri.

SOLO

"First my tyres, now this," I snap, running a finger over the deep scratch on my bike. "This is a total respray." Some dick has kindly run a screwdriver through the fresh paint job on my bike. It was only a few days ago someone also stabbed my tyres while my bike was parked outside the tattooist's.

"Someone's really not happy with you," mutters Viper.

"Yah think?" I snap. "Book it in to the spray shop."

I head back into the club, and Siren hands me a whiskey. I eye up her rounded arse in the tight denim shorts she's wearing. Fuck, it's been too long since my dick got wet. "You okay?" she asks.

I nod. "You in anyone's bed?" I ask, and she grins, shaking her head. "I might need you later."

She totters off, and Viper sits beside me. "You finally giving up on her?" he asks.

"Who?" I know who he means, but I don't want him knowing she's on my mind twenty-four- motherfucking-seven.

"Lara?"

"She got her tattoo covered," I tell him. "She didn't even bother to put something pretty over my name, brother. She had it blacked out." I knock my whiskey back. I ain't used to getting my heart hurt like this, and the tattoo was the final nail in the coffin. "She ain't ready for me right now."

"Meaning she might be in the future?"

I shrug. "Maybe she's right. Maybe we can't ever get over the fact I had her brother killed. Too much shit happened."

"Ain't like you to give up," he says.

"Ain't like me to catch feelings for some bitch who stalked me. It's been a month and she ain't even back at work, brother. I did that to her. I broke her. I couldn't even protect her from a fucking club whore. She isn't safe in this world."

"Kiki was a nutter. You couldn't have predicted the lengths she'd go to."

"But I should have. I used her time and time again. Of course, she was gonna do some crazy shit to my ol' lady. I should have done more." I finish my drink and stand. "Anyway, enough of the heart to heart. We got a club to run and we don't have time for women and feelings. There's a bar that needs to meet my baseball bat."

He laughs. "You're the Pres." And then he whistles to get the guys' attention and orders, "Fall out."

I'm not a fan of micro bars. It's a ridiculous concept that reeks of desperation to claw money using any space possible. When I step inside Mark Huntly's bar, I practically fill it with my large frame. It's not the sort of place I can hide amongst the customers. I take a seat at the bar, and Viper squeezes beside me, muttering words of distain. Huntly, who'd had his back to us when we entered, turns and his smile falters. "Solo . . . erm, what can I get you both?"

"We're not here for a social gathering, Mark. You know that."

"You're a day early," he points out.

I nod. "I'm aware. I was just dropping by to check we're on time."

A woman steps from the back room behind the bar. Sensing the cold air floating around the three of us, she gently touches Huntly's arm. "You okay, Pops?"

I arch a brow in her direction, and Huntly winces. "You have a daughter?"

"Who wants to know?" she asks, not quite as friendly as I expect her to be.

"Careful, little lady. You don't wanna get yourself into any bother," murmurs Viper.

"I'm not scared of you," she snaps pointedly.

"Jaya, leave it," mutters Huntly. "Go out back."

She scowls but does what he asks. Viper's eyes track her every move, and I grin. I recognise that look—it's the same one I had when Suicide marched into my life. "Tell you what," I say. "I'll come back tomorrow. But if you'd don't have what I want, I'm taking her." I point to the door Jaya exited through.

"You can't take my daughter because I can't pay you what I owe," he growls.

I grin wide. "I was clear when I made the deal, wasn't I, Mark?"

"Yes, but I thought I could pay it back and—"

"And now, you can't. So, same time tomorrow, or you get to tell Jaya she's marrying into my club." Viper's head whips around to look at me. "Relax," I say, patting his back. "You need a wife, and I need to settle this debt. It's win-win."

"Solo, please. That's crazy. It's against the law, for a start," begs Huntly.

I laugh aloud. "I *am* the law, Mark. It's why you came to me in the first place. Didn't I sort out your little problem?" I ask, and he nods. "Then, a deal is a deal. Your little girlfriend is a million miles away like you asked. Your wife need never know about the twins she's given birth to. Or the fact their mother is the same age as your daughter. So, same time tomorrow."

We get outside, and Viper shakes his head. "Pres, I thought it was a warning call. A few smashed glasses. What the hell happened in there?"

"I didn't know he had leverage. Anyway, what's wrong? You don't like the daughter?" I ask.

"That's not the point. She clearly doesn't like us. I can't force a woman to marry me."

"Then charm her. You wanna get your kid back, right?" He nods. "Then you gotta offer it a stable life. What's more stable than a wife?"

He throws his leg over his bike. "There are easier ways than stealing someone's daughter."

"Ain't it time critical?" I ask. "The adoption hearing is two months away, brother. You got a lot of people to convince before they'll even consider placing her back with you."

He shrugs. "I guess you're right, man. Maybe it ain't so crazy," he says, looking back at the bar.

LARA

Cheri is different to anyone I ever pictured Solo with. They didn't date. By her account, she was a club girl a few years back, but so far, she's given me nothing gritty to go on. "We never really got told club business," she mutters, twisting her blonde curls around her finger thoughtfully.

"Nothing?"

She shakes her head. "He was always really nice to me," she adds. I give her a sceptical look, but it's lost on her as she smiles wistfully. "He always knew exactly what I needed."

"Cheri, apart from sex, what was your relationship actually like?"

"Put it this way, if he called me tomorrow and begged me back, I'd go running."

"Aren't you married into another club now?" I ask.

She grins. "Don't tell my ol' man. Solo's got a lot of enemies, but I don't think you'll get any dirt on him from club girls like me. We always adored him, even when he was a dick. He's messed up, for sure, and his uncle had a huge part to play in that but—"

"His uncle?" I repeat. He'd never mentioned family to me. Yet another reminder that we never talked.

"Yeah. Not a nice guy by the sounds of it. He lives on the other side of London. He wouldn't dare come near Solo these days. Maybe he'll have something for you."

"Why didn't they get along?"

"I'm not sure. Rumour was Solo slept with his girlfriend. After that, he made his life hell. Most of Solo's family are in that area. He used to drink in the Old Tavern. Solo was very specific about the club not going near that place. Give it a try."

"Absolutely not," snaps Flick. "No way."

"What exactly are you expecting to dig up on him?" asks Robyn.

"Enough to put everything together to take to the police," I say confidently.

Robyn scrubs her hands over her face. "What makes you think they'll listen? You had him admit his involvement in Liam's death and it wasn't enough to take to the police. Whatever Solo did in his past, I'm pretty certain he'd have covered it up well enough to sleep with the ease he does at night."

"Robyn's right," says Flick, rubbing her hand over my own. "You'll never pin anything on him. He isn't stupid enough to leave a trail. He wasn't worried in the slightest when you discovered the truth."

"Because he doesn't expect me to take it to the police," I say.

"Or because he knows there's no evidence to pin anything on him."

I lie to the girls, telling them I'll drop the whole thing about Solo. But as I get into work the next day, I'm already searching for the bar Cheri mentioned, planning to go there after work.

"Look what the cat dragged in," says Adam, looking me up and down. "We really should bring in a uniform policy," he adds.

I can't help but smile. I've missed his catty comments. I look down at my outfit of jeans and T-shirt. "You don't like my clothes?"

"I don't like your face." He checks his watch. "One minute to spare. Anyone would think you'd been off with bereavement," he says, throwing my apron at me. "Clean some tables."

I laugh. "Yes, sir."

My shift passes quickly, but I'm glad I only agreed to a few hours to begin with. I'm shattered as I kiss Betsy on the cheek and head out. I flag down a cab and give him the address to the Old Tavern.

Cheri only knew Solo's uncle's first name, so when I approach the bar, I look around the tables to see if I can spot anyone who looks similar. It's an old man's bar with a stale odour and a real need for a refurbishment. The barman eyes me with interest. "The only people we get in here are regulars and cops, and you're not either."

"I'm looking for someone."

"You probably ain't gonna find him in here, love," he says, wiping a glass.

"Dax?"

He grins. "Dax Emery?"

"I'm not sure of his surname."

"It ain't a name many men have. I can call him, if you like, see if he's around the area?" I nod. "Who shall I say wants to speak to him?"

"Lara. I know his nephew, Solo."

He goes out back to put the call in, and when he returns, he pours me a Coke. "He'll be ten minutes."

I fidget nervously, though I have no idea why. When the door finally opens and a man who looks only slightly older than Solo appears, I'm ready to bolt. He fixes me with a steely glare, making his way towards me. "Lara?" I nod. "Dax. I hear you wanted to see me."

He straightens his suit jacket and takes a seat beside me as the barman hands him a water. "I know Solo," I announce.

"Does he know you're here?" I shake my head. "How do you know him?"

"We dated."

He sniggers. "Solo doesn't date."

"I know that now," I mumble.

"So, what, you're here to get revenge? I'm a cop, lady, not a miracle worker."

I gasp. "A cop?"

He gives me the side eye. "You didn't know? How exactly do you know about me?"

"Someone Solo used to know told me."

"What are you doing here?"

I think about his question. "Honestly, I don't know. I want to dig around and get some shit on him but . . . maybe it's stupid."

"He really hurt you, huh?"

"Not me. My brother."

He turns sideways to face me. "Go on."

"Liam was killed, and Solo was behind it." It's almost a relief to say the words out loud.

"You have proof?" I shake my head, and he sighs heavily. "What exactly do you expect me to do?"

"Cheri said you hated each other. I wanted to know why."

"Family shit. Look, you have nothing I wanna hear. Solo is out of my life, and if he dumped you, be thankful. He brings nothing but problems. It's been that way since he was a kid. Forget him and move on." He stands and slides a business card towards me. "If you get any evidence, you can call me."

"He confessed. He told me himself," I mutter. "I'll never get justice."

Dax lingers a moment. "Give me time to think. Maybe we can come up with a plan to get him to confess again."

"Like a wire or something?" I ask, and he laughs.

"That's so nineties. Put your number in my phone," he says, handing it over. I put it in and hand it back. "Do you have any contact with him?" I shake my head. "Okay. I'll be in touch."

CHAPTER TWENTY-TWO

SOLO

Cheri looks good. Way better than I remember. She smiles up at me, biting her lower lip like a damn pro, and I feel my cock stir. "What brings you here, Cheri?"

"I met your ex," she tells me, resting her hands on my desk so her cleavage is clearly on show. It works—my eyes are glued there. "Lara."

The spell is broken, and my eyes reach hers as my cock instantly deflates. "Huh?"

"She's after some dirt on you. Apparently, you've pissed her off."

"Hold on," I snap, sitting up straighter. "Lara met with you and asked for dirt on me?"

Cheri nods. "Yep. And it got me thinking about you and how much fun we had." She makes her way to my side of the desk and rests against it. "Remember?"

"What sort of dirt?"

She runs her hand over my chest. "You still work out," she points out. "I know a great way to get over heartbreak."

I snatch her hand from roaming further, and she gasps. Her eyes darken with delight and her breathing becomes rapid. "Fuck me, Solo."

"What did she want to know?" I grit out impatiently.

She rolls her eyes. "Just dirt. Any dirt. What did you do to hurt her so badly?"

I get rid of Cheri and call church. The men fill the room, and when they finally settle down, I bang the gavel to start. "I had a visitor earlier," I begin. "Cheri."

"Jesus, ain't she married to a Reaper these days?" asks Duke.

I shrug. "She said Lara's been asking around about me. She's trying to get dirt on me."

Viper sits up straighter, a look of concern showing on his face. "Why is she doing that?"

"I think that's obvious," I mutter, rolling my eyes. "My point is, she's gonna become a nuisance if she starts poking around."

"No one's got shit on you," says Viper. "So, she asked a club whore about you, what exactly can Cheri tell her? The women know nothing, they never have, and Lara knows that. Maybe she's just trying get over her heartbreak . . . occupying her time?"

"I dunno, brother, it just makes me nervous," I say with a sigh.

"Do you think she slashed the tyres on your bike?" asks Breaker.

"I don't think it's her style," I say. "She'd need real strength to get through them. It seems unlikely."

"Pres, if she's not on her meds, who knows what she's capable of," says Viking.

I glare at him, and he looks away. She might not be my ol' lady these days, but I don't appreciate him speaking about her in that tone. "It wasn't her," I snap. "Keep your ears to the ground. I wanna know if this was a one-off, if she's a heartbroken ex kicking up a little dust, or if she's going deeper with this. I'm gonna go see her brother now and have a quiet word."

Lucas is sitting in a booth at Maine's, looking over paperwork and ignoring the heaving bar filled with drunken partygoers. I slide into the booth opposite him, and he looks up. I used to see fear in his eyes whenever he looked my way, but now, he looks at me with contempt and hatred. "What do you want?"

"Nice to see you too, brother-in-law," I say.

"We both know you're not a part of my family, thanks to Lara finally seeing the light."

"I'm here to talk about her, actually."

He sighs, dropping his pen and leaning back. "What a surprise."

"How is she?"

"Great. She's on a date tonight."

I try not to look surprised and force a grin. "Yeah? Anyone I know?"

He laughs, seeing right through my lie. "No. This guy doesn't run in your dodgy circles. He's nice. The sort of man I'd be happy to call brother-in-law."

"All men are dogs, Lucas. Even you."

"I'll ask you again, what do you want?"

"Lara's asking around after me," I say, and annoyance flickers over his expression. "She contacted a woman I used to fuck. Is she taking her meds?"

"Yes."

"And she's getting regular check-ups with her doctor?"

"Why did you contact your ex?" he asks impatiently.

"She said she wanted dirt on me. Now, I'm willing to let this slide if you give me your word you'll speak to her."

"And if I don't? Will you kill her too?"

I stare him in the eyes, choosing not to use words. He nods once, accepting my offer. "Good. It's been great catching up."

It's been a long time since I activated the tracker I placed in Lara's mobile phone. I stare at the flashing red dot telling me Lara is just around the corner from me, in a place I wouldn't be seen dead in. It's posh, with fancy cocktails. Lara loves those places. Glancing around the dull bar I'm in, I wonder how the hell it hasn't been pulled down when everywhere around it is upmarket and fresh. "Another pint, mucker?" asks the barman. I shake my head—one warm beer was enough.

I step out into the busy street, tucking my mobile away and heading in her direction. I won't go in, but I need a glimpse of her. Just one.

As I get closer, a fight breaks out and the door staff jump in to try and break it up. I dodge the chaos, but as I level with the bar, my breath catches in my throat. She's right there in front of me, laughing at something a man said from behind her. She's not looking in my direction, and as she steps out, she almost crashes into me. I automatically take her elbows to steady her, and she freezes, holding her breath before bringing her eyes to mine.

"Careful," I whisper. "Look where you're going."

"Sorry, man, she's full of fruity cocktails," laughs the man she's with. I give him a quick assessment. He's tall, but not as tall as me. He's medium build and a suit-wearer. His hair is cropped short, and he's clean shaven. Completely the opposite to me.

When I look back down at Lara, she's still staring up at me in shock. I run my hands down her arms, dropping one to my side and trailing the other over her hip, she looks down to follow it. I lift her top slightly, hooking my finger into her jeans and gently tugging until her tattoo is exposed. "Hey, man, what the fuck are you doing?" snaps her date, but I ignore him.

I brush the black ink hiding my name and look her in the eyes. "Mine," I whisper.

It breaks the spell she's under, and she narrows her eyes at my word. "I hate you," she whispers back with venom in her voice. Then she grins, turns to her date, and pulls him in for a kiss. He's surprised and doesn't respond for a second, but then his hands grab her arse and he tugs her hard against him. I watch, letting the jealousy envelop me and keeping my eyes fixed on the way she places her small hands to his face and tilts her head to meet his. I watch the fluttering of her eyelashes and the pink flush on her cheek.

"Oh, Suicide, you know I'd give anything to watch the full show, but I got shit to do," I say. They pull apart, and her date looks pleased with himself while Lara looks flustered and maybe even a little turned on. I wanna put her over my knee and slap that look from her, because it ain't for me. "I should thank you," I add, taking a few steps away. "Bringing Cheri back into my life was a good move. That bitch knows how to fuck," I say, winking. "She's the best I ever had." I walk away, angry at myself for being a childish prick, but letting her know I've seen Cheri will make her cautious about trying to fuck me over.

LARA

"I take it you know him," says Kai.

I nod. "Yeah, that's him."

"Shit, your hot biker? He's intense."

Adam stumbles out the bar laughing, but his smile fades when he sees us both. He throws his arm around Kai. "Is everything okay?"

"She just bumped into Solo, literally," says Kai.

"Oh shit."

"And I kissed your boyfriend," I add. "Sorry."

"Did it work?" asks Adam.

I shake my head. "Nope. Why did I do that? I hate him, so why do I care if he's jealous or not?" I wail.

The guys hook an arm each and begin to lead me away. "It's normal to still have feelings. The heart wants what it wants," says Kai.

Adam scoffs. "Bitch, please. The guy is a psychopath. Stay the hell away from him or I'll tell Lucas."

By the time I get home, Lucas has finished his shift at Maine's and is sitting in the kitchen nursing a coffee. "Hey," I say, "how was work?" He glares at me over his mug, and I inwardly groan. "What have I done this time?" I ask.

"Did you stalk him to find out about his ex?" he asks, his voice low and cold.

"Huh?"

"Solo. He came to see me this evening." Now it makes sense as to why I bumped into him in an area he'd never usually be. My heart flickers a little with pain. For a minute back there, I thought he'd been watching me. "He said you're asking questions."

"So, who the hell is he to tell me I can't?" I snap, squaring my shoulders.

"Why?"

"Because I want to know more about him," I say innocently.

"Bullshit. Don't lie to me after everything we've been through, Lara. I wanna know why the fuck you contacted his ex. Is it jealousy?"

I screw up my face. "God, no."

"Then, why?"

I lower into a seat. "I wanna ruin him."

Lucas stares at me for what feels like a lifetime before taking a steadying breath. "Pardon?"

"I want him to pay for what he's done."

"Are you kidding me right now?"

"He killed Liam. He needs to pay for something. Why should he walk around like he's the fucking king and Liam's nothing?"

Lucas pinches the bridge of his nose. "I thought you'd learnt your lesson," he mutters. "I thought, after Liam and your mini breakdown, you'd learned your lesson and you were going to get on with your life. And now, I find out you're planning some fucking revenge attack on the crazy bastard that had our brother killed. *Killed*, Lara. Liam is never coming back because of the choices he made, and now, you're doing the same. What do I do when you're gone too?"

"Solo won't hurt me," I say, trying to grab his hand across the table.

He snatches it back, his eyes bugging out of his head. "Because he fucked you? You think he won't kill you because he fucked you?"

"I know him . . ."

"Jesus Christ, listen to yourself. You knew the man so well that he killed our brother under your nose, and you didn't have a damn clue. You don't know him, Lara. What you do know is he's a killer. He'll wipe you out if you cross him because he did it to Liam and fuck knows how many others. So, I'm telling you now, leave him alone. Stay the hell away from Solo and his club. If I find out you've been near him, I'll take drastic action."

"I'm an adult. I can make my own decisions. Don't you care he's walking free when he should be behind bars?"

Lucas stands abruptly and pushes his face into mine. "I'll have you sectioned under the Mental Health Act, I swear to God, Lara. I'll tell them you're not coping and you're making threats to kill yourself, and I'll have you locked away. I'm serious about this. Stay away from Solo."

I blink the tears that threaten to fall from my lower lashes. "No, you wouldn't," I whisper.

"Watch me. I'll go to any length to keep you safe, and if you're locked away, he won't get to you."

Lucas storms from the room, slamming the door hard, and I let the tears escape.

CHAPTER TWENTY-THREE

SOLO

I open one eye and realise the loud banging is on my bed-room door. "What?" I yell, irritated at being woken.

"Unlock the door," comes Duke's voice.

I grin. "Depends. Are you staying or is this a passing visit?"

Siren stirs beside me, stretching out her naked body and groaning. "What's going on?"

I get out of bed and flick the lock open on the bedroom door. Duke enters, grinning like a lunatic. "It's four in the morning," I say, shaking his hand. "What's so urgent?"

He shrugs from his kutte and lays it over the chair. "I thought you'd be missing me so . . ."

"Are you staying?" I ask again. I climb back into bed, sitting against the headboard. "Cos I could do with my VP back."

Duke sits the other side of Siren and runs his hand up her leg. She automatically separates them, waiting for his hand to travel where she needs it. I guess he still isn't ready to tell me the truth. I watch as he rubs circles over her clit, and she arches her back. "I was thinking of sticking around, yeah. The road is lonely without brothers, and I heard a certain fiery bitch has left the club." He pushes a finger into Siren's wet pussy, and she hisses in appreciation.

"Yeah, Lara's history," I say, rolling Siren's nipple between my fingers. "I'll catch you up on it all later, but she's becoming a real pain in the arse."

Duke lowers his head to between Siren's legs, "Told you she was trouble," he mutters, then buries his face into her pussy.

I release my cock and guide her head towards it. I've missed this.

I watch Duke closely as he's greeted by the brothers over breakfast. Since his return in the early hours, we'd devoured Siren like she was our last meal, something we haven't done for a long time. Sharing women has always been part of club life, so that's not what's worrying me. I'm pissed he won't talk to me. I thought if I gave him time, he'd get his head around the fact he's bi or gay and come talk to me. But he's acting like nothing's wrong, like his life can just go back to how it was. Well, it can't. I've changed, and I want honesty from my brothers.

"So, did you clear your head?" I ask, stirring my coffee. He glances over, then shrugs his shoulders and nods. "From what exactly?"

"Just the general shit, Pres. You know how fucked up it gets in here," he says, tapping his head.

"Meet anyone?" I ask.

He frowns. "Like an ol' lady? No."

"Anyone, not necessarily an ol' lady."

Breaker laughs. "Who else is he gonna meet, Pres, a man?"

I don't laugh, and neither does Duke. Instead, we stare at each other, and something changes in his eyes. He knows I know, and he shuts it down. "There was plenty of pussy out there, but none worthy of bringing back permanently."

I turn my glare to Breaker. "What if he did meet a man? What the fuck's wrong with that?"

Breaker's smile fades and he glances around the table for backup. The other brothers avoid him, and the table falls quiet. "Well, nothing, just . . . yah know. It's Duke. He lives for pussy."

"I don't care who my men bring into this club so long as they're trustworthy. Remember that."

I stand and head for the office. I hear Duke's heavy footfalls behind me, and he slams the office door closed. "What the fuck was that all about?"

I sit behind the desk. "You tell me, brother."

He stares for a minute. "If you got something to say, Solo, just say it."

"You're gay."

He inhales sharply. "What the fuck are you talking about?"

"And it's okay. I just want you to know it's fine by me."

"I'm not gay."

"Duke, I know you," I mutter. "I know you better than you know yourself sometimes."

"Apparently so, if you're telling me I'm gay when I'm not."

I sigh. "Yah know, it fucking stings in here," I snap, tapping my heart, "that my own VP is lying to my face about this. It doesn't change anything. You're my brother, no matter what. I don't give two fucks where you stick your dick. If you're happy, so am I."

I can see his mind working over my words. "It don't fit in this world," he eventually mutters.

"What doesn't?"

"Gay. Bi. Any of it. The brothers won't accept it. Our enemies will use it against me."

I relax back into my chair. "Then we'll kill them."

A smirk pulls at his lips. "You're gonna kill everyone who's got something to say about it?"

I nod. "Yep." I turn my expression serious. "You don't have to be something you're not in this club, brother. If anyone's got a problem with it, they know where the door is. When you're ready to talk, I'm here."

"I'm just not ready to fully be out there, man. The brothers . . . well, they'll struggle. I don't want shit to change around me. Maybe in time, but that ride out got me thinking hard, and I realised I'm okay with keeping my shit private. But thanks, Pres. I appreciate it. And you guessing like that, it's a huge weight off my mind."

"Whatever makes you happy, brother."

"Tell me what Lara's been up to?" he asks, grinning.

I roll my eyes, not knowing where to start. I tell him the truth from the beginning, that I came clean about Liam and my involvement. He groans. "Why'd yah do that, Pres? We had you covered."

"Because with her, it felt different, Duke. Even if I wanted to lie, I couldn't. She deserved the truth, and it worked out for the best because Lara's not for this life. It gave me a reason to let her go."

"And have you?" he asks, arching a brow.

I nod. "Yeah. This bullshit with Cheri meant I had to see her brother, and he told me she was on a date. She's moving on, and that's a good thing."

"Viper tells me things are getting better around this place. You're consulting the guys more, and they appreciate that."

I nod. "We're a brotherhood, right? For a long time, I've been running it as the Solo show. It's time I grew the fuck up and took this club to another level. I want money, Duke. I want to be bigger than we've ever been. I want to expand, and I want some ol' ladies, or men, around the place. We need it to feel like home."

"Sounds like that ol' lady of yours gave you a taste of something you didn't even know was missing."

I shake my head, laughing. "Not me, brother. I'm avoiding the drama. But the guys, they need stability. It's a good feeling to have someone waiting in your bed."

"Speaking of which, Viper told me about some crazy scheme you got going on with Huntley."

"Viper will never get his kid if he don't show he's settling down. Social services are doing a check and home visit in a couple months. He's gotta be ready for that. His eyes lit up when that little bombshell gave him lip. It'll be fun to see him chase her. And it teaches men like Huntley not to fuck me over. When others see I'm willing to take their loved ones, they'll think twice about screwing me over."

"And if they come after your loved ones?" he asks.

"Brother, you know I don't have anyone I give a fuck about."

"Lara?"

"Ain't my problem no more." My phone beeps to show me Lara is at the gym. I slide it into my drawer. "Let's go for a run. It's been too long since I beat your arse."

LARA

The second I step out of the gym, my mobile rings. It's Dax. "Can you meet me?" he asks.

"Sure." He reels off a café address a few streets away, so I make my way.

He's already seated when I go inside. He points to a waiting coffee for me, and I take a seat. "I've been thinking about Solo," he begins. "I can't do much with you on the outside of the club."

"What does that mean?"

"It means you need to get back in there."

I laugh until I see he isn't kidding. "I can't. I hate him. He probably hates me."

"It's the only way. He might confide in you some more."

"He told me to my face that he killed my brother. You said it wasn't enough," I remind him.

"Because Solo would have planned it so there was nothing to lead me to him. Maybe if he tells you new shit that's happening, you can be ahead of the game, taking photos or recording. Confessions are better when they're recorded."

I mull over his words. "So, if I can get stuff on record, we stand a chance of sending him to prison?"

He shrugs. "If it's enough for conviction, sure. We can't pin your brother on him. I checked out the case—it's closed and there's nothing but a medical report telling the world he was a junkie who overdosed. No one's gonna reopen that without hard evidence. It's just not worth the money or paperwork."

Sadness twists my heart as I nod. "Right, I'll try and get something else."

I'm almost at the end of my shift when Duke strolls in. I stare open-mouthed as he grins. "Suicide, long time no see."

"It's not been long at all," I mutter.

Adam appears behind me, freezing at the sight of his secret lover. His eyes dart to Kai sitting by the window, enjoying a coffee and reading the newspaper. "What can we get you?" he asks, autopilot kicking in.

Duke follows the line of sight, leading him to Kai, and his eyes narrow. "Coffee, black."

"Coming right up," says Adam, a little too jovial.

"So, you're back?" I ask coldly.

"I heard you'd left the club, so figured I'd come back to support Solo."

I scoff. "Cos he's so heartbroken," I mutter sarcastically.

"Nah, not even a bit. In fact, I'm sending him on a date tonight. Thought he could do with a real woman in his life."

I narrow my eyes as Adam slides the coffee toward him. "One who can handle a real man," Duke continues.

I take the coffee back. "I think you asked for it to be take-out," I snap, grabbing a paper cup, tipping the coffee contents into it, and securing a lid. "Cash or card?"

He grins. "She's older than you, more mature. She works as a nurse." He whistles, winking. "She's hot."

"I hope he has a great night."

"He said you were dating," he adds.

I shrug innocently. "Yes. Sort of." The lie rolls off my tongue. "He's right over there," I add, pointing to Kai.

Duke laughs hard. "I don't think so, Suicide. That man's gay."

"How the hell can you tell that?" I snap, annoyed he's un-covered my lie.

He leans closer. "I've been there, done that." A strangled noise leaves Adam's throat which causes Duke to look at him. "So, if he's not with her, that means he's with you . . ."

"It's early days."

"Damn right. I've been gone a few weeks, and you meet some fucker who wears hair gel?"

"Me and you were casual," Adam mutters. "I didn't think it was an issue."

"You're about to find out how big of an issue it is. Back room, now!" Duke orders.

I stare after the pair and then look over to where Kai is still oblivious to the drama. Betsy skips through the door, slowing when she spots me. "Oh no, what now?"

Adam managed to get out of Duke the place where Solo's big date was happening. I'm sure the VP dropped it on purpose, fully expecting my jealousy to have me marching on in there to make a fool of myself. He was right. I stare at the Indian restaurant, nerves kicking in. It's the perfect way to put my plan into place. I need Solo to notice me again. I take a deep breath and head inside.

Solo is sitting opposite a blonde. Her back is to me, but I can see she's thin with a fuller arse. Just how he likes his women. He spots me and narrows his eyes. "Table for one, madam?" asks a passing waiter.

I shake my head, smiling and giving Solo a wave. "No, thanks, there's my friend." I head over. "Solo," I say, warmly. He looks confused. I turn to the female, who is shifting awkwardly. "I'm his wife."

"She's not my wife," Solo cuts in. "She's an ex. I'm sorry about this."

"Ol' lady, same thing," I say, shrugging. I pull up a seat, and Solo groans.

"Maybe I should leave," the woman says, picking up her designer handbag.

"No, don't. She's not my ol' lady either. We finished ages ago—"

"After he let one of his whores mess with my medication, admitted to killing my brother and—" Solo grabs my upper arm and hauls me to my feet. He drags me through a back door and a fire exit until we're in an alley, glaring at each other angrily.

"What the fuck, Suicide?"

I bite my lower lip, and his eyes immediately go there. "Seeing you with her . . ."

"Are you stalking me?"

I shake my head. "Duke told me. Bet you're pleased to have your murderous best friend back."

He rolls his eyes. "Of course, he told you," he mutters. "You should go."

"It's been ages since I—"

"I don't care. Go home."

"Fucked," I continue, and heat flares in his eyes. "I hate you, but I can't help wanting to—"

He slams me against the wall before I finish my sentence and his lips crash against my own in a deep, bruising kiss. His hands roughly grab at parts of my body, and I clamber up him until he pulls my legs around his waist. This wasn't part of the plan, but it's the only language we seem to speak when we're alone. His erection is straining in his jeans, and I rub myself against it, panting as sparks ignite me.

"What the fuck are we doing?" he whispers against my lips.

"It's just sex," I tell him, reaching between us to unfasten his jeans. I shove my hand inside and grip his hard cock. He closes his eyes. "I came prepared," I add, using my other hand to pull out a condom from my bra.

His eyes narrow. "Why the fuck have you got that?" he snaps. If I don't think fast, he'll get pissed and the whole thing will end in an argument. I move my hand, gripping his shaft a little tighter, and he hisses, digging his fingers into my thighs.

"I'm not wearing any underwear," I whisper, ripping the packet open with my teeth. He groans. "And I'm so fucking wet, Solo. I need you." I push the condom over his cock and guide it to my entrance.

He pauses. "Are you sure about this?"

"Just one time," I say, feeling him begin to slide inside me. "And then I'll leave you alone."

"You hate me," he reminds me.

"Yep. So, why the fuck does that turn me on more?" I ask, crossing my legs at the ankles and tugging him in to the hilt.

He slams his hand against the wall and rests his head against my shoulder. "Fuck, Suicide. Fuck. I missed this."

CHAPTER TWENTY-FOUR

SOLO

I come so hard, my legs turn to jelly and I can't see straight. I lower Lara's feet to the ground and sort myself out. When I finally look at her, guilt hits me hard. What the fuck did I just do? "You okay?"

"Yeah," she says, smiling, but it doesn't quite reach her eyes.

"Look, Suicide, I promised to let you live your life without me and . . ."

She looks like she's about to laugh. "Oh god, please don't make this awkward. I told you, it's just sex, Solo. It changes nothing."

I frown. "Huh?"

"I needed sex. What's so shocking about that? Have you never been back to an ex for a quick bunk-up?"

"Huh?" I repeat. It's not like Lara, and the last thing I expected was for her to be so cold and unfeeling.

"Listen, get back to your date. And . . . thanks for that." She pats me on the shoulder—actually fucking pats me—and walks away.

I return to the table to find Caris is sitting where I left her. I smile, taking me seat. "I'm so sorry about that. Where were we?"

"I've written down the names of the other two girls," she says, sliding the paper across to me. "Do your checks and come back to me."

"Duke vouched for you, but I'll run the checks. And you all dance?"

She nods. "Yeah. It's how I met your man, Duke." She grins. "He's been visiting me for some time."

"Okay, I'll be in touch once I've had the license approved."

I meet the guys right after. Huntley's bar is brightly lit, but there are no customers inside. Huntley jumps in fright the second I push the door open. "You look like you're on edge," I point out, taking a seat. Viper and Duke linger in the doorway. "Sorry we didn't come back when I said we would. Shit's been crazy. Whiskey, please," I order.

His shaky hand takes down a glass and he pours the amber liquid. "I've almost got the cash," he mutters, placing the glass before me.

"Almost?" I repeat.

"I'm a few grand out," he admits, "but I went to the bank today to ask for a loan. I'm waiting on the decision."

I laugh. We both know the bank won't lend him shit, he's already up to his eyes in debt. "Where is she?" I ask.

"You can't take my daughter," he rushes the words.

"But we can, Mark. I already discussed this with you. Go get her."

"She isn't here."

"Get her," I repeat, more firmly.

"Solo, please. I'll call the cops."

His words irritate me, and I drink the whiskey in one, slamming the glass down. I nod to the back room, and Viper and Duke head for it. Huntley goes to block the door, but I reach over and grab him by the collar, hauling him half over the bar and bringing his face to mine. "I helped you out, and now, you're gonna help me."

"That wasn't the agreement. The agreement was cash," he says, panicked.

"And you broke that, so I re-wrote the agreement. I'm taking your daughter. You'll be a good boy and let me. And if you call the cops, I'll kill her. Deal?"

Viper comes back through holding Huntley's daughter over his shoulder. She's floppy, so he must have put her to sleep. "Meet you at the club," he mutters, heading out.

Duke joins me. "She's a firecracker," he says with a low whistle.

"What are you going to do with her?" asks Huntley.

"We'll look after her, Mark. Don't worry. She'll call you soon." I pat him on the back, and we head out.

"She is fucking hot," says Duke the second we step out. "You sure she's Viper's?"

I laugh. "A few days of listening to her scream and shout and you'll be happy she ain't yours, brother. Now, let's go get this bar license signed."

LARA

"Are you fucking shitting me?" growls Lucas, peeking out through the blinds at Maine's.

"What are you moaning about now?" I ask, wiping down the bar top. It's been a week since my hook-up with Solo, and to be honest, I thought he'd be hanging around more, but he isn't. I haven't seen or heard from in.

"The new owners are next door," he mutters.

"Oooh, let me see," I say rushing over. The building next door is huge and has been empty since Maine's opened. We saw the 'sold' sign go up a few weeks ago. "Surely, it can't be another bar. It's been too quick," I add. That was Lucas's main worry, that a bar would out do him and take his customers.

"Lara, I should warn you," Lucas begins, but it's too late. I'm already looking through the blinds at Solo's smug face as he unlocks the door of the building.

"No fucking way!" I snap, storming out despite Lucas shouting me back. "What the fuck are you doing?" I yell, and Solo slowly turns to me, his smile full and his eyes twinkling in delight at my anger. Duke and Viper flank him like a pair of monkeys protecting their king.

"Suicide, fancy seeing you here."

"Not really a shock, though, is it? Seeing as my brother owns this bar!"

"Yes, we'll be neighbours. Great, right?"

"What will you open as?"

"A gentleman's club," says Solo, and I stare at him dumb-founded. "Anyway, can't stand chatting, I have shit to do." He goes inside, followed by his monkeys.

"That's that then," mutters Lucas from beside me. "He'll ruin Maine's, and I'll have to close. And who the hell will buy this place with bikers next door?"

"Over my dead body!" I snap, rushing after Solo with Lucas hot on my tail.

"Maybe we should come back when you're calmer?" he hisses in my ear.

Solo looks bored when I get down the stairs and into the bar area. I stare wide-eyed. The place is immaculate. "He couldn't possibly have a bar license already," mutters Lucas.

"It's who you know, not what you know," says Viper.

"You're all set to go," I mutter, taking in the fully stocked fridges. Music from the stage starts up and we all turn to see the woman Solo was on a date with, lifting herself up onto the large silver pole in the centre of the stage. "A strip bar?"

"A gentleman's club," Solo corrects.

"It's a fucking strip club. A seedy strip club that we don't want near Maine's. How the hell did you get this passed without telling anyone around here? These things should go through a board of governors at the council. Locals need to be made aware in case there are any objections," I rant.

"It's all above board," says Viper, his tone bored.

"I doubt that," I snap. "I'm going to have you shut down within the month."

Solo sniggers. "Careful, Suicide, remember what happened last time you ran your mouth off."

I feel my cheeks flush pink, and Lucas's questioning eyes are fixed on me. "You're not the only one who knows people in high places," I add, stomping out.

"What was that about?" asks Lucas, following me back into Maine's. I pull out my mobile, ignoring him, and put a call in to Dax.

"Yup?" he answers.

"He's opening a strip club," I inform him. "Right next to my brother's bar."

"I know."

"But how? He can't just open something like that and not tell any of the locals."

"He's Solo. Of course, he can."

I growl in frustration at his lack of interest. "There must be something you can do."

"Have you got anything interesting on him yet?"

"No. I want him closed down."

Dax laughs. "Then speak to the council, love. I deal with law breakers, not slime balls with hands in the councillors' pockets. One of his gang members has a court hearing listed in a few weeks. Something about a kid. He goes by the name Viper."

"Right," I mutter. I didn't know Viper had a kid, so the news surprises me.

"When you lived there, what was he like? Maybe we can put a stop to his custody battle."

My heart twists. I don't want to ruin the other men, just Solo, and maybe Duke. And I certainly don't wanna mess with the kid's life. "I didn't have much to do with him really."

"I don't care. Say you did. I can arrange a meeting with the social worker dealing with the case."

"But he might be a good dad," I suggest.

"I doubt it. He's a biker. They don't make good parents. I'll set it up." He disconnects before I can protest further.

"Can your contact help?" asks Lucas. I shake my head.

"We'll just have to complain. A lot."

The door opens and Solo fills it. "Can we talk?"

"No!" I snap.

"I was actually speaking to Lucas," he says, smirking, and I blush for a second time. "I think we can come to an arrangement."

"He doesn't want to arrange anything that you're involved in," I say.

Lucas sighs. "Let's go to the office."

"Lucas!"

He shrugs. "What choice do I have, Lara? They're ready to open. This has to work."

SOLO

I take a seat as Lucas settles in behind his desk. "Did you do it on purpose?" he asks.

"Yes."

"Why?"

"It's all part of my plan."

"To get Lara back?"

I nod. "One day. She isn't ready yet."

"You're wasting your time. She won't forgive you. Buying up the area, ruining me, it won't help your cause."

I laugh. "I don't wanna ruin you, Lucas. Fuck, if I wanted that, you'd be dead by now." He pales. "One day, we'll be related by marriage, and we'll be running a lot of bars. Your expertise will be invaluable."

"Are you kidding me? You want me to run bars with you?"

"What's so wrong with that? Having the bar next door is perfect. You can oversee both."

He frowns. "I can't run your bar."

"Of course, you can. Ellie is the bar manager, but you'll oversee her. I trust you," I say, passing over a set of keys.

"You're fucking crazy. You can't just come in here and tell me to help run your bar, Solo. That's not how life works."

I take a deep, calming breath. "Yah know, I never had anyone to guide me like you guided Liam and Lara. If I had, maybe I'd know how to do this better. I'm not forcing you. I'm asking. My end game involves Lara. You might not like it, but it does. I'm just starting up our future, so I can take care of her. Help me with that."

Lucas hesitates, his eyes fixed on the keys. "I still don't think it'll work. She hates you."

"Let me deal with Lara."

I find Lara outside staring at the new sign above my bar. "Do you like it?" I ask, wrapping my arms around her waist and inhaling her fruity shampoo scent.

She pulls free, and I grin. "Suicide," she says, glaring at the red sign. "You named a strip club after me. Classy."

"Glad you like it," I say, heading for the door. "Maybe one day I'll get to see you naked, dancing on that pole. Just for my eyes, of course."

"Over my dead body."

"Suicide, you're turning me on, stop."

The yelling from the basement is becoming an issue. The club is set on an industrial park which is no longer used, so passersby shouldn't be too concerned, but it's the guys who are complaining. Since we got Jaya back here, she's done nothing but scream and shout. "Can't you do something?" Duke asks Viper.

"I tried," snaps Viper, pointing to the nail marks on his skin. "She's crazy mad."

I groan, slamming my glass down on the bar and heading in the direction of the cellar. "Pres, what are you gonna do?" asks Viper warily.

"I'm gonna shut her up. Stay here!"

I pull open the heavy door that leads down the stone steps. There's a locked iron gate at the bottom where Jaya is standing. She glares at me with hatred.

"I'm trying to be understanding," I say, unlocking the gate. She takes a few steps back, but her stance tells me she's ready for a fight. "But your noise is driving me insane."

"Then let me go and it'll stop." I step closer, and she smirks. "I'm warning you, I fight."

"It doesn't need to be like this," I tell her, closing the gate behind me. "We can live in peace and harmony."

"Fuck you."

"I will if you don't shut up."

"Try it. Come near me, and I'll bite your fucking dick off."

I snigger. "You have no idea what that does to me."

"I want to leave."

"I want you to behave."

"Why am I here?" she asks.

"Now, I like this kind of thing. Questions, answers, good conversation. If I tell you, will you be more cooperative?"

"Depends on the answers."

"Your dad owed me."

"What's that got to do with me?"

I shrug. "Nothing, apart from the fact you're his daughter. Sucks to be you, right?"

"This isn't a film. You can't take me to punish him."

I grin. "Seems I've done exactly that." She rushes at me, slapping me hard. I catch her wrists and slam her hard against the wall. It knocks the breath from her, and she gasps. "Little princess, I'll give you that one for free. But you raise your hand to me again and I'll cut it off. Am I clear?"

She clenches her jaw but eventually nods once. "Now, you need to help me out, so I can help you. Your dad owes me big, and you're here to clear his debt. You do this with no complaints, and I'll eventually let you go home to Daddy. But you carry on pissing me off and I'll kill you, then your dad will owe me more than he can ever afford, meaning he'll be forever in my debt. Don't you have younger siblings?"

She swallows hard. "What do I have to do?"

"Play wifey."

"I won't have sex with you," she hisses, trying to free her hands.

I brush my nose over her ear, and she stiffens. "I have my own psycho, so I don't have time for another. Viper is trying to get his kid back, but social care won't give him the time of day without the help of a good woman. That's where you come in. Convince them he's a good daddy and we'll have no problems."

"And if I can't convince them?"

"We'll work that out when it happens."

The door opens and I hear footsteps. "Suicide, you can't go down there," yells Viper.

"Fuck's sake," I murmur. "Speak of the devil and she shall appear." I release Jaya and smile wide as Lara comes into view. She takes in the scene before her and narrows her eyes.

"Am I interrupting?"

"Do you care?" I ask. "This is Lara, the psycho I was telling you about," I add to Jaya.

"What are you doing down here?" asks Lara suspiciously.

"I was showing Jaya my sex dungeon," I say, looking around the damp basement. "I never got to show you. Would you like a tour?"

"I came to talk about the club and Maine's."

I roll my eyes, grabbing Jaya's hand and leading her past Lara to go back upstairs. I hand her to Viper. "Keep a close eye on this one. She's been upgraded to the guest suite, but if she tries anything funny, she knows the score."

"Who is she? What's going on?" asks Lara, following me into the office. "I hope you're not going to hurt her."

"What can I help you with, Suicide?"

"You put Lucas in charge?"

"I asked for his help, yes."

"Why would you do that?" I shrug. "Guilt?" she adds.

"Maybe. Or maybe I just wanna help the guy out. He likes bars, and I need an expert. It's win-win."

"I don't believe you. If this is a ploy to get me back into your bed, it won't work."

I roll my eyes. "Lara, we both know it doesn't take a big plan to get you to drop your knickers for me. A week ago, you were begging me, remember? I'm cleaning up my club by investing in business. There's nothing else going on."

"Who is the girl you just gave to Viper? Why was she in the basement?"

"Club business."

"I'll call the police, see what they make of it, shall I?"

I sigh heavily. "I'm trying to give you the space you need, Lara, yet you keep turning up where I am. A bit like when we first met." I move closer to her, and she squares her shoulders, giving me that defiant look I love so much. I gently brush her hair back over her shoulder and stare deep into her eyes. "If you need a fuck, just tell me."

"You make me sick," she mutters, shuddering for added effect.

"Sick or horny?"

"You think you're so fucking—" I cut her off with a kiss, gripping my hands tightly in her hair and tugging hard.

When I pull back, she's panting, and her cheeks are pink. "Get on the desk."

Her eyes glance at the large desk, but then she remembers how much she hates me. "Fuck you."

"Second time I've heard that today. Get on the desk, Lara. I need to taste your pussy."

"No. Not now. Not ever. Get off me."

I tug her hair harder. "Remove your clothes and get on the desk. If you make me ask again, I'll be extra hard on you."

CHAPTER TWENTY-FIVE

LARA

My plan worked, and I slowly unfasten my jeans. He grins like he's won, but I'm the one winning, because every time we do this, I'm a step closer to taking him down.

Once I'm naked, he leads me to the desk by my hair. I climb on to all fours, and he gently pushes my head down until my cheek is pressed against the cool wood. My naked arse is in the air, and he wastes no time circling me like a predator. The anticipation is too much, and when he stops behind me, the urge to cover myself is too real. I squeeze my eyes shut. "You're wet for me, Suicide."

"It's not for you," I snap. If I don't keep up the hatred, he'll be suspicious.

He takes my hand and guides it through my legs. "Touch yourself, see how wet you are for me." I run my fingers through my folds, flinching when sparks ignite. I know the second he touches me, I'll orgasm. "Do you trust me, Suicide?"

I scoff. "No. Not even a little."

He sniggers, opening his drawer and fumbling around. "Good."

I feel cold metal encircle my left wrist. He pulls it back to my leg and cuffs it to my ankle. "This isn't a good idea," I say, even though my heart is beating out of my chest with excitement. He takes my right hand and does the same. "Solo, I'm not entirely comfortable being tied up by you after what you did to my brother."

"Let's not talk about him right now, Lara. You'll kill my mood." He slaps my arse, and I yelp in surprise. "How many men have been here since you left me?" he asks, running his finger up my thigh. I push my forehead against the desk, trying to keep still.

"A lot," I lie.

He laughs, cupping my pussy in his hand and rubbing. I close my eyes, forcing myself to act indifferent. "How many have tasted it?" he asks before his hand is replaced by his mouth. I cry out. The way he holds me to his face like he can't get enough, is causing a heat I haven't felt in too long. He moans somewhere in the back of his throat and then pulls away. "I could live on your taste for the rest of my life and never get bored," he growls. "Fuck, I'm addicted."

"Pity you ruined it all," I say, and he rewards me with another slap on the arse.

"Remember how I used to shut that mouth of yours?" he asks, moving to stand in front of me. His cock is in his hand, and he tugs my hair until my mouth is level with his erection. "Open," he orders. I stare at his throbbing, hard cock and smirk, pressing my lips together tightly. "You wanna play it like that?" he asks, cocking his brow. "I can get Siren in here to do it for you. Just having you looking like that on my desk, with your juices all down your thighs," he takes a deep breath, "it's good enough for me. But you won't come today, Lara. You won't have earned it."

I narrow my eyes. The thought of watching someone else pleasure him sends me into a jealous rage. *I hate him. I hate him. I hate him.* I repeat it as a mantra, opening my mouth and taking in his erection. He hisses, throwing his head back in pleasure as I suck him, occasionally letting him hit the back of my throat. The kick I get from seeing this man come apart is sick. Robyn was right—the line between love and hate is thin. Far too thin.

Solo takes all he can, and I helplessly let him. When he's almost ready to explode, he pulls from me and moves back around to where I need to feel him. He presses his cock to my entrance, gripping onto my arms as he slowly enters me. Once he's fully inside, his fingers dig into my wrists and he delivers a punishing, hard, fast pace. He sends us both spiralling over the edge until we're panting and sweating with an uncomfortable amount of wetness between us. Pulling away, his hand moves between my legs, and I flinch. I'm too sensitive there right now. "You came on my desk," he whispers, rubbing the wetness into my thighs.

"Untie me," I snap.

He sniggers, continuing to rub. "I say when you get free, Suicide. I'm in charge."

"I mean it. Unfasten the cuffs."

"Or what?" Solo's hand finds my swollen clit and he pinches it.

"Fuck," I growl, flinching.

"I could have my guys in here to see you like this. Wet, vulnerable, at my mercy."

"You wouldn't dare," I snap. He rubs the sensitive area until it starts to feel good again. "They'd rip through you like a fucking train," he mutters, using his other hand to touch my nipple. "Now you're not mine, it might not sting as much to share."

"Solo, stop. Let me go."

"You haven't finished, Suicide. Let me take care of that for you." I have no control. He's holding all the power, and when I fall apart for a second time, he gives another satisfied smack on my arse. He releases me from the cuffs and lifts me from the desk. I'm exhausted as he carries me to the couch, laying me down. "Now, let's talk."

SOLO
Lara eyes me warily, as I lay a blanket over her. "About?" she asks.

"You said we never talk, so let's put that right."

"I said that when we were together. We're not together anymore, so I don't care. There's nothing I need to know about you."

I smirk, folding her clothes one by one and laying them neatly on the desk. "We're talking, Suicide."

She sighs heavily, sitting up and pulling the blanket tightly around her. "Make it quick."

"I'm a classic MC kid. Mum was a drug addict, and Dad hated her. He let her stick around, for far too long really, but I get it now. He couldn't just kick her out to survive. He got her the drugs—"

"So, he had all the control. The apple doesn't fall far from the tree."

I shrug. "Maybe he liked the control. But let's face it, that's something I don't have over you. I never have. You break all the fucking rules, Suicide. Just when I think you're gonna do one thing, you twist it and surprise me. You keep me on my toes."

"What happened to your parents?"

"Dad had a club. It was small and mainly for veterans. I don't think there was a brother under seventy, but he was happy for a few years until he passed. Mum died earlier, when I was eighteen and sick of her bullshit, so it wasn't a big deal."

"This is what I'm talking about," she says. "You have no feelings. It's weird."

"Says who? Society tells you to feel sad when someone dies, and I chose to be happy for her. Not because I didn't love her or because I wanted her dead. I just knew she wasn't suffering anymore. It was an end to her hell. And not just her hell, but my dad's too. He spent years looking after her. He deserved better." I lower into my chair. "Just because I don't show my feelings, doesn't mean I don't care."

"How did you feel when Liam died?" she asks, and I shift uncomfortably. This is not where I wanted the conversation to go. "You wanted to talk, so let's address the elephant in the room."

"Why do you have to pick at it?" I ask. "You can't just let shit go. I tell you the truth and it's not enough. You pick the wound until you bleed again. It only hurts you, so why do you need to know every detail?"

"Wouldn't you? If Duke was murdered . . . if I killed him . . . wouldn't you want to know it all? The last thing he said, or if he begged for his life?" She inhales sharply.

"No. It wouldn't change the fact he was dead." We fall silent, and I picture Liam. "He didn't beg, but he wouldn't tell me why he was stealing the drugs."

She folds her arms around herself, suddenly looking vulnerable again. "I think he was using it to help pay for bills. Lucas always bailed Liam out and used a lot of his savings that were meant for the bar. We struggled for a long time. I think Liam felt bad once he'd gotten himself clean. It was his way of helping out."

I feel a stab of guilt. I hate the feeling, so I push Lara's clothes across the desk towards her. "Get dressed."

"A glance at real emotion and you run," she mutters, standing and letting the blanket drop away. I watch as she begins to pull on her underwear. "When he stopped breathing, were you there?" I shake my head. "Where did he take his last breath?"

"At the docks."

"Alone?" she asks, pausing to stare at me. I nod and tears fill her eyes. "I guess that's a blessing. He wouldn't have wanted to die with you beside him."

"Lara, he knew what he was doing would get him killed. It's the world we're in. He knew the score."

"You all keep saying that like it's a comfort. It doesn't make me feel better," she mutters.

"Then what would, Lara? I don't know what to do to make it better because I'm not used to feeling like this. I can't deal with the guilt ripping me up inside. I didn't know I'd feel like this about you, how much I'd fall for you. And we're not over, we keep ripping each other's clothes off. We can't stay apart."

She rolls her eyes. "It's sex."

"We have a connection. I love you, and I know you fucking love me."

She gathers the rest of her clothes into her arms. "What's the girl doing here?"

I sigh heavily. "She's helping the club. Viper's got a court hearing for custody of his kid. The social workers are planning a visit, and he needs to look like he's got his life together."

"But he hasn't. It's a lie. Is she here willingly?"

"Of course." She gives me a hard stare, and I groan. "She is now. Originally, she took some persuading."

"You took her?"

"We were owed a favour. Her dad owes the club."

"Christ. It doesn't stop. You said you wanted to change, but now you're kidnapping women for your own gains."

I shrug. "I didn't kill her dad, though I could have."

"That's not the point."

I stand as she heads for the door, aware that she's in her underwear. "Lara, put your clothes on."

"Yah know, if you want to change so badly, do it. Be a better person," she snaps, pulling the door open and stepping out into the club.

"It's not so easy when you're not by my side," I admit through gritted teeth. I scan the club, noting there are enough brothers to witness this clusterfuck. "Get back in here and put your clothes on."

"You'll never have a woman by your side when you behave the way you do. I manage to get by in life without killing or bullying."

"Not strictly true—you completely bullied me to notice you."

She spins to face me. "I wanted a fuck buddy, not a psychotic murderer. And for the record, I didn't bully you. I got you to notice me, and I didn't hear you complaining."

The guys are now paying interest in our heated exchange. "Look away," I yell at the men, as Lara marches through the club.

"Take it in," she yells, holding her hands in the air. "Look at what your President gave up." I wrap my arms around her, sweeping her off her feet and bustling her into the bathroom. She fights me, kicking out and yelling in anger.

"You're the only woman to drive me fucking insane," I hiss in her ear, and she stills. "Take me back. You can fuck up my head so much better if you're in my bed."

"You realise how messed up that sounds?"

I release her, taking her clothes and unravelling them. "Don't pretend you don't enjoy stressing me out until I wanna punch shit." I hold out her jeans, and she steps into them. I tug them up her legs with ease, noting she's lost too much weight. "I have a fight tonight. Why don't we go for something to eat after?"

"I'd rather not."

"About nine?" I pull her shirt over her head and then hold on to the end, tugging her against me. "I'll pick you up." I place a kiss against her forehead and then open the bathroom door for her to leave.

LARA

"I need a date," I announce as I enter the coffee shop.

Adam looks up. "Did we change into a dating agency without my knowledge?"

I drop down into a booth. "Nine tonight."

"I know someone," says Betsy, bringing a coffee over and placing it in front of me. "He's a nice guy."

My eyes light up. "Perfect. Can you set it up for him to pick me up at nine?"

"I'll see if he's free." She pulls out her mobile and taps out a text.

"So, why so specific?" asks Adam, joining me.

"Solo thinks he's taking me to dinner. I need him to get a clear message."

He rolls his eyes at me. "Please, you love the chase."

"Maybe. But if I didn't do something like this, he'd get suspicious. What happened with Duke?"

Adam looks away, smirking. "He reminded me what it was like to be dominated by a big, sexy bastard."

"And Kai?"

"Is perfect and everything I need in my life to settle down."

"You heard what Duke said, that he's slept with Kai."

"Maybe one day we can all join in together," he suggests, wiggling his brows.

"He's free," says Betsy. "I gave him your address. Be warned, he's a bit of a player."

"It's fine. I don't plan on seeing him again."

I leave them to work and head home, calling Dax as I walk. "I saw Solo today," I tell him. "He's got a woman at the club. It's against her will, but she's gonna help them in Viper's court case."

"What's her name?" he asks.

"Oh, erm, he didn't say."

"Jesus, you'd make a terrible cop. What the fuck can I do with that information?"

"I'm trying," I yell, and a few passersby look my way. I lower my voice and continue. "I'm not used to this, and if I ask too much, he'll get suspicious."

"I'll ask around to see if anyone has reported a missing female in the area. Have you at least got a description for me?"

I reel it off, and he seems happier. "Try and speak to her. Maybe she'll tell you more."

CHAPTER TWENTY-SIX

SOLO

Lucas pulls the front door open and smirks when he lays eyes on me. "You must be here for Lara?"

"She's expecting me."

"Yeah, I get that now. She's not here."

I roll my eyes. "Course she's not."

"She's on a date," he says.

"With the same guy from before?" Blood rushes around my body, pumping loud in my ears.

"Nope. A new guy. Never seen him before. Big fella, too. Might even be as big as you." He looks smug, and I turn away before I punch him and upset Lara more. Pulling out my phone, I walk back towards my bike. The tracking app shows she's in a nearby bar, so I head that way.

It's a typical Lara bar. The kind I hate. I push my way through the throng of people waiting outside and shake hands with the doorman, who lets me go straight in. I spot her right away. She's at a nearby table, and I stare until she feels me, then her eyes find mine. A knowing look passes over her face as I go over. I take the spare seat, ignoring the guy sitting opposite her. "You stood me up."

"Solo, this is—"

"I don't give a shit," I snap. "Get your shit and let's go."

"Hey, man. What the fuck?" the guy asks.

I turn to him. "Lara is my wife."

"I am not."

"I literally had her naked on my desk a few hours ago. She came on my face, then my cock, and then my hand—"

"Jesus," Lara hisses, her face burning with embarrassment. "Stop."

"You keep playing these fucking games, Lara, and I'm tired," I snap. "I'm so fucking tired. I just wanna eat. I wanna sit across from you and eat while we talk about normal shit. I want you to tell me about your life and what you did with the rest of your day. I don't wanna be chasing you around and fucking up guys every time I arrange to pick you up."

"You ain't fucking up shit," snaps the guy, and my fist hits him square in the face. I stand, ready for the fight as he realises what just happened.

"Solo," Lara screams, grabbing my arm.

"Isn't this what you want?" I yell, shrugging her off. "For me to prove how much I love you?" The doormen rush in, pushing Lara from me and dragging me towards the exit. "I'm tired, Suicide."

We get outside, and they shove me away. "It's fine, I'm going," I snap, heading for my bike.

"Wait," shouts Lara, rushing after me, and I slow. "I want seafood," she adds, falling into step beside me. "Lobster."

We're seated by the window as the waitress takes our drinks order. "Cade Walker's your real name," Lara eventually says, "so why Solo?"

"I do everything alone. Well, I used to. Things have changed recently. I'm pulling the guys in on club decisions where I didn't do that before, and now I want my ol' lady on the back of my bike."

"What else is changing?" she asks.

"Business. I'm making more legit decisions. I'm trying to move away from protection and drugs."

"That's why you got the strip club?"

"The gentleman's club," I correct her. "I'm also in the middle of purchasing a micro-bar, Huntley's on the High Road."

She frowns. "That doesn't seem your type of place."

"It's not, but you like that shit, and I figured they're good money-makers. That place can turn over a tidy profit when I'm not keeping the customers away."

"Why would you keep the customers away?" she asks, sounding confused.

"Because the owner owes me. It's his daughter helping the club out. Mark Huntley's decided to move away, start afresh."

"With some persuasion?"

"A little," I say, smirking. "He's been married for years, but he had an affair with a teenager. She got pregnant, and he needed her to disappear quickly. I gave him the money to make that happen."

"Disappear as in kill?" she asks, alarmed.

"No, Lara, as in relocation. I got them a nice place and gave her enough cash to set her up for a few months. He's now decided he can't live without her. I'm buying the bar for a good price and his debt will be clear."

"And his daughter can go home?"

"Once she's done her part for the club."

"Don't you ever feel bad?" she asks.

The waitress sets down our drinks. "No. It's business. I did a nice thing and helped him out. It isn't my fault he couldn't repay the loan."

"You trample into people's lives and take what you want. It's not right."

"Isn't that what you did?" I ask. "You saw what you wanted in me, and you came for me until I couldn't say no."

"I wasn't hurting anyone."

"What happened to your parents?" I ask, changing the subject.

"They neglected us. Lucas got full custody when he turned eighteen, which is unusual but even social services could see we were better off with him. He'd taken care of us since he was small anyway. I don't know anything about my parents now. They could be dead."

"Don't you want to find out?"

She shakes her head. "No. I don't have any good memories. The only ones I do have make me feel sick. I never felt safe with them."

"That's why I like the club. No matter what, the brothers have my back. We keep one another safe."

The waitress comes to take our order. "Lobster for the lady," I say. "I'll take the shrimp."

"Do you know the effect you have on women?" Lara asks, staring after the waitress.

"I only have eyes for one."

She scoffs. "Please. You've had sex with other women since me, and don't even try to deny it."

"You know I have a high sex drive, Lara. Sex with the club girls doesn't count."

"What about your date from the other night?"

"It was an interview, for dancers at the club. What about you?"

"Loads of sex," she says, "with loads of different men."

I smirk. "Liar."

"Maybe I don't want to get into another unhealthy relationship. You've done enough damage to make sure of that."

"You say I don't feel, but when you tell me shit like that, I wanna rip my own heart out and hand it to you. I didn't wanna fuck it up so badly, Suicide. It all got out of hand."

"Have you ever had your heart broken, Solo?" she asks.

I shake my head. "Not unless you count now, the heartbreak I've caused myself."

"Betrayal is so much worse. Take what you're feeling and multiply it by a thousand. It's like you're in the pits of hell and your whole world is crumbling in on you, yet you have to keep going. You have to keep smiling, working, eating, when all you really wanna do is curl up into a ball and shut yourself away from it all."

"I'm so sorry, Lara."

"I know you are, Cade." Her using my name like that sends a warm feeling to my heart. "And that makes it so much harder. I wish you'd show indifference or act cold. I'd find it easier then."

"I've taken life so many times," I admit. "Names, faces, they all blend into one, and a lot of the time, I shut it off. I switch something off inside and get on with it. But falling in love with you means I can't do that with Liam. I relive it, over and over."

"It's your guilt."

"It's knowing I hurt the one person I love. The one person I'd do anything for. And I can't make it better. I can't talk my way out of it or make you see it from my point of view because I was wrong. It was wrong. I didn't mean to kill him." She stares at me in disbelief. "My intentions were no better. I made sure he was given heroin. He told me he'd been stealing the drugs for himself, so when I told my man to shoot that shit into his arm, I knew he wasn't using but I thought it'd break him. I thought he was working for Charlie Reed and that he'd tell me the truth. He didn't cave. He didn't give me what I wanted. But I didn't know he'd die."

"He was taking prescription methadone to keep him off the real thing," I say. "You over-dosed him." She holds her head in her hands. "You could have got him hooked on it again. Do you know what hell we went through to get him clean?"

"I don't think of the consequences, Lara. That's the fucked-up shit I do. I see my end goal and I get it any way I can."

"I hate that people think he went back to his old ways. That was the hardest part for me, the look of disappointment in people's faces at the funeral. I knew he wasn't using again. He wouldn't have put us through that."

"I never see my target having a family. I don't think about the grief I'm causing. But with you, I have no choice. I see it first-hand." I groan, rubbing my face in frustration. "I don't wanna be like this. It's the path I chose and it's too hard to get out of. I warned you. I told you to walk away."

She shrugs. "I never was good at taking orders."

Just then, our food arrives. "I didn't know you liked lobster."

She smirks. "I've never tried it. It's expensive."

I laugh. "You know I have money, right."

LARA

We finish the meal with light chat about my work and other boring stuff. After, we head out to the bike, and he passes me a helmet. "Your place?" I suggest.

He frowns. "Huh?"

"Are we going back to your place?"

He smirks, shaking his head. "No, Lara. I'm taking you home."

It's not part of my plan. When Solo stormed from the bar earlier, I thought I'd lost him. It's why I ran out of there after him. He's never reacted like that before. And now, I need him to take me back to the club, so I can meet the woman he's holding there and talk to her. "But the night's still young," I say suggestively.

"I've fed you and now you need sleep. I wanna see those dark circles gone from under your eyes," he says sadly, rubbing his thumb over my cheek.

"But the club is closer to walk to," I say, pointing to the flat tyre on his bike.

He stares down at it. "Fuck. I'm getting sick of this shit," he growls, looking around.

"It happened before?"

"Yep. Tyres, paintwork, you name it. Some fucker's got it in for me."

"I imagine there's a list of people all wanting to get back at you." I hand him the helmet back and head off in the direction of the club. "Your place it is, then."

Once there, Solo orders a prospect to go and sort his bike out. Duke saunters over, looking me up and down. "You're back," he states. "And this time, you're fully clothed."

"It's only right you see me half-dressed, like when I saw you," I say, arching a brow. He narrows his eyes.

"You saw Duke half-dressed?" asks Solo. "When?"

I grin. "Long story, right, Duke?" He mutters something and walks away. I spot the woman sitting beside Viper at the bar. I catch her eye, and she immediately looks away. "Are you getting me a drink?" I ask Solo, and he rolls his eyes and goes to the bar. I follow, take a seat beside the woman, and smile. "I'm Lara," I introduce, holding out my hand.

She looks at Solo and then Viper as if to confirm she can talk. "Jaya," she eventually says, shaking my hand.

"Why don't you boys go and have a catch-up. Jaya and I can get to know one another," I suggest, taking the vodka and lime juice Solo hands me.

He grins. "Nice try, Suicide. Not happening. Drink that and I'm taking you home. Viper, I need to use your bike."

"Home?" I repeat. "Why?"

"I told you, you need sleep."

"I know what I need, and it isn't sleep," I say, smirking. I turn back to Jaya. "How are you finding the club?"

"Suicide," mutters Solo, a warning in his tone.

"I'm being friendly."

"Jaya ain't here to make friends," he says firmly. "Drink up."

The ride home is short. He stops outside and takes the helmet from me. "Thanks for dinner," I say. "Take care." I turn to walk up the path to my house, but I'm pulled back against his hard chest.

"Take fucking care," he repeats in my ear. "That sounds like a goodbye."

"What did you want me to say?"

"See you first thing for a workout."

I smirk. "Depends what kind of workout."

"One involving a gym. Be ready for seven, and don't get me chasing you down, Suicide. My patience is running thin over that shit."

He turns me in his arms and brushes the hair from my face. "I'm not sure we should be spending so much time together when I hate you so much," I mutter, staring at his lips.

"Seven," he repeats, placing a kiss on my forehead. "Goodnight, Lara."

"He found you then," says Lucas, closing the blinds as I enter.

"Yep. Punched my date and forced me to dinner."

"You looked really unhappy out there," he says sarcastically.

I frown, realising he's right. I didn't pull away or shrug Solo from me. "He'll get bored eventually," I mutter, kicking off my shoes.

My mobile rings and I answer, running up to my bedroom and closing the door. "Dax," I say in greeting.

"You two looked pretty cosy," he says.

"You're watching me?"

"Outside. The black BMW." He disconnects, and I stare at the blank phone. He's more like his nephew than he knows.

"Lucas, I'm just nipping out. I won't be long," I shout as I pass the living room.

"Out where? You just got back."

"Five minutes," I say, rushing out.

Dax stares straight ahead, and I resist the urge to laugh as I climb into the car. It feels like something from a movie. "Tell me you got something," he mutters.

I smile proudly. "I did, actually. Mark Huntly, who owns the bar on the High Street, Huntley's, he owes the Devils money. They took his daughter, Jaya, and she's helping Viper by pretending to be his girlfriend. She's there by force. Solo must have threatened her or something. Anyway, Mark Huntley is now handing his bar over to Solo to repay his debt."

Dax nods. "Possible kidnap charge. Did he say why Huntley owes him money?"

"Something to do with a secret pregnant girlfriend. He didn't want his family to find out, so he borrowed cash to relocate her. He couldn't pay back."

"I'll go talk to him, see what he can give me. If he'll talk, maybe we can get Solo on a couple of charges."

I twist my fingers together. "He said he didn't mean for Liam to die."

"Course, he did. He'll say whatever it takes to get himself out the shit."

"You think he's lying?"

"Has he proved to you he's honest?" He sighs. "Solo will do and say whatever to get what he wants. When he's bored of you, he'll cut you out his life like you never existed. He takes what he wants without thinking of the consequences."

"Did he do that to you?" I ask.

"Do yourself a favour. Whatever you have going on with him, break it off."

"There's nothing between us," I say innocently. "I'm trying to get as much dirt as I can to get him sent to prison."

Dax smirks. "Keep telling yourself that, princess, but I saw how you two were just then. You're not that good an actress."

CHAPTER TWENTY-SEVEN

SOLO

I stare down at Lara sleeping soundly. I lift the sheet and see she's completely naked. Fuck, I'd give anything to jump right into her bed and wake her up the way I used to. Instead, I tug the sheet hard, and she wakes with a start. "Morning, Suicide. It's seven-oh-five."

"What the fuck? I didn't know I was in the Army," she snaps, trying to snatch the sheets back.

"Let's get the workout done so I can feed you. I hate seeing your ribs," I say, running a finger over the visible bones. Her nipples immediately react, and I tweak one. "Now, Suicide, or I'll scrap the plan altogether and spend the entire morning fucking you."

She jumps up and heads for the bathroom, which surprises me after the way she was last night. The option of morning sex is something I'd expect Lara to pester me for. When she returns, she's in her gym gear.

We go to her usual gym, which is busy with people getting in their workout before the day begins. Lara goes to the cardio machines, and I go for the weights, but I watch her the entire time. I don't miss the way the men look her way with need. It reminds me how badly I've fucked up. All she'd have to do is click her fingers and she'd have a date with any one of these men. When she begins squatting in front of the mirrors, I can't take it anymore, so I join her, standing right behind her to hide her perfect arse from the rest of the gym. She eyes me in the mirror. "You okay?"

"Uh-huh."

"Are you sure? You look pissed off."

"We should shower and head for breakfast before you go to work," I say, checking my watch.

"I'm not hungry. I'll grab some fruit once I'm at work."

"Lara," a man calls, a huge smile on his face. He ignores me as my eyes burn into him. Lara stands straight and smiles back.

"Hey, long time no see."

"Right," he agrees. "I've been taking the late sessions to work around my shifts."

"I usually take the women's hour now," she tells him, and I relax a little. At least I know she's not always around these sex pests when I'm not around.

"Still getting over that twat then?" he jokes, and Lara's eyes dart to me. She sniggers.

"I'm the twat," I introduce, glaring at him.

He almost laughs, which only pisses me off some more. "Catch you later, Lara," he says, walking away.

"You told other men about me?" I snap.

"Men are suckers for a sob story," she replies, winking.

I slap her hard on the arse. "Go and shower. And know that I'm buying a gym for you to use. It'll be women only," I tell her as I head for the showers.

LARA

The second we step out into the fresh air, Solo takes my hand and leads me next door to the health kick place I usually avoid. "I told you, I'm not hungry," I mutter when he gets in line to order. He ignores me, and when we get to the front, he orders two breakfast smoothies. We sit down, and I rummage in my bag to find my tablets. He watches in silence as I pop one in my mouth and swallow it down with the smoothie.

"Things all good?" he asks, nodding to the pill packet.

"You'd be dead by now if they weren't," I say, and he smirks. He eyes the second pill, and I shrug. "Antidepressants," I tell him when he frowns. "Just to help me get out of bed."

"Since when?"

"Since I discovered the man I loved had killed my brother."

He looks away guiltily. "Lucas never said."

"What are you doing with your day?" I ask. I never knew what he did with his time when we were a couple.

"Club stuff," he says vaguely.

I sigh, grabbing the smoothie and standing. He watches, confused. "I should go."

"Lara, you know I can't tell you what I do. It's club business."

"Fine. Whatever." I head out, and he follows, cursing under his breath.

"A couple of collections nearby. I don't usually do them unless they're being difficult, but seeing as I'm already out this way, I said I'd take care of them. This afternoon, I'm signing for the new bar."

"Why did Mark Huntly go to all that trouble of sending his lover away, only to give it all up and join her anyway?" I ask. "It makes no sense."

"She's younger. It's taken him some time to accept it all, I guess."

"Does Jaya know the truth?" He shakes his head. "Because she wouldn't help you if she knew?"

"Because she thinks her dad is in danger if she doesn't help Viper."

"And is he?"

"Yes."

Something about his brutal honesty is refreshing. "Do you have any family? Siblings, aunts, uncles?"

He frowns. "No." Seems like some things he still doesn't want to share. "Let me get you to work," he mutters. "I can't take you for dinner tonight. The gentleman's club is opening, and according to your brother, I have to be there."

Robyn comes to see me at work over her lunch. It's been a long time since we lunched together, so I take my break too and we sit together by the window. She pops a fry into her mouth and asks, "So, how's things?"

I prod my salad with my fork. "Fine."

"Do you have dirt on him?"

"Some. Not much."

"Oh no," she mutters, dropping half the fry back onto her plate. "Oh, fuck."

I look up in alarm, "What?"

"You're sleeping with him."

I blush, and she groans. "It's not like that, Robyn. It's . . . I need him to trust me. It's not intimate, just . . . fucking."

"That's worse," she wails. "Why can't you just stay away from him?"

I wince. I've been asking myself the same question since I saw Dax last night. Part of me is swallowed by guilt for telling him about that stuff, and the other half is working hard to convince myself I'm doing it for Liam. "It's not as easy as I thought," I admit. "The sex wasn't meant to happen, but when I'm around him, I don't think straight. He crowds me and—"

"Lara, did he force you to have sex?"

"No! God, no," I rush to say. "Nothing like that. I just feel different around him. Like I'm . . . I dunno . . . safe." I drop my fork and it clatters onto the table. "How ridiculous is that, after what he did? But I've never felt this safe, not ever. Not even with my brothers. I just know he'd do anything to protect me. It's overwhelming, yet freeing. When I'm with him, I don't have to pretend. He can handle me, all of me, even the crazy part. And I hate that."

Robyn grabs my hand and gives me a sympathetic smile. "You love him, I get that. Even after Liam, you can't just switch it off. But look at everything he's done. Look at the heartbreak and destruction he's caused. You took that stupid leather jacket of his and nothing's been right since."

"I know, and I'm not losing sight of the end goal. It's just not as simple as I thought it'd be. He's doing all the things I wanted him to in the beginning. Why was Liam even involved in all that after the work he put in to get clean? I wish I could speak to him one last time, so I could ask him why he'd do that to us."

Robyn shrugs. "It's the world he knew."

"Solo asked Lucas to help run his strip club," I tell her, and she scowls. "Lucas agreed. It's the opening tonight."

"We should go. I'll ask Flick, too. We'll put Solo in his place."

SOLO

Running a gentleman's club is harder than I thought. Between Ellie and Lucas, they seem to have it all under control, much to my relief. I'm using my own brothers to provide some of the security, and the rest are from a company I know well and trust. Everything seems to be in place, and in just under one hour, the doors will open and we're praying for a good sign-up because after this evening, it will be members only.

I check the tracker and see Suicide isn't home where I need her to be so I can concentrate on things here. She's in a bar not too far from the club. I go over to Lucas. "What's Lara doing tonight?"

"Not a clue," he mutters, signing off on an order and handing the sheet back to the delivery driver.

"She staying home?"

He sighs impatiently. "I think she's going out. She was getting ready as I left. Why?"

I walk away, pulling out my mobile to call her. She doesn't answer. Instead, she sends me to voicemail. "Suicide, Lucas tells me you're out. Be good. I'll call by later."

At exactly ten, I stand at the entrance to the club and I'm relieved to see a line of potential members. Ellie spent a small fortune on advertising and it paid off. I shake a few hands of people I know as they pour inside. "It looks promising," says Duke.

"This place is only the beginning," I tell him.

I walk along the line of people, stopping when my eyes land on Lara and her friends. "Hey," says Robyn, waving. "I can't believe we have to stand in line when she's fucking the owner," she slurs, and Lara slaps her hand over Robyn's mouth, both of them giggling.

"Sorry, she's drank too much."

"I called," I tell her, unclipping the red rope so they can step out of line.

"I'm having girl time." She smirks, following me to the front.

"Duke, these ladies can go straight through," I say, and Duke smiles, stepping aside to allow them access.

"Aren't you coming?" asks Lara. It's the first time she's looked at me like she wants me around, but I shake my head, choosing to let her have her girl time.

Later, the stage is lit up red as two dancers work their bodies around the poles. It's the third dance, and each time, they've been a hit. I'm feeling more relaxed knowing this venture is going to work. Ellie's already updated me to say she's had an overwhelming interest in sign-ups. I sip my whiskey, keeping my eyes on Lara as she watches the women on stage. Her cheeks are flushed pink, the way they go when she's turned on, and I wonder how she'd feel about having another woman join us in the bedroom. Something tells me she wouldn't be entirely opposed to the idea. I'm about to go over and suggest she join me in the office when a hand lands on my shoulder. I spin around angrily cos no one fucking touches me without announcing themselves first, but my words fall short when I stare into Dax's eyes.

"Cade Walker," he says coolly, like he doesn't already know me. "You need to come with me."

I stare at the line of police officers behind him and wonder how the fuck they got in unannounced. "Why?"

"You're under arrest for coercion under section twenty-one of the Theft Act 1968. You do not have to say anything, but anything you do say may be used against you in a court of law." He nods to another cop, who grabs my arms, tugging them up my back and cuffing me.

"Are you fucking kidding me?"

"What's going on?" comes Lara's voice.

"Nothing, baby, it's fine. I'll get Duke to get you home safe," I say.

"Lara, you might need to come to the station tomorrow to give a full statement," says Dax, and her eyes widen in panic.

"Lara?" I ask, waiting for her to explain.

"I'll be in touch," adds Dax, pulling me away from her.

"Lara, what the fuck's he talking about?" I yell as she watches me being dragged away with tears in her eyes.

"Careful who you trust, Cade," Dax warns, grinning.

Duke steps in the way of our exit. "What the hell's going on?"

"I'm gonna have to ask you to move," says Dax.

"Why's he being arrested?"

"Get Specs to meet us at the station," I tell him, and he nods, moving to the side. "Update Vipe," I add, a subtle warning to hide Jaya before the cops sniff around.

I'm shoved roughly into the waiting cop car. There's no fucking way Lara has anything to do with this. She doesn't even know Dax. I've never talked about him. I rest my head back and stare hard at the roof. "Long time no see," says Dax, climbing into the front passenger seat.

"What is this all about?"

"We'll get to that at the station."

"Yeah, right. After you've held me in a fucking cell for twenty hours."

He grins. "You know how it works."

"How do you know Lara?"

"She's been very helpful, telling us all about Liam. Seems you've been a bit sloppy lately."

"I don't know what you're talking about. Liam was a drug addict."

"We know. We also know what happened to him and why, but seeing as we can't pin that on you, we'll settle for the charges we've got."

"Good luck with that," I snap.

LARA

"Tell me that had nothing to do with you," yells Lucas, pacing back and forth in the office.

"I can't lie to the police," I snap in defence. "He asked me about Solo, so I had no choice."

"Bullshit! No way did that cop just approach you out the blue."

"Not entirely. Apparently, Dax is related to Solo. Uncle, I think."

"Jesus, you stupid, stupid girl. You know we're gonna have to leave. We can't stay here now you've screwed him over."

"He screwed me over first," I shout. "He deserves this."

"Is that right?" asks Duke from the doorway, and I spin to face him. "I always knew you'd be trouble, Suicide, but never did I think you'd put yourself in so much danger."

"He killed my brother," I mutter.

Duke rolls his eyes, slamming the office door hard. I jump. "I am so fucking sick of your whining. It happened, get the fuck over it. If the Pres goes down for this, you'd better listen to your brother and get the fuck out of here, cos I'll come for you, Suicide. Then you'll get to spend eternity with your junkie brother."

"Let's just relax," says Lucas, stepping between us. "She's grieving, and let's not forget your Pres's girlfriend meddling with my sister's drugs."

"If I was you, I'd get her out of here. Solo's gonna lose his mind when he finds out what she's done. And there's no way she can give a statement to the police."

"It's not up to you," I snap, and Duke grabs me by the throat. I panic as the whooshing sound in my ears blocks out Lucas's yelling.

"You're not safe because he fucked you, little girl. This isn't a joke. Solo will want blood when he gets out, and you're the first person he's gonna visit. Don't be there waiting like an idiot. Get the hell out of the area."

When I get home, I rush to my room and call Dax's mobile again. I've tried him ten times since Solo's arrest, all to no avail. "You know what time it is?" he answers, sounding sleepy.

"You're in bed?" I almost yell.

"Where else would I be at three in the morning?"

"At the station, speaking to Solo. What's happening?"

"Nothing. He's safely locked away in a cell. We're interviewing him tomorrow."

"His vice president threatened me. Said I need to leave thanks to you outing me like that."

"Don't leave before I get that statement. And he would have discovered it sooner or later."

"You're not listening. He said Solo will want my blood."

"Lara, it's not like you didn't know who you were messing with. What exactly do you want me to do?"

"Help me. Can't I get protection?"

He laughs. "No. It's hardly the crime of the century. We searched the club and there was no sign of Jaya. Mark Huntley is coming back first thing to finish his statement and then we'll charge Solo. If he's found guilty, he could be facing fourteen years."

"And if he's not?"

"Then we'll have to release him. Just lie low for a few days. If you go missing, at least I know where to look."

"Great," I mutter, disconnecting the call.

I tossed and turned all night. Guilt is keeping me from sleep and fear is not far behind. A part of me wonders if Solo will be able to look me in the eye while he takes my life. Another part of me wonders what it will be like, that final moment knowing I'll be at peace. Knowing I won't cause Lucas any more worry. Maybe death isn't the worst option.

I call in sick to work, partly because I can't concentrate on anything right now and I don't want to risk bumping into Duke. I rub my bruised neck where he grabbed me last night. Lucas interrupts my thoughts by bringing me breakfast. "We need a plan," he tells me.

I shake my head, and he lowers onto my bed. "No more plans. No more running. I'll face Solo if I have to."

"You promised me you'd leave it," he mutters sadly.

"I'm sorry. I always disappoint you. Just like Liam did."

He gently touches my cheek, the way he did when I was little. "I'm not disappointed, Lara. I'm hurt you ignored me and did what you wanted. I tried hard to give us a better life, but somehow, you and Liam always came up with a way to derail it. You both take after our parents, self-destruct mode always on. I'll talk to Solo, make him see sense. Maybe now, with the club and stuff, we can work it out."

"It's my mess. I'll take care of it."

I must fall back into a light sleep because when I open my eyes again, it's after lunch. I stretch out and check my phone, seeing a missed call from Dax. I sit up and scream in fright. Solo is sitting in the chair by my window, staring out at the dreary day. "Solo," I whisper.

"You were right," he mutters gruffly. "Betrayal hurts way more."

"I—"

"Duke wants you dead."

"Oh . . ."

"A few months ago, I'd have squeezed your neck and stared into your eyes while you fought for breath," he mutters. *At least that answers one of my questions.* "I'd have let my men take turns on that magic pussy of yours as punishment for crossing me."

"I'm not sure—"

"But you've done some voodoo shit to me, and I can't hurt you. Even now, after spending hours in a fucking cell, with no decent food and having them watch me take a fucking piss, after lying awake for twenty hours thinking of all the ways I want to watch you suffer, I can't do it. I can't fucking hurt you because I already did, didn't I? I already did the worse thing. I've already seen the pain in your eyes and the life leave it. I've watched you starve yourself, barely living. So, we're quits." He stands. "We're even. I walk away, and you get to live."

"What happened at the station?" I ask, confused by his behaviour.

"Jaya told them she's at the club willingly. Mark Huntley left London after withdrawing his statement. No charges." He heads for the door. "Take care, Lara."

"Take care," I repeat. "That's goodbye. You said those words were a goodbye." He stares at me for a few seconds, his eyes full of mistrust and pain. I shouldn't feel bad, what he did to me was way worse, but the panic I feel at the finality of his words controls me. "Is it final, Solo. Is this goodbye?"

"When you pushed your way into my life, you irritated me. You asked too many questions and were far too confident. I tried being horrible. I tried being blunt. Fuck, I even fucked you like I hated you, but you loved it. And I thought to myself, what kind of woman keeps coming back for that? How messed up is she to want that? You crave toxic, and I'm done. It's too hard, too tiring, and I have too much to lose to continue this fight of love and hate. You're hard to love, Lara. You make it hard. So, yeah, this is goodbye. Take care."

I stare at the door as it closes. My heart hammers in my chest. Hard to love. Those words haunt me over any others because it's what Liam used to say whenever our parents let us down. We were too hard to love. I inhale a painful breath, followed by another, and the lump in my throat keeps building until tears roll down my cheeks.

CHAPTER TWENTY-EIGHT

SOLO

I stare up at the new sign hanging above the gentleman's club doors. It's been a month since I walked away from Lara. I deleted the tracker and avoided the places I knew she hung out at. Now, seeing the words 'Riding Solo' over the club, I feel like a weight has been lifted. It's the final piece of her to go. Rubbing my hand over the new tattoo on my chest—the one covering her design, her name—it stings, thinking about her. Even more so when the sale went through for Huntley's. I'd planned to gift that to her, so she could set up her own business. I thought she'd like the independence from the club.

Lucas joins me and mutters, "Looks good." None of this has been easy on him, and I recognise that, so I've released him from managing the club. We came to a mutual decision that he'd offer my members VIP access to his bar with discounted drinks, and I'd recommend his place to my customers. My girls drink and eat there before starting their shifts at the club. It's a win-win situation and means I don't bump into his sister.

His mobile rings and he takes a couple of steps way. "Lara, you okay?" I pretend not to listen in, but it's hard when I know she's right at the other end of the phone. "What do you mean? All four of them? Right, okay, I'll come now." He disconnects.

"She okay?" The words tumble out before I can stop them.

"She's been having trouble. Someone keeps letting her tyres down, scratching the paintwork on her car. Now, it seems they've gone a step further and slashed all four tyres. It's costing a fortune. Last week, paint was thrown over the house windows. I don't know what the fuck is going on."

Alarm bells ring. "I had some problems similar to that a few months back."

"Maybe kids in the area then," he says, shrugging. "I have to go and rescue her."

LARA

I'm aware that Solo went through this too, but there's no way I can call him to ask about it. It's possible the same person is targeting us both, and I've picked up my phone a hundred times to call him but bottled it each time before I've dialled. I found a new gym, a quiet back street place. It's cheaper monthly, and it's females only. The only downside is, it's down by the docks, which is a creepy place to be at this time of night with no one around. I pace, waiting for Lucas to pick me up, as a car pulls into the car park with the headlights on full-beam and I shield my eyes. It slows in front of me, so I move around to the passenger side, but as I pull the door, I realise it's not Lucas's car. I laugh and bend to see the driver. "I'm so sorry. I thought you were—"

I stare at the gun pointed at my face. "Get in," snaps Kiki.

"Kiki?"

"Now!"

I slide into the passenger seat. "What's going on?"

"I hear he's done with you," she says, grinning. She begins to turn the car around, keeping the gun on me.

"Yeah. We're over."

"You grassed him to the cops."

"We're moving forward from that," I mutter, pulling my seatbelt on. "Can I ask what this is all about?"

"He let me back to the club."

"Oh." I can't hide the surprise in my voice.

"I had to grovel and, of course, it involved hot sex. He never could resist me," she brags.

I ignore the pang of jealousy. "So, why am I here?"

"I can't believe you fell for it. You're so easy to manipulate."

"What do you mean?"

She laughs. "Dax. Cheri. I put them in your path, and you took it. Dax isn't his uncle, but you didn't even question it."

"He's not?"

"No. I mean, his mum made him call him Uncle Dax, but he wasn't a real uncle. They were fucking. When she died, Dax blamed Solo and his dad. There's a deep-rooted hate there. Dax became a cop because of it."

"Right." I'm angry with myself for falling for more bullshit.

"But now things are going well, I can't risk having little miss crazy pop back into our lives and fuck it all up."

"I won't," I say. "I'm done. I'm glad to be out of it all."

"Right now, yeah, but when you see him moving on, having a family, settling down, you might be tempted to shake your arse in his direction, and I can't say he wouldn't chase you. He's been sad since he dumped you." She sighs heavily and it feels like she's talking to herself more than me. "I try to keep him busy, but he's a little lost."

"Kiki, I swear, I'm over him. I don't want him. You're welcome to him."

She glances at me. "It's just easier this way. I hope you understand."

SOLO

Lucas rushes towards me. "She's not there," he says, panic in his eyes. "I went to the gym, and she's not there. The car is, but she's not."

"Maybe she walked?"

"Her mobile was in her bag in her car. She wouldn't leave it behind."

"Lucas, she's probably at home. Have you called around?"

"Yes. I stopped at home, but she isn't there. I called Robyn and Flick, and they haven't heard from her. I think something bad has happened."

I roll my eyes. "Right, fine, I'll get some of the guys looking."

He nods. "Thanks, Solo. I appreciate it."

It's been two hours since Lucas came to me to say Lara was missing. Two hours and there's no sign of her. There were tyre tracks leading away from the gym, but they could have been anybody's, and they soon disappeared on the road. I've been to every bar I could think of, all the places Lara loves, and she's not in any of them. The guys have searched fields, places around that stupid gym she joined by the docks, and even amongst the shipping containers.

I stop my bike outside the club and remove my helmet. A few of the club girls are outside smoking. "Where's Kiki?" I ask, getting off the bike. Siren shrugs. She's pissed I let Kiki back, but I figured she couldn't do any harm with Lara gone. I freeze. *Lara's gone.* "Have you seen her at all in the last few hours?" I ask more urgently.

"No. She left about eight and hasn't been back since."

I put a call into Duke. "Have you got her?" he asks.

"No, but Kiki's been missing the last few hours. Do you think that's a coincidence?"

"No, Pres, that's a fucking sign. I'll let everyone know to look out for her."

"Her car's gone too," I tell him.

"Kiki's car is out back," says Shorty, another club girl. "Near the killing barn." It's what everyone calls the empty barn out back. We haven't ever used it to kill anyone, that's what the basement is for, but it's a creepy place and the floors are stained with blood from when the farmers would slaughter their animals years ago. I relay the information to Duke and rush to the barn.

The door creaks when I open it, and Kiki spins around with a gun in her hand. Lara is on her knees with a gag in place and mascara staining her cheeks. My heart stops beating for a second as I take in the scene. "What the hell are you doing?"

"She turned you in to the cops," snaps Kiki. "Why do you look upset?"

Lara shakes her head slightly, warning me. I take a calming breath. "I'm not upset, Kiki. I just want to know what's going down in my club without my permission."

"She needs to be gone from our lives forever. I don't want her turning up in a month's time and ruining what we have. And she needs to face punishment for grassing the club up to the cops. If she were a man, she wouldn't have gotten away with it."

I frown. I haven't been near Kiki since she returned, so there's nothing between us to ruin. "I dealt with her for that. It's done."

"Why do you care so much about this bitch? All she did was cause you trouble." Kiki waves the gun around carelessly.

"Alright," I almost yell, putting my hands out in a placating manner. "Stop waving that thing around before it goes off. I'm not with Lara anymore, Kiki. We're over, so I don't understand why she's here, gagged, on her knees like some damn sacrifice."

A strangled growl leaves Kiki's throat and she stomps her foot in frustration. "I told you. I don't want her ruining what we have."

"What we have?" I repeat, my brow furrowed in confusion.

"What we will have once she's gone. I know she's the reason you're sad." She moves closer to Lara, pointing the gun at her head, and I try to calm the panic in my chest.

"Kiki, you can't just take people and kill them. It's not how I do things now. I decide who dies at the hands of my club. I have an agreement with Lara's brother. We can't kill her."

"You still love her?" Kiki yells, pushing the barrel of the gun hard into Lara's temple.

LARA

I squeeze my eyes tightly, waiting for the bang. "Jesus," hisses Solo, and I detect fear in his tone. "I don't love her. I never fucking did." I open my eyes and stare at him. I know he's saying it to end this charade, but my heart still twists. "She's not cut out for this life," he adds, and I know he's now speaking the truth. "She never was. I need a woman who can ride or die for me, and she ain't it."

Kiki eases up the gun slightly. "Really?"

"Yes," he whispers, reaching out his hand to her. "I didn't see it at the time, but you're right, you're ol' lady material. I never should have let you go."

He keeps his hand reaching out to her, but she doesn't take it. "Prove it," she says. "Kill her."

"Kiki, come on," he murmurs, letting his hand drop to his side. "You know I wanna take this club in a different direction. You have to share my vision too, babe, if this is gonna work."

"I do," she says, "and once she's out of the way for good, I'll never pick up a gun again. But I need you to prove it to me, Solo, or it's just words." She adds a cute smile, reminding me of a child using charm to get her own way.

"The guys are gonna be here any minute, Kiki. When they see you waving a gun around, it might end badly. Put it down. Let's talk."

"I knew it. You're talking shit to stop this happening, but it won't work. If I can't have you, neither can she!" The gun presses harder, and Solo takes a step closer. Kiki turns the gun on him, and he freezes. "You can't save her," she screams.

"This is madness! I'm not with her," he yells. He takes another step, and Kiki places her second hand on the gun, raising it higher. "Put the gun down," he orders. "This is gonna get you killed."

I see the opportunity to lunge. She stupidly didn't tie my hands or feet, and while she's waving the gun in his direction, I charge, knocking her forwards and straight into Solo's arms. A shot rings out and I look up as Solo falls to the floor, taking Kiki with him. The door opens and Duke runs in, his gun already drawn. Kiki pushes back from Solo and her gun clatters to the ground. She screams, falling back onto her arse. There's so much blood, I can't see where it's from, but when Solo doesn't get up, dread fills my stomach.

"This is your fault," she screams, and her eyes land on her gun. I make a lunge for it at the same time she does. It all happens so fast, Duke doesn't have time to react. My shaking hands squeeze the trigger, and a second shot echoes into the stillness of the night. Kiki makes a gurgling sound before slumping over. Duke puts his gun away and drops down beside Solo, just as Viper and some of the other brothers rush in.

"Call an ambulance," orders Duke, ripping open Solo's blood-stained shirt. "Check if Kiki is breathing."

Viper lays Kiki onto her back and presses his fingers to her neck. I'm shaking so hard, I can't disguise it. Viper shakes his head once, and I slap my hands over my mouth to muffle the sobs. "She's gone, VP," he says.

"Then get her out of here before the ambulance arrives," snaps Duke.

Viper scoops her up, and I stare helplessly as her limbs dangle at a funny angle. "Suicide, get over here," Duke demands. I shake my head, unable to find words. "It's an order! I need your help to save Solo," he yells.

I crawl over to where they are. Solo is pale as I place my shaking hand over his cheek. "Oh shit," I whisper.

"Hold this over his wound," says Duke, grabbing my hand and pressing it hard over a screwed-up shirt he's pushed onto the wound. "It needs pressure," he adds, and I get onto my knees and press both hands onto it.

He checks for a pulse. "It's weak, but it's there. Where the fuck is the ambulance?" he yells.

"They're coming, VP. I'll go out to flag them down," says Thor.

CHAPTER TWENTY-NINE

LARA

Solo died. His heart stopped twice in the ambulance, but they fought and so did he. And now, he's hooked up to machines that beep constantly to keep him alive. Duke sits one side, and I sit the other. We both stare at Solo's pale face, praying in our own way that he pulls through. Praying for a miracle.

"You can get some rest," Duke mutters. "I'll call if there's any change."

"I'm good." He doesn't want me here. I can tell by the irritated looks he keeps throwing my way. "Why was she even back at the club?"

"She'd been sleeping rough. Pres didn't want her on the streets, so he agreed she could come back. He didn't see the harm since you were gone."

I trail my finger over Solo's bare chest. An eagle now sits where my nickname once was. "Everything's such a mess," I mutter.

"He was trying to change for you," admits Duke, "and you screwed him over."

"I thought I wanted him to pay. It got out of hand. What happened to Kiki?" I ask in a low voice.

"Don't worry about that."

"What if the police come asking?"

He narrows his eyes. "Then maybe I should tell them the truth." He rolls his eyes when he sees my panic. "Relax. Solo wouldn't want me to. The cops won't come looking. As far as we know, she had no relatives who cared about her. No one will come looking."

"I shoved her onto him. I didn't mean to. I just saw an opportunity to push her, and I thought she'd drop the gun . . . but she didn't. It went off and then he—"

"Lara," he hisses. "Shut the fuck up before someone hears you. Lucas knows about Solo. I told him Kiki took you and she did this. As far as he thinks, Solo saved your life by jumping in front of the gun. We stick to that. Kiki took off when I came in, and we both tried to keep Solo alive. We're each other's alibi, okay." I nod.

A few days pass and there's not much change in Solo's condition. The doctors tell us he'll wake in his own time and his body needs time to recover from the surgery to remove the bullet. I haven't left his side except for when the nurse sneaks me into the showers when the staff nurse isn't looking. Duke spends a lot of time here too, but he's also had to take care of the club.

He hands me a sandwich, and I take it gratefully. We've reached a truce. One where we can sit in the same room without sniping at one another. "How's he doing?"

"No change," I mutter. "They're coming to give him a bed bath in a minute. I said I'd do it instead."

"You?" he asks, arching a brow.

"Yes. What's wrong with that? He might not want strangers touching him."

Duke sniggers. "He definitely would. The nurses might be able to wake him up with some gentle prodding and poking."

I narrow my eyes. "I'll do it." So, when the nurse comes five minutes later, I take the bowl of warm, soapy water and insist everyone leaves, including Duke.

"I think you're enjoying this," I mutter to Solo whilst I squeeze the cloth. "I feel bad for shoving Kiki into you. God knows why, because if it wasn't for you, I wouldn't even know her. You called me psycho, but she, well, she really was."

SOLO

I hear water trickling. "I don't even know how to do this." Suicide. It's her voice. "Am I supposed to wash your bits? I mean, if it was me lying there, I'd want my bits washed, but it seems weird to touch someone when they're out of it." I smile at her ramblings. "I don't think you'd find it weird. Look, I'll wash your bits, but we'll never talk about it. It's a real low point for us both." I feel a damp cloth sweep over my cheek. "I wish you'd wake up, Solo. It's not right seeing you in this bed so lifeless."

"Are you gonna work your way down to my bits or not?" I ask, my voice raspy. I cough, desperate for a drink.

"Jesus, you're awake!"

I blink a few times, and she comes into focus. "Don't they have nurses to do this sort of thing?"

She smiles, cupping my face in her hands. "You gave me a scare."

I'm checked over by the doctor, who tells me I've lost a lot of blood and had a bullet lodged in my lung. They removed it and repaired the lung. I also hit my head when I hit the ground, causing a small bleed on my brain, which is the reason I've been out for days. "You'll need rest for a few days, but other than that, you've been very lucky." I shake his hand, and he leaves.

Duke comes in and fist bumps me. "Fuck, Pres, we thought you were a goner."

"You can't get rid of me that easily," I say as he takes a seat.

"She's been here day and night," he tells me. "Lara."

"Yeah?"

"Her brother tried to make her go home, but she refused. The nurse has been sneaking her in for a shower, and Siren brought her a change of clothes. I came in here this morning and found her curled up beside you on the bed, fast asleep."

"Careful, you sound like you like her."

"I could think of worse ol' ladies. Take Kiki, for example." We both laugh.

"She lost her mind," I mutter. "She was talking like we were together, demanding I kill Lara. It was fucked up."

"We should have kept her away from the club."

"I should never have messed with her in the first place, man. From now on, we're careful about who comes into the club. Everyone is checked and then checked again, and we don't risk giving false hope to the club girls. They're there for all the brothers, it's what they sign up for. We make that clear."

"Got it."

"Anyone ask about Kiki?"

He shakes his head. "She went to the incinerator. Cops came asking, and I sent them away. Said your ex showed up, attacked you, and ran. I told them you wouldn't wanna press charges, but fuck knows if they'll listen. I didn't give them Kiki's name. Said I didn't know her real name."

"Where's Lara now?"

"She spoke with the doctor, then said she was going back to the club to make arrangements. She said she'd be back later."

"I need to speak to her. Get her back here."

LARA

I place my hands on my hips and look around Solo's room. I've cleaned every inch of it, and I'm admiring my hard work when the door opens and Duke pops his head in. "Why aren't you with Solo?" I snap. "You said you'd stay until I came back."

"He's not a baby. He's fine. Besides, he sent me to get you. He wants to talk."

"About what?" I ask, unable to hide the panic in my voice. It was the reason I left as soon as I got a chance, to avoid talking.

"Did you clean his room?" he asks, looking around.

I smile proudly. "He needs rest, and he can't relax in it when it's filthy. And trust me, it was filthy. It looks like he was living off noodles."

"Not many of us men can cook, Suicide."

"That's why I'm moving in."

"Moving in?" he repeats.

"Until he's feeling better. I'll cook some proper dinners, maybe add in some vegetables."

Duke smirks. "Right. I'm sure he'll love that."

I sigh. "Do you think he wants to get a restraining order on me?"

Duke laughs. "Why would you ask that?"

"I don't know if I can take his rejection again," I admit, and Duke gives a sympathetic smile.

"One thing I know about you, Suicide. You can handle Solo and whatever he throws your way. You were meant to be his ol' lady. Trust me."

Solo is sitting up in bed when I get back to the hospital. He's chatting to a nurse as she checks his blood pressure, and for a second, I feel a stab of jealousy, but when he spots me, his wide smile reassures me he's happy to see me. "You ran out on me, Suicide."

"I had things to do." The nurse leaves, and I take a seat by the bed. He taps the space beside him, so I move, loving the heat from his body. "It's good to see you sitting up."

"You owe me a bed bath."

I laugh. "Trust you to hear that part."

"The doc thinks I need to take the next few weeks easy," he says, twisting my hair around his finger. "I was wondering, seeing as you pushed Kiki onto me, if you'd mind helping out." He smirks, and I laugh.

"I guess I could cook a few meals now and again."

"Anything but noodles."

"Solo, I'm sorry, for everything."

He shakes his head. "You have nothing to be sorry about."

"We spent too much time playing games and I almost lost you."

"Nothing like a bullet to the chest to make you realise what you really want," he jokes.

"And what do you want?"

"You, Lara. Just you. No more games. I want you and your ridiculous questions, your crazy outlook on life, and the way you nibble the chocolate from the Snickers bar so you can eat it all separately. I want to spend the rest of my life being a better person for you. Because I love you. More than anything."

My smile is watery as I nod in agreement. "I get it wrong all the time, and I know I'll drive you crazy most days, but I'll get better at loving you and allowing you to love me. I know what life is like without you and I hate it. Seeing you bleeding like that, it was awful. I really thought you were gonna die."

He strokes his hand down my hair. "I'm never leaving you, Suicide. Never. We're gonna grow old together, running The Depraved Devils the way it should be run."

"I'll have to speak to Lucas."

"Lucas knows. I've been telling him all along we were gonna marry and we'd be related."

I laugh. "Yeah, what did he say to that?"

"When it comes to you two, I don't have any say," comes Lucas's voice from where he stands in the doorway. "I just want the whole thing to be over, and if it means you two get married and spend the rest of your lives annoying the shit outta each other, be my guest."

I go over and wrap my arms around him. "Thank you," I whisper. "I love you."

"You better take good care of her," he says to Solo. "Or I'll find a bigger person to take you out."

Solo grins. "You don't even have to ask, brother."

"Brother," repeats Lucas, smirking. "Fuck's sake." He turns to leave. "Oh, and don't rush back to work. I've got Riding Solo covered."

Solo grabs my hand. "I'll never ride solo again."

I smirk, leaning in to kiss him. "I'm gonna spend forever riding Solo."

THE END

A note from me to you

If you enjoyed Riding Solo, please share the love. Tell everyone, by leaving a review or rating on Amazon, Goodreads, or wherever else you find it. You can also follow me on social media. I'm literally everywhere, but here's my linktr.ee to make it easier.

https://linktr.ee/NicolaJaneUK

I'm a UK author, based in Nottinghamshire. I live with my husband of many years, our two teenage boys and our four little dogs. I write MC and Mafia romance with plenty of drama and chaos. I also love to read similar books. Before I became a full-time author, I was a teaching assistant working in a primary school.

If you'd like to follow my writing journey, join my readers group on Facebook, the link is above. You can also use that link if you're a book blogger, I'd love you to sign up to my team.

Printed in Great Britain
by Amazon

10496641R00154